Apocalypse

The Redemption Chronicles:
Book III

Glenda C. Finkelstein

Final Destiny Press
Plant City, FL

Final Destiny Press
Plant City Florida 33565

Edited by Dr. Tammy L. Ferrante

Cover Art used under Royalty Free License:
49084122@GORG66/Dreamstime.com

Cover Design by Tony E. Finkelstein

ISBN:13-978-0991409068

Library of Congress Control Number: 2013931627

DEDICATION

This book is dedicated to all the United States Veterans past, present, and future. Thank you for your service to the people of this nation.

CONTENTS

Apocalypse

ACKNOWLEDGMENTS

All the people that have encouraged me in my dreams.

PROLOG

Prince Horeb, with his small band of men and dwarfs, stands in disbelief at what their eyes observe. The sky is as dark as pitch over the Wilderness of Desolation. Lightning and thunder rage from rainless clouds above them, their water dumped in full upon Navarre. The noonday sun is blotted out with no hint of its existence due to the thickness of the clouds. It's as if the atmosphere itself is on fire, glowing like a blacksmith's forge. They jump out of the way of a barrage of fierce lightning bolts. The hair on their bodies stands on end from the electricity being discharged in such close proximity. They run headlong into the wilderness seeking refuge, but little can be found. The storm continues to drive them forward like a shepherd herding sheep.

The lightning continues to light their way as they continue down a rocky path with no regard for the evil that lies within. At this moment, they're more frightened by the certainty of death from the storm than the legends that permeate this evil domain.

The ground beneath their feet begins to rumble causing rock slides that cascade down the hills to the right of them. They jump out of the way, but the forest in front of them is becoming denser with each passing step. Prince Horeb spies something moving up ahead and he slows their pace until he can discern what is coming towards them.

Suddenly, and without warning the evil that lives inside this Wilderness bursts forth from its realm summoned by a cataclysmic sound that nearly rupture the eardrums of Horeb and his entourage. They quickly dismount their horses and drag them forward towards the trees to find a hiding place from the approaching hoard. The evil creatures and fiends rush toward the Granite Castle paying no attention to their clumsy attempts to hide. They are focused only on answering their master, the Dragon's, call.

"Hide!" Horeb commands as he pushes some and pulls others into the thick foliage lining the narrow path from the oncoming hoard of nightmarish creatures and phantasms.

The images become clearer and fiercer with each new lightning strike. All with Horeb are seasoned warriors, even young Andrew is no newcomer to terror, but all of them cower and shake like frightened children as the unholy masses pass by. He looks over at Andrew and can tell that he recognizes many of these beasts as the color runs out of his face like fresh paint in the rain. Horeb puts his hand on his shoulder to steady him. He's certain that they were seen by the creatures, but they don't seem to be interested in his scouting party.

Just when it appears that the danger of these ghastly creatures has passed them by, a lone figure stands at the head of the path. His form is that of a human, but its eyes are made of fire flickering brightly amid a body made of ash and cooling lava. Andrew is captivated by this solitary form carefully surveying its surroundings. Horeb is quick to note that his young knight's expression is no longer one of terror, but of familial recognition. Horeb snaps back around and studies what has captured Andrew's attention and realizes that he's looking at his former Army Commander, Mathias, who was also Andrew's uncle.

"Unc…" Andrew begins to call out but is silenced by Horeb placing a hand over his mouth.

"Be quiet," Horeb whispers into Andrew's ear as he holds the young knight firmly in his arms. They hold their collective breath, their hearts pounding in their chests, hoping beyond hope that this ghostly apparition will pass them by.

The brief sound of hearing Andrew's voice catches this being's attention amid the thundering clamor of the storm. Mathias walks forward slowly studying the trees and then stops right in front of Andrew's position. He pauses, peering into the trees, and locks his gaze with that of Andrew's wide eyes. The next few seconds that transpire seem like an eternity, but another bolt of lightning behind this creature of fire and ash renews the pull of the Dragon's call upon him, and he moves reluctantly along. It looks back only once but continues at a brisk pace to catch up to the others.

"That was my Uncle Mathias!" Andrew announces to Horeb. "He's alive!"

"Was, being the operative word, Andrew. I doubt that what we saw would be considered alive. I agree he looks like your uncle, but he was not made of flesh," Horeb informs.

"Listen to him, young knight," Quimby, the Dwarf leader adds, and then continues. "Evil has been called out along with all the dead that were not raised on the first summons. Everyone, human and dwarf alike, that reached the age of twelve before their deaths have been raised to do the Dragon's bidding. This time, however, they are creatures of fire and ash, rather than dust and bone, and you won't be able to kill them."

"What did you say?" Horeb asks in disbelief.

"You can incapacitate them where they can't fight, but you can't kill them," Quimby repeats.

"Why not?" Horeb inquires further.

"Partly because when they are ordered into battle, they will seek out their kin. Their kin, recognizing them as sons, daughters, sisters, and brothers, will be filled with pity rather than fear just like Andrew was. Those who have become fire and ash, have no will of their own. They will carry out the Dragon's command. Secondly, even if you dismember them, they will remain until the Redeemer makes his sacrifice. Their cries will not and cannot be silenced."

This small group takes a few moments to ponder and comprehend all that Quimby has just shared with them. They soon begin to understand the ramifications of what this will mean to those they have left behind. Each of them is summarily gripped with an overwhelming urge to return and help their loved ones, but it's the prince who unwittingly verbalizes his thoughts.

"Rachel's in danger from Seth! I have to protect her!" Horeb quickly announces without thinking.

This is the first time that he has given any indication to his human scouting party of having feelings for her or any woman. Although Sebastian has suspected for quite some time that Horeb has feelings for the woman, he has tried to grant his prince his privacy. They all know that Rachel, the Healer, saved Horeb's life, and her village, Tierney, has been through a lot. No one would argue that, but it was out of character for Horeb to put any individual above his military objective.

The simple truth is that Horeb can't bear the thought that her dead husband could come back and kill her, but not just Seth, her sister, Hannah, is also a danger. All eyes turn to him, curious as to why he would yell out her name above the people he is prince over.

"Why should this person be more special to a Northern Kingdom Prince than all his other subjects?" Quimby asks.

"Firstly, we are one kingdom now, and I am Prince of Navarre. Secondly, I owe her my life," Horeb quickly answers explaining the reason he would say her name so quickly. The statement is true, but the tone confirms to Sebastian his suspicion that there is more to his statement than his words convey.

"My apologies if I insulted you, but all those we love are in equal danger. However, unless she is a warrior, she is safe for now. This final battle will take place on the Plains of Galeed," Quimby adds.

"It's as if hell has been unleashed upon us again. How can we stop it?" Horeb asks.

"We can't stop it, but we can finish it if we persevere to the end. We have entered the time of the Apocalypse, and the winner will take all including our souls," Quimby enlightens the uninformed humans.

"Our souls?" Horeb questions in horror.

"Yes, our souls, both the living and the dead will belong to the victor," Quimby confirms, then turns his attention to Andrew.

"Despite what you believe, young knight, about the creature you just saw. It may resemble your uncle, but make no mistake his will belongs to our enemy. You need to understand that he no longer has a choice. He will do the Dragon's bidding and his alone. Any affection or bond you may have had with him before he died no longer has any meaning to him."

"He sacrificed his life to save me," Andrew defends.

"If you love him, then should you meet again cut off his arms or his legs so he can't harm anyone else. Should we win the day, he will receive his reward and be freed from this ghastly existence."

"I can't kill him," Andrew replies.

"I already told you that they can't be killed," Quimby corrects.

"I can't harm him either."

"Then the Dragon has already won," Quimby informs.

"Right now, those creatures are not our objective," Rastus reminds.

"Rastus is correct. The Dragon has called all the evil out of this wilderness which should aid our quest," Horeb interjects attempting to change the subject. He must focus their energies back to the task at hand of finding where the Dragon's eggs are so they can destroy them before they hatch.

"You're beginning to understand. Any evil creature that is alive within the four realms must obey him and respond to his summons. Except for the lightning, this forest is safer now than the land of Navarre," Quimby states.

"The four realms?" Horeb inquires.

"Yes, earth, wind, water, and fire. My people acknowledge the life force held within each," Quimby explains.

"Andrew, the rest of us couldn't help but notice that you recognized many of the creatures. Can you confirm if there are any left?" Sebastian asks.

"Only one, it lives in the swamp at the northern border of the wilderness. It should be the only obstacle left, and I know the safest path through its lair."

"Then this creature you speak of is not evil, it just is," Quimby comments.

"You didn't see it kill your companions Dwarf," Andrew responds sharply.

"True, but there's a difference between an instinctive need to kill for food and one that just kills for sport or to inflict pain. Evil focuses on the latter."

"Think what you like, but it'll be a miracle if it doesn't take one or more of us when we pass by," Andrew responds. His previous experience with the creature clouds his ability to discern its true nature and attributes evil intent in place of raw, mindless instinct.

"Very well, mount up. The lightning seems to be subsiding. The faster we find what we seek, the sooner we can help those we love to fight the Dragon," Horeb orders.

"But it's pitch dark now. How will we make our way through without killing ourselves?" Oleg, one of the dwarfs, asks stroking his braided brown beard.

"We'll use the remaining lightning to our advantage moving forward as it lights the way ahead of us," Horeb orders.

The group moves forward. They lead the horses instead of riding them as they are too upset to be ridden, but even this is not ideal. Horeb takes advantage of a tree caught fire by a lightning strike by fashioning makeshift torches, allowing them to make better progress through the dark. They travel through the night and although they can't discern the sunrise the next morning the sky is a brighter gray than the blackened night sky.

As they make their way, Horeb's mind reflects back on that stormy night long before they knew about the Dragon when he awoke to consciousness and there before him was the most beautiful creature he had ever seen. Rachel was beautiful in body and spirit. Horeb now understands that what he feels for her is much more than lust, attraction, or even appreciation for saving his life. He loves her more than anything, and for the first time in his life, he truly cares about whether he lives or dies. He intends to fight until the last bit of evil has been vanquished from this land. Although quite willing to sacrifice himself to rescue her, he desires to hold her in his arms and make her his wife should they survive these perilous times.

In his heart, he makes a bargain with the Most High, most would call it a prayer, but Horeb is too worldly to become spiritual now. He vows that should the Most High grant him this one singular wish, that his love will be enough to bring joy back to Rachel's spirit. He knows that he can never replace the memory of her dead husband, Seth, but hopes against hope that her heart is big enough to love two men in her lifetime.

CHAPTER 1

Princess Sabrina awakens from a sound sleep to the storm raging outside Ophir's Castle. Her husband, Prince Robert, hasn't returned in his allotted 90 days with any dead dwarfs to prove his loyalty to the Dragon, nor did she expect him to. Robert's plan was to ally himself with them should he find them in hopes of joining forces to defeat the Dragon, Lucius, and his hoards. The long wait is finally over, and she knows that her pretense will no longer be tolerated. As of this moment, she is of no further use to Lucius, and her life is effectively over.

She stands to her feet, grabs a robe, and puts it on. She takes a quick glance into the mirror to fix her hair and face before getting dressed, but a smudge on the glass makes it difficult to see. Sabrina tries to wipe the spot with the sleeve of her robe, but when it starts to move back and forth, she suspicions it's not dirt. Suddenly, the spot extends out from the mirror and she recognizes the demonic intruder.

"You have no business in my room Gorkon," Sabrina informs curtly.

"I was just watching over you. We can't have anything happen to you prematurely. I wouldn't want to deprive my master of any pleasures."

"Like you care… You've been spying on me to see if I'll give away any secrets. Get out!" Sabrina orders.

"So you do have secrets. Your tantrum gives you away," Gorkon counters.

"I said get out!" Sabrina orders.

The demon departs her room without another word as a cold chill runs down her spine. She expels a sigh of relief thankful that her blouse was still buttoned high enough to cover the amulet which is now her only protection from Lucius. She glances over at the clock and realizes that the Dragon has called his wrath down early. She quickly finishes getting dressed and makes her way to the castle balcony where she once waited to see her former husband, Horeb, return. Now she hopes to catch a glimpse of Robert with an army of dwarfs behind him but would settle for just another friendly face.

As she steps on to the balcony, she sees hoards of evil creatures and beings of Fire and Ash gathering below. Drums pound out the rhythms of the marching ranks as they fall into rows awaiting their orders. Sabrina attempts to count them and soon realizes that there are thousands upon thousands of them, and no sign of her beloved Robert. Her heart sinks to her feet wanting one more glimpse of him before her time is ended. She strains her eyes to see the hope of daylight peeking through a cloud bank, but alas, they are too thick for that. Her hope drains from her with each peal of thunder rumbling through the sky. A few lightning strikes hit close by her position causing her to jump and withdraw from the balcony's edge. The light from the bolts, however, allows her to see her people running south for safety.

Suddenly, she feels very alone. She recollects her night terrors that plagued her for so many weeks. Dreams that the Oracle confirmed were visions of her destiny. She should be feeling afraid, but in actuality, she feels relieved that the time of waiting is over. If everyone has run away, then there is no one the Dragon can use to force her to surrender the amulet. This will buy her the time she needs to remember the incantation that Rainah gave her and enable her to take control of these horrid creatures. The injury she sustained at the hand of her mother to deflect any guilt away from her because of the dwarfs' escape, rendered her memory at the moment preceding the assault shaky at best. She knows that once the Dragon discovers she has the amulet, she can't let any sensibility dissuade her from acting at the right moment for the greater good.

"What are the words?" she asks herself aloud, straining to

remember. "Rah, Gah, Tah, Ba…Ba…Ba what? Sabrina, you're an idiot!" she comments aloud to herself. No one, however, can hear her over the clamor of the storm.

"Princess," Shaman, the Dragon's second in command, addresses. Sabrina jumps and is noticeably startled by his unannounced arrival.

"How long have you been there?" She snaps.

"I just got here. Our master wants to speak with you."

"You mean your master," Sabrina corrects.

"Whether you acknowledge him or not, he is in control. Are you coming or do I have to drag you?" Shaman inquires when he notices her not following behind him.

Sabrina glares at Shaman then catches a glimpse of Lucius in his full Dragon splendor atop the castle. She realizes that she must capitulate and turns to follow Shaman up the stairs to the top of the castle. The moment she sets foot on the roof, the Dragon turns its head and lustfully glares at her. At this moment she doesn't know the true fate of her beloved Robert, nor is she about to afford this hideous creature even the smallest of victories. She, therefore, stands before her enemy defiantly proud and confident completely unmoved by his sexual overture. After all, in the absence of all the royal males, she is queen and must place the needs of her people above her own no matter how few may remain.

"Your husband didn't show," the Dragon Lucius informs.

"You violated your word and went early. He may still be on his way. This violent storm that you conjured undoubtedly hinders any progress he could be making to return with your prize."

"I believe we both know that your husband never planned to return."

"You're impatient," she accuses.

"I've waited over a thousand years that's hardly impatient. Besides, I already know he was successful. The wind turned when I called forth the storm. There are thousands of detestable dwarfs marching to their defeat. Their stench is an offense to my nostrils. The Trolls I sent with your husband have returned to me as Fire and Ash. So it is he who first violated our agreement."

"You gave him no choice."

"Yes, I did, but he chose them over you. Poor little princess, always a pawn and never the loved one," Lucius mocks.

"Would it surprise you to know that I encouraged that choice?" Sabrina proudly submits for the Dragon's consideration.

"Pity, there may be more to you than spoiled entitlement after all, but I haven't the time to devote to turning you."

"I'm not my mother. I would never allow myself to be turned," Sabrina defends.

"Every human has a price, my dear. It's just a matter of finding the proper motivator," Lucius responds. He then pauses to survey his growing army below. He smiles wider as each new legion is completed and finds their place in his ranks.

"What do you want from me?" Sabrina asks in aggravation. She is tired of being toyed with and wants him to get it over with.

"I want you to die," the Dragon states simply then blows fire at her. Sabrina doesn't even flinch under the Dragon's fiery breath as the amulet creates a bubble of protection around her. After expelling his full fury upon her, he opens his eyes expecting to see a pile of ash in a heap at his feet. His surprise is evident upon his face when he finds her standing in front of him unharmed and defiant as ever.

In this moment, although alive, Sabrina is now in a different kind of danger. The Dragon discovers the amulet he's been looking for has been under his nose and on her person the whole time. He steps back to see that not even a hair on her head is singed nor does she smell of smoke. He steps back from her alarmed that she knows the incantation which would stop this war before it begins. Sabrina notices a slight, passing look of dread cross ever so briefly across his face. She now faces in reality, the fear that paralyzed her in nightmares for months. The only thing Lucius can do to harm her now is to hurt others around her.

"Shaman, bring me the human servants," Lucius commands.

"Right away, master."

Sabrina stands firm and erect with shoulders back waiting for
him to do his worst. In a manner of moments, twelve servants
stand before her and Lucius unaware of the danger they are in.
Lucius looks over at the quarry and licks his lips like a dog eagerly
awaiting a juicy bone.

"Give me the amulet or I will kill them."

"No," Sabrina responds calmly, defiantly, and succinctly.

Lucius lunges forward with the lightning fast reflexes of a
snake striking their prey. He snaps up the first servant in line and
munches on him like a cracker. The other servants scream and
draw back in fear. Shaman keeps them from retreating back inside
the castle. Sabrina remains unmoved and emotionally cold.

"You surprise me, princess, I expected you to be far more
compassionate toward your own staff. Now, hand over the amulet
or I shall do worse to the remaining servants."

"No," Sabrina responds again.

Lucius burns the rest in a fit of rage eating them in the midst
of their agony. Sabrina stands defiant and resolute to the greater
cause. The Dragon is surprised by this reaction especially in
comparison to his previous encounters with her.

"Your composure and defiance surprises me. I expected you

to cave quickly."

"You forgot one thing. Those were Ophir's servants. He had them conditioned to die to protect him and the royal household. Their rescue would have insulted their sworn duty. I know my purpose, and I know its cost. I shall not be pushed into acting prematurely or be bribed to give it over to you regardless of who you threaten, maim, or kill."

"Indeed, what do you know of the power than hangs around your neck?"

"I know you're scared of it, and you should know that I'll never give it to you."

"Use it," Lucius demands, calling her bluff.

"As I've already told you, I shall choose the time, not you," she counters boldly.

"You don't know how to use it, or you would have already done it. Seize her! Be careful not to harm her, but place her in Ophir's cell. Keep a guard on her day and night until we leave for the Plains of Galeed."

Shaman and Lucius' guards standing nearby obey and place her in Ophir's cell. She goes willingly into the cell. The fear that she struggled with for so long is gone. The determination to undermine everything that Lucius does has taken its place. Her first duty is to remember the incantation that Rainah had given her and being in a cell will help her concentrate. The noise, however, that fills the air around her is full of unholy sounds. She does her best to block them out each time they crescendo to an ear piercing force holding her hands upon her ears to make it more bearable. Yet, it does little good.

Lucius gives orders to Shaman to discover a way of undoing the magic of the amulet. Shaman knows that his task is an impossible one, but he'll do everything he can to appease his master. He knows that their success will depend greatly upon the amulet being rendered useless and he'll exhaust every spell, curse, and incantation that he knows towards that end.

CHAPTER 2

In the village of Tierney, the town folk huddle together inside the main structure they had rebuilt. The ferocity of the storm is beginning to wane, but a thick fogbank has rolled in blanketing the coast and stretching into the forests. The people fear the return of the Fog Wraiths and dare not go outside. These hideous creatures, although small, are ravenous and no one wanted to be attacked by them. The howling wind blows through the trees that bend and creak under pressure making a sound like baying wolfs in the forest.

Mark's dog, Snootzer, hears something moving outside amid the tumult. His ears perk up and cocking his head sideways he listens for danger. Detecting something out of place, he suddenly stands to his feet, walks to the door, and begins to draw attention to himself. His hair stands straight up on his back and begins to growl while rapidly scratching at the door. His whimpers grow to barks which catches Mark's attention as well as those around them.

"What is it boy? What do you hear?" Mark asks. The dog simply barks, growls, and continues to scratch at the door. A loose plank gives way, and the dog jumps out of the house like a shot. "Snootzer, come back!" Mark yells as he feverishly tries to unbolt the door to follow. The last time he failed to keep Snootzer in check, it cost Seth his life. He wasn't about to let that happen again.

"Oh, no you don't. You're not going out in this," Rachel informs coming up beside him taking hold of his arm so he can't bolt after the dog.

"I can't let him wander alone in the fog," Mark explains.

"I don't intend to let him I just won't allow you to go out after him. You are too valuable," Rachel corrects as she grabs a trident leaning near the door.

"Nor are you going out there alone," Jonathan adds as he grabs a trident to join her. Rachel smiles in response, appreciative of the company.

"Papa, lock the door behind us," Rachel instructs her father, Laban. He shakes his head in the affirmative.

Rachel and Jonathan slowly emerge from the house and follow the sounds of Snootzer's barking. They can see things moving in the fog the size of an army. Individually they appear larger than Fog Wraiths who always remain below the fog, but they can't make out what or who is coming towards them. These days, one always assumes the worst and she and Jonathan immediately go on the defensive.

"Stop and identify yourselves!" Rachel calls out into the thick mist. It's so thick that the trident she holds in her hands is becoming slippery and hopes that she'll not have to use it.

"Halt!" commands an unfamiliar voice from the mist. The company of troops comes to a stop. Then that same voice responds back to Rachel, "Identify yourself first."

"I'm Rachel, Healer of Tierney, you are on our land."

"Rachel, it's I, Prince Robert. I come with a new ally, the Dwarfs," Robert announces drawing close enough to be identified. His familiar voice relieves their fears.

"You gave us a fright!" Rachel acknowledges amid Snootzer's frantic barking who is now running back and forth between Rachel and Jonathan. "Snootzer, be quiet! These people are our friends."

Snootzer stops his barking and whines slightly. Then his hair lies flat, and his tail begins to wag going from dwarf to dwarf looking for dried cheese.

"You are Rainah's people," Rachel surmises.

"Yes," the lead dwarf answers.

"How many Dwarf troops do you have?" Rachel asks.

"We are 500,000 strong," the Dwarf responds.

"I think introductions are in order," Robert informs and continues. "This is General Rasmussen, commander of the Dwarfs. The men that are with me are few, but I'm hoping there will be more waiting further inland."

"This is Jonathan, one of Tierney's warriors who served under the command of Prince Horeb. We can offer your troops no shelter or food as we have little left these days," Rachel informs apologetically.

"We have our own provisions. Besides, we'll not be stopping here. Half of us will be continuing on to Togarmah's castle to join with the warriors that are in the south, the other half will be first to face off against the Dragon on the Plains of Galeed."

"The Plains of Galeed, but that is reserved for the final battle," Rachel comments.

"Yes, the end of things as we know them is quickly coming to pass," Rasmussen confirms.

"I'm glad you came out, we may have walked right past and missed the road we needed," Robert interjects trying to keep a hopeful mood alive.

Slowly the villagers emerge from the main house to see Rachel and Jonathan conversing with Prince Robert and a stranger.

They know that they must be Rainah's people by their stature. Mark runs along the beach chasing after Snootzer now that it has been confirmed safe for him to do so. He finally closes the distance and picks up his furry friend with mud caked paws. Then in a moment of reflection, he gazes upon these beings knowing that many of them will be lost in the upcoming battle.

"Chief Laban, how are you doing?" Robert addresses seeing Rachel's father drawing close.

"I'm recovering. Who is this?"

"General Rasmussen. He brings 500,000 dwarf warriors to help us fight the final battle against the Dragon."

"Welcome to my village such as it is. I'm thankful that you are more than myth and are an ally. I was beginning to think we were mistreated for no reason."

"The Dragon hates us more than you. We would have come sooner, but the council was afraid of upsetting the prophecy and losing our one opportunity for victory," Rasmussen explains.

"I understand about prophecy and the fullness of time in which they come to pass. I'm still glad that you're here now," Laban extends his hand in greeting. Rasmussen takes hold of his hand and notices the deep scars on his arm. "Jonathan, show his men the road."

"Yes sir," Jonathan obeys. "Follow me!" he calls out to the dwarfs. They pause and glance over at Rasmussen who nods his approval. They follow this human through the fog to the Frontier Road.

"If you'll excuse us, we are on a tight time schedule, and I must see that my men understand their orders," the General informs.

"Of course, I shall remember you in my prayers," Laban adds.

"We'll need them," the General admits.

"I, too, must go. It's good to see you again," Robert conveys.

"Success my friends," Laban calls after them which concludes their brief conversation.

As Rasmussen and Robert walk toward the road, the general leans in to ask a sensitive question. "What happened to him?"

"He was tortured for information by the Dragon's minions."

"What kind of information?"

"If he knew where any of your kind was hiding. Those scars on his arms are minor compared to the rest of his body. He was burned in unspeakable places and didn't break."

"He did this for my people? He didn't know us. Not even the Dragon knew where we had gone."

"His brother-in-law was blinded for the same cause. He didn't break either."

"He has a warrior's heart, and we shall fight all the harder to honor such a sacrifice on our behalf," Rasmussen vows.

"I would expect nothing less from those as honorable as yourselves," Robert comments. His relief that the dwarfs have joined their cause and are so committed is evident upon his face.

Rachel watches them until she can no longer hear or see them while Laban stands quietly by her side contemplating the past, the present, and the future. When the last of them march out of sight, a tear runs down Rachel's face. Laban takes his finger and wipes it away.

"We shall never see any of them again. Will we, papa?"

"Maybe not in this world, but we will see them again."

"In this world…Papa, you have a gift for understatement. I know what the Chronicles of Destiny says about the last days. We shall all be sifted regardless of our faith or disbelief. It is the end of all things, and nothing we do will stop it. Yet we march towards oblivion just as if we were ignorant of our fates."

"My daughter, your beautiful countenance is so downcast. Do you not also remember the hope that is promised to come after? A new beginning awaits the Remnant that remains and those redeemed during this time of tribulation. There will be joy and peace again, but this time it will be a lasting peace."

"How can a thing so fragile emerge after such strong darkness?"

"It begins in our hearts. We must hold on to the promised goodness to keep ourselves alive during this time of despair."

"I can't see or feel it like you can. My heart is numb, papa."

Laban goes to hug his daughter, but she shrugs him off and turns to go sit on top of the bluff overlooking the northern edge of their village. He doesn't pursue her but turns to find his sister Agatha standing behind him. She overheard their conversation.

"Give her time brother."

"We don't have time. She needs to snap out of it and be a leader."

"Her strength came from Hannah and Seth, she'll find it again. She maintained very well when you were gone in the face of adversity. I couldn't have been prouder of her."

"Thank you, Agatha, but I just can't help but worry about her. She is too young to be so hopeless."

"To be honest brother, I think even Hannah's energy would be muted in these days."

"I just wish she could focus on the hope," he adds.

They walk back to the main house in silence and begin to prepare the only meal of the day. The fish have become scarce, but they found some muscles to supplement the lack of fish. They also pulled up some potatoes that they had planted a few weeks ago. There wasn't many left to plant, but they are making the rations last. They spend a good portion of their day foraging in the forest for mushrooms and wild turnips. The people continue to survive on meager portions, but Laban isn't aware of food located anywhere else believing that everyone is just as hungry as they are.

Laban's heart is still concerned over Rachel. He knows that Rachel dealt with a lot of tragedy while he was away, but she hasn't seen what he has seen. Laban knows that the worse is yet to come, but he also has faith in Mark, the Redeemer, to vanquish the darkness and give birth to a new golden age. Laban puts on a brave face, but inside he's just as scared as she is, but for the good of his people he dare not show it.

CHAPTER 3

Beverly and Beth remain indoors in the abandoned village of Elim taking care of the infant boys. They anxiously await the return of Beverly's adult children, Sasha and Tubal who went in search of their captured village. Beverly hopes that they have been successful in freeing their people from the Trolls that took them away. She is all too aware, however, that Trolls are not to be trifled with and are difficult to overwhelm or kill. Both Tubal and Sasha are skilled fighters, but their skill alone isn't sufficient for the task against larger numbers. Beverly's hope remains with their intelligence and not just their combat techniques. Trolls are not known for strategic thinking, they are the Dragon's bullies that he uses to pummel his enemies into submission. This ability to think is where her children's true advantage lies.

It's been several days since they left to try and rescue their people. Beverly knows that the violent storm will impede their progress, so she isn't too concerned that they haven't returned yet.

Even though Beverly has the gift of sight like her daughter, Sasha, she has refrained from using it for multiple reasons. Firstly, the Dragon's powers are now at their strongest, and he can hitchhike upon her power to see them, and secondly, if the news is unpleasant, she wants to put off dealing with it for as long as she can.

In the meantime, she focuses her energy on keeping Lady Beth, her infant son, and the infant prince that Beth has become a wet nurse for calm during the storm. The young prince is the son of Princess Sabrina and Prince Robert. The Princess demanded that her son be taken away and hidden from her and her husband until the Dragon has been vanquished. One of the last prophecies in the Chronicles of Destiny speaks of an infant prince that holds the key to the future of Navarre. This responsibility fell to Sasha and Tubal, and should they fail, the future of Navarre will die with him.

The young prince, who has yet to be given a name, remains fussy. Beth has done everything she knows to comfort him. In desperation, she hands him off to Beverly, the Matron of Elim. She gladly takes the boy, and he's immediately soothed by the tender touch and voice of this elder woman. Instead of crying, he begins to coo.

"How do you do it?" Beth asks, shaking her head in disbelief.

"Do what child?" Beverly questions not realizing that what

she did contained any special magic.

"I've been trying to calm him for the last half hour, and you simply touch him, and he's calm."

"That's because I'm calm. Babies are smart and pick up on your emotional state," Beverly explains.

"You're right. I didn't get much sleep last night, my mind is a muddle of worry, and my nerves are shot. The storm was so violent I jumped with every thunderbolt thinking that was going to be the end. I'm at a loss to understand how you can remain so steadfast with all that's happened."

"Wisdom and experience are the only difference between us. Storms always pass, and this one seems to be calming down. We're still here and no worse for wear save lack of sleep. I only hope that Sasha and Tubal will be successful, find shelter from the storm for all of my people, and return soon."

"Forgive me, I've been thinking only of myself and my son. I can't imagine the worry you must be experiencing with your children and village missing. You don't know their fate. Yet, you seem to be at peace as if you know that they'll be fine."

"I'd be lying if I said I wasn't concerned, but I also have faith in my children's abilities to make good decisions. Besides, unbridled worry does nothing but make one ill and its practice changes nothing. And to answer your unspoken question, I have no special insight. It's the result of years of practice at being a mother," Beverly elaborates to the amazement of the young Beth.

"I have a lot to learn about being a mother," Beth admits. Suddenly, Beverly shushes her as she hands back the now sleeping infant. "What is it?" she whispers.

"Quiet, someone's coming," Beverly insists. "Go hide in the back room." Beth nods her understanding and retreats to the back room.

Both women listen intently to the sounds outside. The thunder has subsided, and they can hear footsteps coming closer. At first, Beverly believes that it could be the enemy coming back, but then there is a familiar rhythm to the steps and rapping at her door. She pauses only a moment to insure that her ears have not betrayed her by peeking through the slats in the door to confirm her suspicions of who is at her gate. She expels a sigh of relief as her eyes confirm that it's Sasha and Tubal. She flings open the door and hugs them both passionately.

"My children, you're safe!" Beverly announces. Her white teeth shine brightly amid her grinning dark face. Overhearing the conversation, Beth emerges from the back room leaving the sleeping infants on the bed.

"Yes, mother, and we were successful in retrieving our people. All are present, but many need care."

"I'll take care of it immediately," Beverly responds. Before she can take her first action, she is surrounded by the village children.

"Mama Beverly," they call as they crowd around her hugging her small frame.

"I'm happy to see all of you, but I need your help with the others. Now run along and fetch water and food so that we can eat and strengthen those that have become weak."

The children immediately disperse to do as Beverly commands. In a matter of seconds, she organizes the village so they can treat those who are injured or sick. She enlists the aid of the stronger ones to carry those who can't walk on their own and sets a guard to maintain a lookout for the enemy. The children pass out food and water to the rest after refreshing themselves first. Sasha and Tubal assist her following her every instruction without question.

***

Later that evening, after everyone's needs have been met and are resting comfortably, Sasha calls a village meeting to order. Beverly is curious as to what her daughter is up to. They have not had an opportunity to catch up on what happened nor share what they learned on their rescue mission about the enemy. Tubal stands beside his sister as she addresses the village.

"My people, we have entered a time when no one on this world is safe. The time of the apocalypse has come. We must join forces with the people of Navarre to help them hold back the enemy until the Army of Light arrives. In my visions, I have seen many things that confirm that we are in the last days. I also know that we possess the only defensive weapon to protect them from what is coming."

The villagers begin to murmur among themselves. This thought is highly unpopular among her people. They are not citizens of Navarre and feel no obligation to assist. At first, Sasha just looks at everyone giving them a moment to ponder her statement while Beth observes from the sidelines. Sasha knows that what she is about to say will be difficult for them to accept especially on the heels of their recent ordeal.

"I think you're overreacting. This fight is for Navarre!" a villager responds to the group. The village erupts into loud cheers for the statement made. Tubal steps up to silence them with a wave of his hand then steps back to allow his sister to address the comment.

"You weren't taken captive to be slaves to the Dragon. You were taken to feed his offspring!" Sasha announces. The crowd gasps in disbelief. "We may not be citizens of Navarre, but the Dragon declared war on us! We can't let that attack go unchallenged."

"Listen to my sister!" Tubal insists. "Are you blind to ignore the signs in the sky? Do you wish to forget how the Trolls were raised back to life after we killed them? Don't be fools. We join the fight, or become food for Dragons!" Tubal's passions begin to sway the crowd.

"What are you proposing?" asks a village elder.

"We raid our vaults and bring out every shield we have. The dragon scale shields will be the only thing that will protect the warriors from their fiery breath," Sasha responds.

"Remember, a dragon is lethal from birth, and has a ravenous appetite," Tubal adds.

"So what will it be? Will you join my brother and I to defend our children and elders against the Dragon and his minions, or will you just sit by and wait to be captured again only to be ripped to shreds by his voracious children?" Sasha challenges.

The village grows quiet while they ponder and discuss the decision amongst themselves in guarded whispers. Beth sits nervously knowing that her people are outnumbered and need all the help they can get. She utters a prayer that they'll join the cause. Finally, one of the village elders stands up to give a response.

"We can't deny your words. You did rescue us from certain disaster, and since you have seen these events in your visions, we will take the only logical step and join the people of Navarre. We will not, however, be hasty. Our people are not nearly as numerous as we were millennia ago. We ask for two days to rest from our recent ordeal and prepare for war. We also need to repair the wagons from storm damage to transport all the shields."

"Agreed, in two days time all those that can, will join us and head for Castle Togarmah where we shall join the women warriors of the old Southern Kingdom. We'll leave behind four warriors and enough shields to provide protection for those of you who can't fight should his young come this far. There's not much left in Navarre for them to eat which is why the Trolls were seeking quarry this far south. The Dragon won't be hemmed in by the borders of man so we'll draw the line in the sand that will not be crossed," Sasha informs.

The meeting is dismissed, and the people disburse to their own dwellings. Beth follows after Sasha and Tubal who return to their mother's house. Sasha opens the door to find Beverly changing the infant prince's diaper, but before entering the house, Sasha stands their watching her mother care for the baby in silence. Sasha appears to be deep in thought, but Beth can see that she has something to say.

"There that's a good boy, you'll be much happier now with a dry diaper," Beverly informs the cooing infant.

"Mother," Sasha begins after taking in a deep breath for extra courage.

"Yes, dear," Beverly responds walking towards her daughter while holding the baby. "I'm pleased with your choice to rally the village to help Navarre. It's the right thing to do. This fight belongs to all of us."

"I need you and Beth to travel south to the Port of Salt and stay there until this is over."

"Why? I've never run away from a fight in my life. Nor have I deserted my village for any reason and I don't intend to start now," Beverly informs sternly.

"Because nothing and I repeat nothing, can happen to that child."

"What did you see in your visions?" Beverly asks.

"This child, the son of Prince Robert and Princess Sabrina, will rebuild the land and unite the world itself. He'll be raised by another couple after their deaths. If he dies, even if we win, our future dies with him."

Beverly is not surprised by this revelation knowledge, but it catches Beth off guard, and she plops down on a nearby chair despondent at what she hears.

"What's wrong with you?" Sasha inquires.

"What happens to my lady, his mother, and his father?"

Sasha looks into Beth's eyes and turns away without uttering a word. A tear runs down her face as she walks out of the house. Her gift of sight isn't always a pleasant one. Beth stands up with her son in her arms to go after Sasha. Tubal reaches out and gently grabs her elbow stopping her.

"She didn't answer me," Beth explains looking up into Tubal's chocolate eyes.

"I think you know the answer, don't make my sister's sorrow any worse by speaking it aloud," Tubal whispers. Beth shakes her head not wanting to believe it, but knows they have no reason to lie.

"Not my lady," Beth expounds and then begins to weep.

"Your Lady is an incredibly brave woman and both she, and Prince Robert's sacrifice is to secure the life of their son. Will you dishonor that sacrifice by not doing everything in your power to safeguard their child?" Tubal submits for consideration.

"No, I could never dishonor them. It's just hard to know what might happen."

"It's what will happen. My sister is never wrong. Her gift is both a rare joy and a terrible responsibility. Time has already been written we can't change the future any more than we can change the past. All we can do is to make the wisest choice we can in the present."

"That's not always easy to do," Beth admits. Beverly puts the infant prince who has nodded off in her arms to bed then starts a pot of tea.

"The right choice is never easy, but it's the only path that leads to life," Tubal adds as he turns to follow after his sister. The two have been and are virtually inseparable.

"How does she sleep with such burdens?" Beth inquires of Beverly.

"It's not easy. The position of Oracle got too much for me to bear, so I passed that burden to my daughter. It saddens me that I wasn't strong enough to keep the mantle a bit longer, but she has held up well. She, too, has given up much to see us through these last days."

"Other than her sanity, what else has she given up?" Beth inquires believing that only her Princess has sacrificed something priceless.

"She had to give up the love of her life, your own Prince Javan. She had to release him so that he could fulfill his destiny and become Anak, Commander of the Army of Light. If she hadn't, we would already be counted among the dead."

"Is there nothing left of my king's house?" Beth asks aloud.

"Never forget that the child sleeping upon that bed is of the house Togarmah. He will possess the inheritance of all that was good and noble about your late king."

"I never thought of it that way. I vow that I shall not let them down."

"Very good, now have some tea then try to get some sleep. We have some hard days ahead of us," Beverly entreats. Beth takes her advice, sips her tea, and then falls asleep next to the babies. Beverly soon follows her own advice pulling out a mat and some pillows onto the floor. She then curls up in a blanket and sleeps through the night at peace knowing her children are safe for the moment. The next couple days will be busy and require much planning. They'll need every ounce of their strength to meet the coming challenge.

CHAPTER 4

Across the sea, Javan, in command of the Armies of Light, battle the forces of nature set loose by the Dragon's incantation. When the armada first began their journey, the ships glided effortlessly across the surface of the ocean unfettered like a canoe gliding across a mirrored lake. The storm's ferocity had no effect on them with the hail, rain, and wind passing through them as easily as a butterfly flits from flower to flower. Yet with each passing moment, the resistance they face from the unleashing of nature grows worse. Gale force winds howl whipping the sails into a frenzy nearly tearing them to shreds, but the crew manages to secure them before they're damaged.

"What's happening?" Javan asks Anak as he reaffirms his footing to stand up straight against the squalls.

"Hard to port!" Anak yells without responding to Javan. The ship turns into an oncoming swell to avoid being capsized. "Hang on!" He commands. The crew braces for impact as the swell curls over the bow of the ship pounding the deck with thunderous force. Another ship several yards away is doing their best to avoid a water spout that sprang up from nowhere and dissipates just in a nick of time. Everyone breathes a sigh of relief, but must quickly prepare for the next danger.

"Our ships are being pummeled. Why are we facing such resistance? The storm was worse than this when we set out, but we cut through it like a hot knife through butter without issue. Now it's pounding at us as if we were a walled city," Javan comments again looking for an explanation.

"We are transforming the closer we get to Navarre."

"Transforming? Into what?" Javan asks nervously, uncertain as to what may be coming next.

"Mortal beings!" Anak yells so he can be heard over the noise of the storm. "It took a man of faith to command us, but to fight the Dragon and give your people hope, we must become mortal."

"What are you saying?"

"I'm saying that for us to help your people, we have to lay down our immortality. If we are killed in battle, we will die. Our only hope of life after this sacrifice is the Redeemer."

"I didn't know that. I thought that the Army of Light was

invincible," Javan admits. His facial expression drops to that of a scorned child who wasn't told to stay out of the garden then got in trouble for wandering in there.

"It's not surprising. You haven't known much about anything," Anak jabs with a sly grin.

"Thanks, you really know how to instill confidence in someone," Javan's conversation is cut short as their ship comes off another swell and plunges toward the sea below them. Water and salt spray them down saturating them to the bone. The salt begins to sting Javan's eyes. He blinks to evacuate the foreign mineral. His hair drips with water, and the wind adds a cold chill to his drenched clothing. He looks over to see how the Firecats are doing and are starting to resemble drowned rats rather than a fierce winged predator.

"Answer me this Anak. If I'm so ignorant, why did you agree to follow me?"

"Because your cause is greater than yourself and the purpose of our existence is to supply help when it's most desperately needed. It's our destiny and the reason we were created."

"So again, my life has no meaning, only the cause," Javan states with disappointment. Anak looks at him then slaps him in the back of the head. Javan's eyes narrow scowling at Anak for slapping him. It's clear he still doesn't understand the true meaning behind Anak's statement. "What was that for?" he asks yelling to raise his voice above the tumult of the storm.

"For being an idiot," Anak yells back then continues, "You twisted what I said. You were created for a time such as this. You are the only one found worthy to lead us. You were destined from birth to lead an army that no other human could lead. Without us, your people and the dwarfs would fail, and both races would be doomed to enslavement by the Dragon and his progeny."

Javan ponders Anak's words while another wave crashes across the bow dousing them again with cold salty water. He wipes the excess water away from his eyes so that he can look Anak in the eye.

"You're right, I am an idiot. I kept looking for some moment of glory and honor not realizing that it's my sacrifice that is worthy, not my life."

"Now, my friend, you understand in full your destiny and purpose."

"My father always said I was too hard headed for my own good."

"Yes, but at least you won't break on the first punch," Anak playfully jabs.

"Thanks, for the love."

"What are brothers are for?"

This is the first time that Anak has referred to Javan as family. This fills Javan with pride that although he may have given up much to pursue this quest, he is embracing a new family and destiny worth more than gold, fame, or inheritance. It's a relationship that is built on trust and on a love that can't be undone.

Their transformation continues to accelerate. Javan gazes out over the bow beyond the immediate storm to look in on his sister before he loses his gift of sight. He can see that she has been placed in a cell, but can also see the protective aura of the dragon's amulet protecting her. In this moment, he feels neither sorrow nor fear. He recognizes that she, just like himself, are where they're supposed to be. Safety is not a word that applies to anything or anyone at this point in their journey. He can perceive her resolve to protect their people and defy the enemy. He's proud of her for she has come to the place of embracing her destiny without fear and he has confidence that she will do what she must to defeat the Dragon.

Javan switches his gaze to that of Sasha who is currently preparing her people to join in the final battle. He watches with approval and knows that although their love would not be on this side of heaven, a new world awaits them both where that relationship can endure for eternity. Slowly his vision dims, and his sight returns to that of a mortal man, but the hope he feels in these last glimpses of those he holds most dear galvanizes his will. Defeat is not an option.

Suddenly and without warning, a wave comes crashing over the rail and knocks Javan's feet out from under him. Anak reaches down and grabs his arm keeping him from washing away with the water. Javan reaffirms his hold on the railing and secures himself with a rope around his waist. He smiles nodding his head to acknowledge his appreciation to Anak for keeping him from going overboard.

CHAPTER 5

Several days later at Castle Togarmah, Cassandra the Brave comes upstairs to check on Connor, her Dwarf commander, and his wife, Rainah. She's been helping Mary, Andrew's mother, with their care ever since they escaped from Ophir's castle where the Dragon tortured them for several days. She knocks softly so she doesn't wake them should they be resting.

"Come in," Connor authorizes in a low, soft voice.

"I was just checking on how you and Rainah are doing," Cassandra informs. "I noticed that the violent storm has finally subsided, but the clouds are a funny color, and the air smells of rotten eggs. The women warriors are on edge about what this means. Do we need to prepare for another attack?"

"It's the signs of the last days. We shall not see the sun again until the Dragon is vanquished."

"Do we need to prepare for another attack?" Cassandra asks

again since Connor failed to answer her question. He looks up at her. His eyes reflect the weariness within his spirit as if answering her question would expend what strength he has left, but takes in a deep breath as if gathering strength from the air around him to do so.

"No," Connor answers but then recants his statement. "Yes."

"Which is it?" Cassandra inquires for clarification.

"Yes, we must prepare for another attack, but it won't happen here. The last battle will take place on the Plains of Galeed. Prepare the women for battle and be sure they have enough rations for three days."

"The Plains of Galeed are two days travel from here. Three days rations will not suffice."

"Yes, they will. We go to win, or we go to die. If we don't win, there will be no survivors."

"Are you able to lead us again, or must I, alone, lead?"

"I will lead you when the time is right. You just get ready."

"What about your wife? I doubt that she's ready to go with us."

"She'll remain here," Connor informs. A groan comes from the other side of the bed as Rainah turns over.

"It'll be a cold day in hell before I let you march off without me," Rainah informs. She then attempts to sit up on her own but doesn't quite have enough strength to do so. Cassandra rushes to her side and supports her attempt while Connor steadies her.

"If we had more time for you to recover, then I would agree, but you can't even sit up on your own," Connor advises.

"If I would stop hurting, I'd make sure you eat those words, but I ache all over," Rainah admits.

"I'll go fetch some eucalyptus tea, and bring some liniment for your aching muscles," Cassandra volunteers.

"That would be lovely thank you," Rainah responds.

Cassandra turns to leave when something catches her eye outside the window. She stops and walks across the room towards the balcony to get a better look.

"What is it?" Connor asks with concern.

"I'm not sure. Something or someone is coming down the Castle Road."

Connor props Rainah up with some pillows and joins Cassandra on the balcony. In the distance just clearing the tree line, he sees a contingent of dwarf warriors coming over the hill. This was a sight he thought he'd never see again. His heart leaps in his chest and starts jumping up and down like a giddy schoolboy.

"Who is it?" Rainah questions with confusion. She is having trouble reconciling Cassandra's worry with Connor's jubilation.

"It's the Brigade of Verdoon," Connor utters in both amazement and relief.

"The who?" Cassandra asks.

"The Brigade of Verdoon contains the finest dwarf warriors in the world. No one is their equal," Rainah answers on Connor's behalf and continues. "Can you see who's in command?"

"Commander Soba," Connor answers. The two of them were best friends when they were young boys.

Suddenly, Mary comes bursting through the doors. "Warriors are coming!" She exclaims in alarm having never seen the likes of them before.

"Yes, we know," answers Connor with a big grin across his face. "They're here to help us," he explains further.

"Thank the Most High! I was beginning to think we were forgotten," Mary exclaims in relief.

"Never, my good woman, never are we forgotten. Please make some small preparations to welcome the officers."

"Yes, by all means. I doubt we have enough to feed that many soldiers, but I'm sure we could put something together for the officers," Mary informs.

"That'll be fine," Connor confirms.

"Connor I need to lie back down. I'm getting dizzy," Rainah calls.

"Of course," he runs back to her bedside and helps her lay down.

"I'll go fetch that tea and liniment," Cassandra mentions as she slips out.

"Rainah, I..." Connor begins.

"Go and meet them. I know Soba will be glad to see you."

"Thank you, my love," Connor kisses her gently on the forehead and virtually runs down the stairs. Although he, too, has some wounds that are still healing, the adrenaline rush of seeing an old friend that brings the best help in the world with him lightens his heart, step, and mood. He breaks into a run hampered by a slight limp sustained in their escape from the Dragon. It neither slows him down nor dampens his joy.

Commander Soba sees what appears to be a dwarf running toward him. Never expecting to find his childhood friend alive, he breaks ranks after handing command to a subordinate and runs closing the distance between them. Nearing one another, they slow down enough to bump chests like they used to do as children. They break out into a deep belly laugh over their instinctual greeting and hug each other while tears of pure joy roll down their faces.

"Connor, you stiff necked mule! I never thought I'd see you again."

"Soba, you trouble maker! I never thought you'd be part of the Brigade. I'm proud of you!" Connor exclaims while patting him on the back in a congratulatory manner.

"I'm thankful to find you. Is Rainah with you?"

"Yes, she's still recovering from a torturous ordeal, but she'll be all right."

"Thank the Builders!"

"How many are you in numbers?" Connor questions getting straight to business. Being outside and smelling the foul air brings him quickly back to the realization that time is a luxury none of them have.

"We're about 150,000 strong. General Rasmussen has taken the larger contingent of 350,000 troops to the Plains of Galeed. What few humans are left are with him and Prince Robert. We understand you have women warriors here."

"Yes, about 5,000 are left after our first encounter with the

Dragon's forces. We lost many, but they're fierce fighters. If they weren't so tall, they'd make a Dwarf army proud," Connor explains with a sly grin forming on his face.

"Have you received any word about the Army of Light?"

"Only that Prince Javan has gone after them. We have no knowledge of when they'll arrive, but I do know that Prince Javan is a man who refuses to fail."

"When... Don't you mean if?" Soba submits for consideration.

"I refuse to give in to doubt, so yes, my friend I choose to use the word when. Prince Javan may be human, but he'd have made a fine Dwarf."

"Where can my men set up camp?" Soba asks.

"There in the valley. Don't approach the trees north of the valley there are still active booby traps amongst them that we made in preparation for the Dragon's first attack."

"Sound advice."

"Do you think the Dragon's army will come this far, or stay on the plains?" Connor asks.

"I'm told by our scribe, that the council made us bring, that all will remain contained on the plains. They also say that the General's group will take the heaviest casualties and we'll be there to provide support and replacements when the time is right."

"How do we know when the time is right?" Connor asks. Soba holds up his right finger silencing Connor so he can give instruction to his approaching troops.

"Make camp in the valley below and don't venture into the northern forests they've been booby trapped." The troops nod their head and in an orderly fashion begin making camp. "To answer your question, our signal to move out will be when we hear the Horns or Hell sound."

Connor swallows hard. Legend states that the Horns of Hell will make a sound so loud that it will travel around the world itself before ceasing. He shakes off the impending dread to take advantage of this brief moment to spend time with his best friend. He asks Mary to bring them a pint of ale and a leg of lamb. It's a delicacy that is not easily come by these days, but the occasion warrants such an extravagance. Soba's officers are also provided pints, but the lamb is intended for Soba only due to the meager rations available.

"I'm honored by your offering of meat, but if there is not enough for my officers then I must abstain," Soba informs.

"I understand," Mary responds withdrawing the offer.

The two friends spend the rest of the night regaling one another with tales of their adventures. Each story becomes more outlandish with each pint of ale downed. It's not until they can't sit up straight in their chairs that they realize they must call it a night.

It's late at night and having laughed yet once more over childhood days, they settle down into a more somber mood. They look into each other's eyes. Neither of them knows what the next few days will hold, but they will face it together. They embrace each other as brothers and part ways to get some sleep. Connor quietly sneaks into his bed and snuggles up beside Rainah. She roles over grunting slightly and kisses him.

"I thought you'd be asleep by now," Connor whispers.

"I was too busy listening to you and Soba laugh like children."

"We didn't mean to keep you up."

"On the contrary, the laughter was very cathartic. With everything we've been through its good to remember what it is we're fighting for. My heart is lighter than it's been in a long while."

"I guess the old saying is true, a merry heart does good like a medicine," Connor reminds noticing that his strength has returned to him. Rainah manages a smile.

"Good night, my beloved," Rainah whispers.

"Good night," Connor whispers back as he carefully embraces

her. She drifts off into a peaceful and sweet slumber.

***

Deep inside the dwarf domain, Marisa is tossing and turning in her bed. Her arms are flailing about, and she pushes Leopold on the floor. After he hits the ground with a thud, Marisa sits up screaming their daughter's name, "Rainah!"

"Marisa! Wake up!" Leopold pleads desperately trying to get her to wake up.

Marisa's green eyes pop open. Her white streaked long brown hair is tussled like a bird's nest, and her arms are trembling violently. Leopold returns to their bed and attempts to console her by taking hold of one of her hands. She looks over at her husband and begins to sob upon his shoulder. He pats her gently on the back.

"My darling wife, you mustn't allow yourself to be so tormented."

"I'm so scared. The earth has shaken violently for days, and my baby is out there amid that evil. We should be there to protect her."

"Over 500,000 of our troops are out there filled with our friends' sons and daughters. Don't you think they, too, worry? We are not alone, and neither is our daughter."

"Why is our generation the ones who must endure the Apocalypse?"

"Marisa, I don't disagree that these are treacherous times, but there is a hope on the other side of this terrible time. We must stay the course so that the Dragon will be defeated and we can live free without fear of evil for thousands of generations to come."

"I just wish it could all be over," Marisa explains. Leopold gently wipes away her tears.

"It will be very soon. Come on, let's go back to sleep. We, too, have much to do here. Rainah will be okay. I promise."

"You've never broken a promise to me," she reminds.

"That's how confident I am. We have a smart girl who is a highly skilled fighter. She knows how to survive."

"You know I never approved of you teaching her to fight, but I'm very thankful that you didn't pay me any mind on that point. Why did you teach her?"

"Because being the historian of our people, I was privy to documents that most are never taught. When you gave birth to a daughter, and I saw that fiery red head of hers and heard the name you had chosen for her, I knew that her path would be different than any other daughter born to our people."

"You never told me that."

"No, because I didn't think you or anyone would have believed me. I didn't want to believe it myself, but I couldn't ignore it either. I wanted to give her every chance and allow our people the beauty of life without the threat of disaster for as long as I could. Now, you need to get some sleep. We must keep up our strength."

"Good night, husband," Marisa bids.

She and her husband fall back asleep. This time her sleep is less fearful, and she is encouraged that there is a hope waiting on the other side of this present darkness. She vows under her breath to acknowledge his wisdom going forward as he has a unique perspective.

CHAPTER 6

Now that the fury of the storm has abated, Prince Horeb and his men proceed unhindered through the heart of this deep and evil forest. The Dragon's summons, calling all evil entities unto himself, freed the Wilderness of Desolation from this well earned moniker making it as safe as any other forest in the world. The only exception is the creature living in the swamp. The swamp is on the northern most border of the wilderness with the Canyon of Woes only a day's journey beyond.

Prince Horeb places Andrew in the lead since he has been this way before. The torches are no longer necessary because the lightning has retreated to the cloud tops lighting them up from behind casting a green iridescent glow on the forest below. They can also see a break in the clouds beyond the forest in the distance. Caution, however, is still required to traverse the last few miles of this wilderness as evil isn't the only treachery in the forest. These woods are filled with quicksand, wild beasts, and poisonous plants.

Andrew manages to keep them on the safest path, but it's narrow and slow going. They must keep the horses calm as any vibration could awaken the creature that waits patiently underground for its prey to fall into its trap. Andrew slows the men to a stop while he surveys the myriad of paths that lay before them. He signals to them to bring their ranks close, to come across in groups of three, and to silence any conversation. The horses neigh nervously, Andrew is the first to reassure his beloved Marzipan while Quimby holds tight to Andrew. As the leader of his small party of dwarfs, it's his duty to go first.

"Easy girl, we'll be through this in a moment," Andrew encourages. Once the horse calms down, he goads her forward ever so slowly taking great care that each step is as solid as it appears. The others follow behind in turn with Prince Horeb bringing up the rear.

After an hour of careful travel, they finally reach the other side of the swamp. Only three left to cross over. Two of the mounts support double riders, one human, and one dwarf. As they slowly make their way across, a loose goatskin filled with water falls from the horse's saddle. It drops with a thud to the ground. Everyone freezes in their tracks while the others waiting on the other side hold their breath knowing that the creature will show itself at any moment.

Suddenly, a tentacle erupts forth from the ground, then

another, and another flailing about in all directions until one of them wraps around Rastus' waist yanking him from the horse. Sebastian tries to grab his foot, but the creature is too fast for them. Rastus cries for help while the others in their party continue to dodge the remaining tentacles. Sebastian tries his sword, but it just bounces off the creature's outer skin.

"Hurry and come across before it takes you too!" Andrew yells waving his hand in the air. They spur their horses on save Horeb. He waits to see if they can save Rastus before leaving him behind while fending off a tentacle of his own. Instead of his sword, he uses a dagger to stab the creature's extremities which seems to be giving it pause before striking again.

"My prince! What are you doing? Hurry!" Sebastian urges.

"I'll not leave anyone behind to be eaten by this foul creature," Horeb responds. In this moment, his character and honor is proven to the dwarfs in their company. They have never heard of a human that was willing to risk their life for that of a dwarf.

In the meantime, Quimby grabs his ax from Andrew's saddle and waits for the creature to open its mouth to gorge itself on its catch. At that precise moment, he lets the ax fly guided by expert hands, a keen eye, and a deadly aim producing the same precision that a crossbow would afford a hunter. The ax, much heavier and sharper than the human swords, strikes its mark killing the beast.

In gasping agony and chaotic movements, the creature drops Rastus who lands in a deep quagmire of thick mud. The more he struggles to get back to Horeb, the deeper he sinks. Horeb jumps down off his horse retrieving a rope. He ties a loop in it big enough for the dwarf and ties the other end around his waist. He then tosses the rope to Rastus.

"Take the rope, put your arms through it, and then I'll pull you out!" Horeb orders.

"Okay," Rastus responds but struggles with the rope. He finally succeeds, and Horeb slowly pulls him through the mud trying to keep his head from sinking into the quagmire.

"You're heavier than you look," Horeb comments while readjusting his feet to get a better stance and continues to pull him toward the safety of the path.

"You can do it!" Oleg yells out like a cheerleader while Rastus hits a pocket of slimy water and starts to sink deeper. He struggles to breathe as he doesn't know how to swim.

"Oh, no you don't, you're not going to get out of this quest that easy," Horeb informs as he gets down on his hands and knees in the slippery mud lining the grassy path where his horse remains. He reaches out plunging his hand into the murky water grasping for the dwarf and barely manages to take hold of his collar with his fingers and pulls him up. Cheers erupt from the men on the other side. Horeb drags Rastus across the muddy ground to the grassy path. He tries to help by wiping off some of the mud that is caked upon his face, but there's too much of it to make much difference and his black beard, saturated by the mud, is turning a mucky brown color.

"Is he alright?" Quimby asks to be sure.

"I'm capable of cleaning myself off," Rastus protests against Horeb's assistance.

"He's okay," Horeb announces to the anxious crowd of men.

Horeb hoists Rastus up on his horse and walks the remainder of the way to the opposite side where solid ground is plentiful. Oleg immediately tries to see if Rastus has sustained any injuries, but has to stand on his tip toes to see. Rastus shoos him away. He's covered in mud from head to toe but is in one piece save his nerves and pride.

"We need to keep moving," Andrew informs.

"I think we're all in need of a good night's sleep," Horeb responds, but is not oblivious to the nervousness of his otherwise brave young knight.

"Not here, if we go just one more hour and reach the other side of the glen, we'll be far enough away from the swamp to be safe."

"Safety is a luxury, but we shouldn't invite danger," Rastus adds as he wipes away a cake of mud from his brow. The whites of his eyes glow like pearls amid the mud still on his face. Rastus' comment is enough to convince the Prince to move forward and make camp elsewhere. They move forward for another hour before making camp.

"Allow us to stay here and enjoy the comfort of the trees tonight. When we reach the plains tomorrow, there is nothing but rattle snakes, scorpions, and sand under the hot sun. Even the curse that the Dragon called forth can't overshadow the scorching sun over the Canyon of Woes," Andrew requests indicating that they should be safe.

"Then I shall stand watch over you this night so you can get some well deserved rest," Prince Horeb advises.

"Sire, there's not much left, but wild beasts at this point and our fire should keep them away for the night," Andrew suggests. His prior nervousness is no longer present in his mannerisms.

"Your mind is too stuck in the past, Andrew. Do you forget why we are here?" Horeb pauses. Andrew shakes his head no. Horeb then turns his attention to the group and continues, "I doubt that the Dragon would leave his progeny unguarded. I shall take watch."

"You are our prince, and it is I who should take watch,"

Andrew announces wanting to redeem his prior weakness before his sovereign.

"You are very brave, and I have heard of no one willing to go to the Wilderness of Desolation twice, but you're not experienced. I have little to offer anyone since the Dragon has invaded our land, but I can offer you comfort. It'll probably be the last any of us will see in a long time, I'll not be deprived of my right to offer it to my warriors."

The group capitulates to Horeb's orders and makes camp. Sebastian and Oleg build a good size fire which will keep them safe from wolves and the like. Their time to complete their mission grows short, but in the coming days and hours, stealth can't be compromised for any reason. They're too few in number to risk premature discovery, but the denseness of the forest will conceal even their fire this night. Without further argument, the men settle into a solid sleep resting in the knowledge that Horeb will keep them safe throughout the night.

CHAPTER 7

In the village of Tierney, Rachel walks along the beach contemplating their future which at the moment appears bleak at best. She watches as the elders and the young patch the damage done by the storms to the only shelter left to them. Gorham, Jonathan's little brother, and Mark are playing fetch with Snootzer amid the ruins of homes that used to be. She then sees Jonathan and Courtney strolling arm in arm toward the valley with baskets probably to forage for berries. They should just be starting to ripen if the storm didn't pluck them from their briars. Other villagers forage through the dirt where gardens used to be looking for forgotten potatoes and shuffle their feet in the surf for muscles. After taking in the entire goings on, Rachel's gaze returns to that of Jonathan and Courtney.

Laban comes up beside her and gently places his hand upon her shoulder. At first, she remains fixated on the sight of her friends and the lighthearted nature of the moment that they're enjoying. Her heart yearns to feel that again for even a few seconds, but it seems so far off right now. Laban is patient allowing her to acknowledge him in her own good time rather than interrupt her contemplation.

"Good morning papa," Rachel acknowledges then continues with an inquiry. "Taking a break from your supervisory duties?" Rachel asks after the objects of her gaze disappear into the valley.

"No, I just noticed you walking alone along the beach. Your countenance saddens me. The fierceness of the storm has finally subsided, and we can finally see the occasional sunbeam breaking through the clouds over the sea. I would think that deserves a smile at least."

"What would be the point? Today is just another stop between now and oblivion," she admits in her hopelessness.

"What's gotten into you?" He asks, with both offense and anger.

"Excuse me?" she questions, wondering if she is the only one who sees the signs that are all around them.

"I didn't stutter. In times like these, you take pleasure and rest when it presents itself. You must allow yourself to be light hearted and thankful for the gift of the moment."

"But these are the last days of this world," she defends.

"Of this world as we know it? Yes, but that's not what's really bothering you. Is it?" Laban asks with that penetrating fatherly wisdom of his. He realizes what's really going on with her then continues to drill down until she admits it to herself. "You're still grieving the loss of your husband and wondering if he, too, has become a pawn of the Dragon."

"Yes, Papa, again you see through everything. I miss Seth so very much, and to think that he's become like Hannah not knowing me or remembering our love. It makes me so angry that neither of them is able to rest from this madness. I'm filled with such grief and rage I can barely contain it without lashing out at everyone and everything. Then I see Mark, and I'm reminded of Seth's sacrifice which was for the greater good, but it leaves me empty. Clairese mentioned nothing about this terrible pain that doesn't go away! Where was her prophetic vision then papa?"

"But she did mention it. She said it would get really bad before things would turn around and that you had to hang on to your hope so that despair didn't overtake you like it is right now."

"Hope, Papa? What hope is there? The dwarfs and what remains of our warriors are marching to the final battle. In just a few days, everything we have, including our future, will belong to our enemy."

"I don't think your giving the Most High enough credit. He has extended to us mercy, wisdom, and grace. You helped this village survive in very difficult times. That wisdom could have only come from him."

"Mercy, you call this mercy? Have you looked at your scars papa? Have you looked at the ruins of our village and the condition of our people? Where is God's mercy in this? Tell me, Papa, if you can."

"I'm alive, as is many whom you healed over this past winter. War is never easy, but life goes on. I clearly don't have all the answers you seek, but you must let go of this rage for your own sake."

"I do find moments of escape from the pain briefly, but they don't last long. Then when I see Courtney and Jonathan together, I'm reminded of all that I've lost. Then the rage comes back because I yearn to love again and I know that I won't. Don't misunderstand me, papa, I'm happy for them but sad for myself at the same time. I've lost more than I can ever replace."

"Replace? Do you think that's what I've done with your mother or your sister?" Laban's offense is blatantly unrestrained. His face turns red with anger at his daughter's accusation.

"No, of course not…" Rachel stammers trying to take back her statement. She is surprised by her father's reaction of anger rather than his usual compassion.

"I could never replace your mother or your sister nor would I try, but it doesn't stop me from enjoying special moments with those I still have. This life gives and takes away, and gives back again. Don't be so focused on what was taken, that you fail to see what awaits to be given."

"What is there to be given? The land lies in shambles, the sea has little left to sustain us, and our people are gaunt and weak. I'm spent and poured out. I've nothing left to give, and my future is non-existent."

"Stop feeling sorry for yourself!" Laban snaps. "Do you think for one moment that your loss and pain is greater than anyone else in our village?"

"No! Of course, not! I would never think that."

"Then stop acting like it. You are the Chief's daughter. If you can't find something to bring hope to our people, then they'll become despondent also and give up. We can't afford to give up hope on what awaits us on the other side."

"You heard Prince Robert and the Dwarf General. They're massing at the Plains of Galeed to face off against the Dragon in the final battle which doesn't look like we'll win. How can you even suggest a moment of happiness amid these last days?"

"I didn't say happiness or joy. I said, hope. If anything should happen to me, you'll be chief of these people. Hope will lead them to life, without it we lead them to their deaths.

Sometimes you must act in a particular manner whether or not you feel it's sincere because their lives depend upon it. We are responsible for them. We must see them through to the hope that awaits us on the other side of this darkness. And there is something wonderful waiting on the other side. Open your eyes and look toward the future, a future of peace, unity, and one without evil stalking your every move!" Laban completes his passionate speech and finally begins to see a change in his daughter's countenance.

"I never thought of it that way," Rachel admits as her defeatist attitude begins to subside.

"Then perhaps you should start."

"How?"

"Smiling would be an excellent beginning. You know the smile I mean, the one that makes your nose scrunch up like a bunny rabbit."

His words cause her to remember a warm moment from her childhood and her face simply smiles a grand smile without coaxing or pretense. She looks away blushing, surprised that it was so simple.

"Now that's my girl," Laban acknowledges with fatherly pride.

"Papa," she addresses still blushing. She slowly turns to look into her father's blue eyes. They still have that sprite like sparkle that Hannah inherited. "How do you always know what to say?"

"I don't...I just keep trying until I get it right."

Rachel hugs him burying her head upon his shoulder. When she opens her eyes, she notices that the water that was previously cascading gently atop their feet has receded. She pushes him away to take an inventory of their surroundings. He starts to chastise her but stops short as he also becomes aware that something is very wrong. He quickly gazes upon the horizon and sees the sea pulling back like a blanket off a bed.

"We must hurry! Help me get everyone to the road. That may provide us enough altitude to escape it."

"Escape what?" Rachel inquires never having seen such a phenomenon before.

"A tidal wave! Hurry, we haven't much time!"

Rachel runs to the village bell and begins ringing it with all her strength while Laban shouts out instructions to the village.

"Everyone to the road! Now! Children come quickly!"

Rachel joins her father in getting the lagging children to hasten their steps. Jonathan and Courtney run back to the village edge having heard the alarm bell. They see everyone running toward the road although they don't understand why. They instinctively follow their neighbors to the top of the road. While shooing some children along, Rachel notices Agatha is having trouble with Samuel. He's still unsteady not having become accustom to his blindness. She runs to her father-in-law and braces his left side.

"Father," she whispers in his ear. "We must hurry. A tidal wave is coming."

The moment she utters those words a horrific thunderous noise begins to rise in the distance. She glances back for a moment, and she can see a wall of water rising up from the ocean. It hurdles towards them at incredible speed. The women hurry nearly dragging Samuel's feet. His ears pick up the sound of danger, and he tries to hurry. He stubs his toe but keeps going knowing that his toe will hurt a lot less than the wall of water will.

"Hurry!" Laban yells.

Jonathan sees that Rachel and Agatha are doing their best, but aren't going to make it to safety in time. He runs towards them telling them to run, and he puts Samuel over his strong shoulders and runs the rest of the way back to the trees. The moment he reaches the road where the village has taken shelter among the large trees on the opposite side, the others help Jonathan get Samuel secure. Jonathan quickly finds himself a tree to hang on to near Samuel and holds fast so as not to be swept away.

The wave crashes through the rocky shore and covers the entire area of where their village sits with the last tips of this mighty wave licking the village side of the frontier road. It cuts large gullies in the road leading to the village. When it recedes back into the ocean, it takes every stone and wood beam with it wiping away any evidence that a village ever existed. The caves where they previously took refuge and contained their residual food stores remain submerged as the waters settle a hundred yards into what was the village proper.

Everyone is in shock staring in silence at the seashore that was wiped clean in a matter of seconds. Laban performs a head count. He counts 89 souls and one dog expelling a sigh of relief that all are present. He looks over at Rachel and nods confirming that all have made it to safety. She, too, is relieved, but now they have bigger problems, where to find shelter and food for their numbers.

"Laban, what are we to do?" Agatha asks aloud stating what the others are still too stunned to utter.

"My chief," Jonathan interrupts. "If I may make a suggestion, a half day's journey south is the crossroads where there are several Inns and taverns. We passed them on the way here, and they were abandoned, but intact. They should provide temporary shelter and some food until we can find a more permanent solution."

"Excellent idea Jonathan, lead the way."

They follow quietly behind Jonathan as he leads his village with nothing but the clothes on their back to what he hopes are buildings where they can take refuge. Rachel appears stoic but manages an outward confidence reassuring their frightened friends and family that all will be okay. Unbeknown to Rachel or Laban, Mark overheard their previous conversation. As Redeemer, he is granted one favor from the Most High and has reasoned in his heart what that favor will be.

CHAPTER 8

The dwarfs and remaining male human warriors gather on the Plains of Galeed under the command of General Rasmussen and Prince Robert. They begin digging trenches near the towering pines that grow along its perimeter to fortify their position. The plains cover an area two miles long and a mile wide. The ground is covered in knee high crimson colored grass. Legend states that the grass testifies to all the blood that was spilt there over countless centuries back to the beginning of their world. Animals don't graze upon it, and nothing but the grass will grow there. Even insects are not found on this stretch of land. It's a cursed place bearing witness to the treachery of hatred and the pursuit of power.

General Rasmussen and Prince Robert survey the progress of their troops along with their officers. Once the battle begins, the only way to leave the field will be in death or victory. Robert looks across to the opposite side where the enemy will soon gather. Behind where the enemy will gather is the eastern most end of the

Sentinel Mountain range with its craggy walls of granite jutting up from the ground below like teeth in the mouth of a shark. In contrast, gently rolling hills mark the horizon on the southeastern side of the plains.

"The Dragon will have an advantage. The elevation is much higher above the battlefield than our position," Rasmussen comments aloud.

Prince Robert looks at the general wondering if he read his thoughts. He glances briefly over at Joss, his second in command, with a knowing look silently soliciting suggestions. At first, Joss replies with a blank look as both commanders begin to scrutinize more closely their side of the battlefield.

"Sire, what about the tree tops?" Joss submits for consideration.

"Yes, we could make use of some of these trees. They're strong enough to support a man's weight. We could climb up into the branches for a better view," Robert adds.

"That's part of a good idea. It would take a great deal of strength and time to climb up. If we hammer spikes into its trunk, we can climb up and down it more quickly," Rasmussen suggests.

"That's good. Once up in the tree, the branches are more than sufficient to support more than one person if needed. We should be able to get a really good look at the battle's progression,"

Robert states in agreement.

"There certainly are enough of them so that we can have more than one lookout tower. The branches are lush enough to provide some protection from enemy attack," Rasmussen adds.

"Joss, see to it that we have at least four trees for this purpose spaced at intervals along our side of the battlefield."

"Yes, Sire," Joss responds and immediately grabs some men to get to work on it. Now that he has been given his assignment, Mordecai, who has become Robert's third in command, stands close by to execute any additional orders Prince Robert may give.

"General, the only drawback I see is that it won't be easy to communicate," Angus, the general's second in Soba's absence, adds. Angus is short even for a dwarf, but his steely eyes and fiery red hair and beard containing the medals he's earned intertwined in several braids demonstrates that there is more to him than meets the eye and should not be underestimated.

"That's true, but we can get around that by using signal flags. We're already going to use them to deal with the width of the battleground," the General informs.

"Excellent idea, but we'll need a different color for our communication, so we don't accidentally order our troops to the wrong place by accident," Robert adds.

"Agreed…Angus, take care of that for me."

"Yes, General, right away. I'll have something for you within the hour."

As they continue to survey the area, Robert catches a glimpse of something odd and out of place on the other side of the field. He's never seen the likes of it before. He pulls out his spyglass and peers through it. He sees a purple cloud which seems to pulsate and keep pace with them moving slowly back and forth directly opposite them.

"What on earth is that?" Robert asks aloud pointing in the direction of his observation. Rasmussen squints trying to make it out then takes out his own spyglass and looks over to where Robert is pointing and studies it a moment.

"I don't have a clue," he responds.

"Its name is Desolation," Mordecai interjects. He recognizes the creature without the scrutiny of a spyglass.

"Desolation? How do you know that?" Robert inquires further.

"It's the demonic creature that abides in the Wilderness, and where the Wilderness of Desolation got its name. It's a sinister demon that preys upon fear. It's drawn here just like the vultures and the jackals are, but where they feed on the dead it feeds upon your fear while you're still alive. The Chronicles of Destiny states that it eviscerates its victims from the inside out killing them while consuming their fear and terror. With each kill, it'll become stronger and larger."

"Aren't you full of good news?" Robert states sarcastically.

"Look it disappeared," Rasmussen interrupts.

"It'll be back. Trust me when I say that if you don't control your fear, it'll take you out in a matter seconds then move on to the next victim," Mordecai somberly explains.

"How do we defend against it? Once the battle starts it's only natural to be afraid," Prince Robert asks.

"True, but your duty and your training control that fear allowing it to feed your strength without paralyzing you. Anyone who doesn't have that control will die and quite possibly cause the deaths of others around them. Anyone who witnesses a kill like that is not likely to maintain their courage for long."

"The men have been through so much already. How do you think they'll cope with this new weapon?"

"I think they'll be okay so long as you keep them focused on a task. That way they won't have any time to let their mind wander," Mordecai suggests.

"How do you know so much about this?" Robert asks as he

doesn't recall anything from his own training about the creature.

"I'd like to know also as this knowledge has never been given to the dwarfs either," Rasmussen requests.

"I'm a prophet, or I used to be. Not much use for my kind in these last days, but to answer your question; rumors about what that young knight, Andrew, the nephew of your former Commander Mathias, saw traveled fast amongst the peasantry. It's said he didn't say much about his experience except through night terrors. He didn't see the attack on the other knights, but his description of what was left of them that covered their entire company matches what the ancient texts described in vivid detail."

"I wish I hadn't asked," Robert mutters under his breath.

"It's important to know what we're facing. Otherwise, how can you protect against it?" Mordecai submits for consideration.

"He has a point," Rasmussen adds.

"Other than Desolation over there, what can we expect?" Robert asks.

"General, I would think your people would know more than ours," Mordecai comments.

"We probably do, but we didn't know about that which makes me wonder how many other things may come up that we're unprepared for."

"I think it's best that we share information about what else we'll be facing before the enemy arrives," Prince Robert suggests.

"Do you have any other tidbits to add before I begin?" the General inquires.

"Only what the ancient texts say that the first wave of the last battle will be a battle against ourselves, but I have no idea what that means," Mordecai responds to the General.

"It appears that the General knows what that means. Don't you?" Robert asks, surmising that the General has knowledge about this by the green color that just entered his face.

"Yes, I know what it means. The first warriors the enemy will send against us will be the beings of Fire and Ash. These will consist of your own kin who perished in the initial invasion and will include all the dwarf dead from the time we tricked the Dragon to return to the abyss until now. Unlike the first raising of the undead who were human warriors, the second raising of the dead will include everyone over the age of twelve."

The General's information causes the color to drain from Robert's face. He has fought in many battles, but only against other warriors. His father, King Ophir, had taught him to show the enemy no quarter regardless of age or sex. Robert always thought that approach was too harsh, but for this battle, that tactic may finally be appropriate.

"What possible use could children be to the Dragon?" Robert asks.

"It'll cause us to hesitate," Mordecai surmises.

"Yes, you'll be overcome by pity. What they won't realize is that the only thing remaining is their image. Everything else is guided by the Dragon's will," Rasmussen clarifies.

The other men overhear the conversation as there is no privacy on the plains and begin to speak in hushed whispers amongst themselves. Fear begins to move through the camp. The General and Robert recognize that they need to stop rampant rumors in their tracks or this battle will be shorter than they anticipate. They quickly call the troops to order so that they can prepare them for what lies ahead.

"Dwarfs and humans…Listen to me!" General Rasmussen begins. "As you may have overheard, our first encounter with the enemy will be with the beings of Fire and Ash. These will appear to you to be those that you once loved, but know this, that is all they have in common with them. They will try every means to distract you from attacking so that they can kill you. Once the battle starts, you'll fight until you can no longer fight. There is no next battle. This battle will be the last one.'

"You must resolve in your spirit now to remain steadfast to the purpose of destroying the enemy no matter what form it takes so that you'll not be moved whatever comes against you. Hesitation to strike because your opponent seems familiar will only get you killed. You must be braver than you've ever been before. You must not allow the beings of Fire and Ash to invoke your memories or your emotions. They're no longer your loved ones. You can't give quarter to them. Mercy has no place on this battlefield. Legend states that this will only last four days once it begins. You'll not rest, you'll not eat, if you stop to quench your thirst, you may not survive your first swallow."

The troops look at him, and their countenance falls to one of horror and shock. Although Prince Robert feels the same as these men and dwarfs, they can't enter battle in this frame of mind, or it will be like lambs to the slaughter.

"We fight for our very survival and for those we love. We can do nothing for those that have preceded us in death, and allowing yourselves to be killed will not help them or bring them back. You must fight for those currently living," Prince Robert adds.

"That's right!" Mordecai interrupts. "On the last day, the Redeemer will show himself and free our kin both living and dead from the curse of the Dragon! We must prevail until that time at any cost so that our surviving kin will continue to live and that those that we have lost can be rescued from their ghastly existence. We fight! We live! We fight! They live!" He shouts.

"We fight! We Live! We fight! They live!" the troops chant

back. The chant continues for a few more moments. Prince Robert notices that the General wants to address the men again. He holds up his hand to silence them.

"We are losing the sunlight. We need to finish the trenches to provide a defensible position to keep the enemy here. Nothing gets through our line. When the enemy sounds their mighty horns, it will summon our support and the next wave of our warriors will come to us. Until then we must hold this ground," General Rasmussen orders, and then shouts, "Victory or death!"

"Victory or death!" the troops respond three more times then they busy themselves with preparations for battle.

***

Back at the palace, the Dragon is waiting for word of where the enemy is before he releases his army of Fire and Ash. Shaman enters the Dragon's presence with the confirmation that the enemy has gathered.

"Master, we have confirmed reports that the humans and dwarfs are massing on the Plains of Galeed."

"How many dwarfs have been counted so far?"

"At least 8 legions have been counted, but there are probably more. They outnumber the humans 4 to 1."

"How poetic that we shall finish where we started in our

struggle against the Most High. His poor choice in allies has led him to this end. It's no wonder he cowers in the caves of Mt. Tiras entrusting his least loyal and weakest creatures to defend his honor. Victory is surely ours."

"I agree, master. The humans haven't been loyal to him. It's no wonder that he sits back and watches from a distance. I doubt that he even sent the Redeemer. We will be victorious," Shaman adds.

"Yes, well, I have plans for the humans and dwarfs. Those that aren't killed by the sword will leave the battle through the bellies of my offspring."

"Yes, Master, and according to my calculations from the information you provided me, the first eggs should be hatching in just a few days. After they arrive, it'll be easy to conquer the rest of this world and send the Most High packing. Even if the humans were successful in obtaining the help of the Army of Light, they'll be no match for your children."

"My plan is working out brilliantly," Lucius comments aloud to himself. He smiles an insidious grin then gives his first orders. "Send out the troops of Fire and Ash first. Tell them to find their kin and kill them before engaging random targets."

"As you wish," Shaman acknowledges, bows, and turns to leave.

"Wait. Give those orders to Captain Morbius and have them leave immediately. You are to prepare the princess for travel. I want her to watch the destruction of her people as she is unable to release the power of the amulet."

"But Master you know I've not been successful in breaking its power. It's too dangerous to take her to the battlefield. She may be lying about not knowing how to use it," Shaman cautions.

"Are you not a purveyor of dark magic?"

"Yes, Master, I'm well schooled in the arts, but I don't have the power to undo Dwarf magic. I've tried more times than I can count. I don't think anyone can undo the spell."

Lucius is shocked at Shaman's confession. He takes his front claw extending it out as light glints off its mirrored surface and knocks the half troll, half human on his back. He then pins him underneath his front foot like a cat would pin a field mouse in its claws.

"I didn't mean to anger you, Master. Have mercy on me," Shaman pleads like the squirmy rat he is.

"Do as I say. If you can't find a way to undo the spell, then find a way to keep her from using the incantation. I don't believe she knows it or she would have already used it."

"I'm not convinced of her ignorance," Shaman restates his

concern.

"Either way, I'll not deprive myself of a single moment's pleasure in my victory. She will suffer the loss of her people and watch them bleed, burn, and die," Lucius snorts the words into his face then lets him up. After he releases him, Sharman falls prostrate before his master.

"I implore you to leave her behind. The magic of the amulet is too strong to risk it should I fail."

"Are you still challenging my orders?"

"No, Sire. I only wish to serve you and help make your victory a success."

"Then stop questioning me. Bring her and refocus your energies on breaking her since you can't break the spell over the amulet."

"But Sire, she's stronger than she appears. She has a habit of lying to you. If she gains control of your armies, it would be disastrous."

"So what if she does," Lucius counters shoving Shaman under his claws again pushing his face against the dusty floor. "The beings of Fire and Ash are just pawns, and the amulet will have no affect on my children or the Trolls. They'll finish the fight," Lucius informs.

"Of course, Sire."

"Now go and carry out my orders."

"As you wish my master, I shall do as you command," Shaman capitulates even though he knows he'll not succeed. Lucius lets him up, and he immediately prostrates himself again briefly in obedience to his king to warily dispatch his orders.

"Now!" Lucius orders having grown impatient with this minion's hesitation.

"Yes, right away!" Shaman exclaims rising to his feet. "I'll have them place a gag over her mouth to keep her silent."

"No gag."

Shaman doesn't make an effort to counter his master's reckless orders and makes a hasty retreat. He soon enters Ophir's quarters where Princess Sabrina is being kept. He scowls at her studying her carefully. He feels that his master is being over confident, but he has no choice than to obey him. Regardless of his personal opinions, he has no desire to risk the fate of his predecessor, Felix.

"Unlock the cell and shackle her hands and feet. Our master wants her taken to the Plains of Galeed to witness his victory. Be sure that poles are erected on the bluff so we can secure her and she can watch her people perish."

The guards immediately obey. Sabrina casts a look of disgust at Shaman, but she doesn't resist. She hopes that she can find a window of opportunity and perhaps remember the magical words given her by Rainah. The cell door clanks and screeches as the troll guards open it. Shackles are placed upon her ankles and wrists. They are weighed down with heavy iron chains, and she is secured to a troll for the journey.

Shaman grabs a potion of subjugation and anoints her head with it. The potion simply boils off her skin vaporizing into the air. Now he's even more concerned with bringing her with them. He knows that there are two incantations; one that will subdue his master, a second that will take control of his armies. She has played dumb before, and he's hesitant to trust her supposed ignorance.

"I've not had a meal or water today," she informs.

"The time for pleasantry is over. You'll get what you need to keep you alive, but nothing more." Shaman picks up a nearby basin of water and tosses it on her.

She licks the droplets left upon her skin to relieve the dryness of her mouth, but her thirst remains unquenched. Her mind reflects back upon her nightmares. At this point, she feels more numb than afraid. She knows from the prophecies she read in the ancient texts when her and Mary stood up until dawn looking for answers, that the daughter of the Returned One will perish. She is determined, however, not to perish alone.

CHAPTER 9

Sasha and Tubal, along with 500 warriors from their tribe, set out on foot for Castle Togarmah. The air still stinks of rotten eggs, but they continue on in hopes of joining the women warriors they know reside there. Two of the wagons pulled by a couple of mules contain about 3,000 dragon scale shields. These will provide them protection from Lucius' lethal offspring. The third wagon is reserved for Beverly, Beth, and the two infants. It's paramount that they get the young prince to safety before the final battle commences. They arrive at the crossroads about noontime where the southern path will lead the quartet past Mt. Tiras and beyond to their destination, the Port of Salt. It'll take them a couple days to reach the port.

The siblings pause to give a proper farewell to their mother. They each kiss their mother's cheek in order of their birth. She, in turn, takes hold of their faces cradling them in her hands. She stops before kissing their foreheads to gaze with motherly gratification and concern into their eyes. She conveys through her thoughtful gaze what words are incapable of. Beverly's face beams with pride in her children's demonstration of bravery having put her fear away. She releases each one with a special blessing. After receiving her blessing, Sasha takes an extra moment to whisper some instructions to her mother in hopes that it'll keep her safe in these last days.

After saying their good-byes, Beverly turns the team of mules toward their destination and drives them forward. Sasha and Tubal wave farewell following her with their eyes until they can no longer see their mother while the warriors continue on their path. A tear falls down Sasha's face as her mother's image disappears below the horizon. Tubal is also concerned about their mother's safety, but he's not moved to the level of sorrow that his sister appears to be experiencing. This usually means that she has withheld some critical piece of information about her visions from him.

"Out with it," Tubal demands.

"Out with what?" Sasha questions feigning ignorance as she wipes away a fresh tear cascading down her face.

"You know what. We will see our mother again, right?" Tubal inquires.

"She'll be fine, and yes, brother, you will see her again,"

Sasha answers. At first, Tubal is satisfied by her response, but then realizes her careful choice of words.

"I will see her…" Tubal grabs his sister by her shoulders and looks her square in the eye. "You believe you're going to die!"

"Lower your voice, I don't want to panic our warriors. My vision is unclear about my own well being in the coming days. I didn't want to say anything. Everything must proceed as it's supposed to."

"My sister, the selfless martyr," Tubal expounds sarcastically as he throws his arms up in the air in frustration.

"I don't see myself as a martyr," Sasha defensively protests.

"You've all but resigned yourself to it. This is so like you. Your interpretation can be wrong you know, but more powerful than a vision is someone who believes they're going to die. I won't let you."

"Why? Because it's your job to protect me? You know as well as I that all bets are off in this war."

"I'm hurt that you think I protect you because it's my job. I protect you because I love you. We're family, and that's what family does."

"We're falling behind," she points out attempting to change the subject.

"We'll catch up, but not until you promise me that you'll do everything in your power to stay alive." Tubal looks her in the eyes. She avoids his gaze, but he won't allow it.

"You're pushy, you know that?" Sasha accuses as she steps back and attempts to walk around him.

"Promise me," Tubal insists. He steps into her path refusing to allow her to pass until she responds.

"I promise, but you know as well as I that fate will not be cheated," she utters reluctantly.

"Look me in the eyes and say it!"

"I promise," Sasha relents staring him down.

"What have you seen?" Tubal ardently inquires. She takes in a deep breath before responding. "And don't give me that, I might change the future nonsense," Tubal informs. His insistence on knowing her vision is not just in relation to the fate of his beloved sister, but also may hold a strategic advantage against the enemy.

"All I know right now is that at some point in the battle I'll be captured by the enemy. I'm not being hurt just restrained, and then the vision grows foggy. Considering the battle that we're embarking upon and that no prisoners will be kept for long, I simply follow the next logical conclusion."

"You're certain that's all you see," Tubal verifies staring her square in the eye looking for any sign that she is holding back.

"That's it. I swear it. Perhaps my vision will clear in the next day or so. Now let me go so we can catch up to the group," she insists as her forehead furrows displaying her agitation.

Tubal realizes that he may have pushed his sister too hard. He knows from experience that she is still keeping something from him. Yet, for her to maintain her silence so intensely, he understands that what she knows may still be too frightening for her to deal with and so releases her. They pick up the pace to rejoin their small contingent. His sister's promise does little to ease his worry. He makes a promise to himself to keep an extra close eye on her from now on. The air grows heavier as they near their destination and they have to pace themselves. They also keep a wary eye on the horizon, so they're not caught unprepared with the pending assault from the skies.

The warriors are not oblivious to the tension between Sasha and Tubal. Tubal picks up on this uneasiness. He knows that it's important for everyone to keep their focus and not be dragged down into the muck and mire of wandering thoughts that lead to uncertainty about the future. Tubal begins to recite one of their tribes' ancient victory chants. Some thought it odd that he chose a victory chant rather than a war cry, but no one lingered upon it too long. The power of the song's ability to stir up confidence in those who sing it is desperately needed to raise the spirits of the warriors and himself. He knows that one who is confident in the outcome of an uncertain situation is more likely to get the results they desire.

***

Hundreds of miles away on the plains surrounding the Canyon of Woes, Prince Horeb and company, have completed the arduous trek across the scorching desert plains and have found some welcome shade among the rocks surrounding the canyon wall. The prince pulls out a spyglass and surveys the canyon. He discovers that it's teaming with troll guards and hundreds of secured human hostages.

"This isn't going to be easy," Horeb shares with the group.

"Did you expect it to be?" Quimby asks.

"No, I didn't," Horeb responds. Out of ideas, he solicits them from the only survivor known to have returned from this cursed place. "Andrew, do you have any suggestions?"

"No, Sire. I didn't make it this far. Only my uncle made it this far."

"I might be of service," Rastus informs. "According to the depictions of this time emblazoned upon the walls outside the Great Hall. I believe we'll find a hidden path on the south side of the canyon. It should provide us cover in order to slip into the camp unnoticed."

"We humans may be able to slip in unnoticed, but you dwarfs won't," Horeb informs. "No offense intended," Horeb continues after seeing the looks on their faces after his first comment.

"None taken, but we are surprisingly stealthy," Rastus answers for the group. He, specifically, has a special respect for Horeb and knows the prince would never insult someone he risked his life to save.

"We'll sneak into the caves while you and yours provide the needed distraction," Quimby adds.

"What distraction?" Horeb asks inquisitively.

"Why, the escape of the human prisoners. The troll contingent is too large for a frontal assault but small enough to be overwhelmed by something unexpected. While they're busy catching the escaping hostages, you can kill them in the chaos. My comrades and I will kill the guards at the cave entrance and start destroying eggs," Quimby informs.

"Sounds like a solid plan. Let's do it. We'll leave our mounts here so their neighing won't give us away."

The men secure the horses in the shade of the rocks with some water. They follow Rastus' lead down the hidden path to the bottom of the canyon. The path is well hidden from the valley below, but they proceed with caution in case there are any guards posted along the path. They make it all the way to the bottom and stop. The sun is too bright, and they'll be seen the moment they step out into the open. They'll need to hold their position until nightfall when they can sneak in more successfully.

Several hours later after the sun sets, Prince Horeb and the dwarfs make their way into the camp. The prince goes to make a comment to Quimby, but the dwarfs have already disappeared. He listens for them and can't hear anything either.

"Stealthy, indeed," he comments aloud under his breath.

The only light available this night comes from the campfires built by the troll contingent. They sneak through the camp slowly going from boulder to boulder. When they reach the hostages, they quickly shush them to keep quiet. They share their plan with them, and they agree to run in as many directions as possible while making as much noise as they can. Horeb, Andrew, and Sebastian go from prisoner to prisoner cutting the ropes that tie them together. It takes several minutes to free enough of them to provide the greatest success.

On the count of three fingers and a flick of the hand, the prisoners start running in all directions and make a great shout. Some run towards their captors, and even though they are unarmed, they quickly subdue them and take the troll's weapons from them. The prisoners are only too happy to dispatch with these cruel prison guards. The captives that are not yet free see what's going on and start jumping and shouting in place creating as much confusion as possible.

The trolls guarding the cave entrances above release their crossbows into the chaos below with little effect. They only get one volley off before the dwarfs make quick work of their knees chopping clean through them with their axes. Quimby is currently using a sword since he lost his ax in the swamp. He misses it fiercely as he has to work twice as hard to take out the trolls as his comrades do. In a matter of seconds, the trolls are neutralized, and to everyone's relief, they don't reanimate.

Now that the Trolls have been taken care of, Horeb and his small band of men begin the process of freeing the others. The hostages lift up a cheer for their good fortune. Horeb's heart is moved to joy by the sight of these men, women, and children being released. This feeling is reminiscent of the moment he discovered true love in the face of his beloved Rachel and in the lives of her people. He is briefly transported back in time to that moment. How he desires to hold Rachel in his arms again? He can't begin to fathom the answer to his own question. While lost in thought, he doesn't realize that the hostages have started to kneel before him.

They recognize Prince Horeb despite his beard and hair growth and bow before their sovereign. After returning to the present moment, he motions for them to rise to their feet. They seem well fed which supports the intent that they were going to be dragon food. Horeb instructs them to free the rest of the captives. This allows Horeb and his group to carry out their mission to find the various clutches of eggs hidden in the myriad of tunnels and caves lining the canyon walls.

"Thank you for rescuing us. We thought we were dragon dung for sure," a spokesman for the group relays not wanting their prince to leave without showing their gratitude.

"You rescued yourselves and it does me good to see that you're healthy," Horeb remarks. "We've marked a safe path through the Wilderness of Desolation. I ask that you make your way back to Navarre and report to my brother on the Plains of Galeed as your numbers are sorely needed on the battlefield."

"We're happy to fight in your service, sire."

"Be sure to take as much food and water with you as you can. I suggest you leave now so you can cross the plains before sunrise, then rest at the edge of the forest before you continue."

"What do we do about the evil creatures in the wilderness?" someone asked.

"There is none left. Your countrymen await you on the Plains of Galeed."

"Aren't you coming with us?"

"No, I must make sure that the dragon's eggs are destroyed, or we may still wind up as dragon dung."

"Sire," a man amongst them calls out. He steps forward and kneels before his prince. His unkempt mousy brown hair and beard detracts from his determined demeanor. "My name is Argo, please allow me to stay with you and destroy the eggs. You should also be aware that we overheard the trolls saying that there are more prisoners coming in the next day or two. You'll need fighters to defend against the new arrivals and watchmen to make you aware of their approach."

"Very well, Argo, you may stay. I'll allow six more to join him. The rest of you must return and join my brother. You women and children should return to your homes. If they're safe, stay. If not, try to find shelter and stay together."

"Sire, there's nothing left of our homes. The trolls destroyed them when they captured us," a woman explains as she steps forward out of the crowd. Her appearance reminds Horeb of his beloved Rachel as her dark brown hair looks black in the firelight.

"What's your name?" Horeb asks.

"Elaine," she responds.

"Then find a safe haven for yourselves and the children in

your company to wait out the battle."

"Yes, Sire. Come, children," Elaine encourages. Horeb watches her. She is aware of his gaze but isn't aware that he's actually seeing Rachel in his mind's eye and not her. Elaine does her best not to blush and focuses her attention on the other women and children.

"Horeb!" Quimby calls from above. "We found them."

"On my way... Go now and tell my brother that I'll join him soon," Horeb instructs the men.

"Yes, Sire," they respond and depart with haste to fulfill his orders.

Horeb joins the others with Argo and four of the new recruits in tow. The other two he posts to keep watch for this additional group that should be arriving any day now. After posting guards, Horeb walks into a cave that is covered a foot deep in dragon eggs. They begin stomping them under their boots and crushing them with clubs, axes, and swords. After a while, the slime from the eggs makes walking and climbing very treacherous. They slip and slide across thousands of eggs colliding with one another as well as landing on their backsides a few times.

"I would expect the eggs to be more advanced by now," Horeb comments aloud.

"That's what worries me. According to the ancient texts, the Returned One will have laid thousands of eggs at a time across several weeks. I believe that this batch may have been the last one laid," Quimby adds.

"They stink too, like sulfur, but they don't appear to be rotten," Andrew comments.

"More work, less talk," Prince Horeb orders.

"Rastus, go and see how many other clutches you can find and mark them," Quimby orders seeing that Rastus face was beginning to turn green from the acrid smell of the crushed eggs. He didn't want vomit added to the aroma of the cave.

"My pleasure," Rastus responds.

"Take Argo with you. It may make the search more productive," Horeb orders.

"Well come along. Don't dawdle," Rastus entreats of this new human.

"Yes, sir," Argo acknowledges as he quickens his pace. He's never seen a dwarf before and stares at him instead of looking for dragon eggs.

"Stop staring at me and look for eggs," Rastus insists.

"Sorry, I meant no disrespect. It's just that I've never seen a dwarf before," Argo admits.

"Now you've seen one. Your eyes are better served by looking for more clutches. We can't allow these creatures to hatch."

"You'll get no argument from me on that," Argo responds and begins searching the caves and crevices in earnest.

CHAPTER 10

The villagers from Tierney find the Tavern and Inn buildings abandoned just as Jonathan said and begin to settle in. The tavern contains a cellar which is still stocked with provisions. Most of the food is still good and includes a stash of valuable salt, pepper, and other spices. Luckily, the hearth is large enough to hold the large kettles needed to cook a meal for their numbers. Agatha helps Rachel get the pots cleaned and a fire going while Jonathan and his little brother, Gorham, round up some of the goats and sheep that have been wandering loose. They placed them in a nearby pen which needed some minor repairs and was quickly made sturdy enough to keep the animals secure.

Laban takes one of the lambs they caught and butchers it so that they can have lamb stew. It's a delicacy that they haven't had in a year. Most of his people are beginning to show signs of malnutrition having had only enough rations to survive, but not thrive. Although the tidal wave was devastating, Laban views it as a blessing in disguise to move them to a place with more abundant rations. There are several buildings which they have yet to inspect and should be large enough to shelter them until the final battle is over. He hopes to find additional cashes of food and bedding in those buildings to sustain them beyond the battle.

It's odd for them not to hear the ocean, but there is a babbling brook nearby that is fresh, cool, and surprising clean. They surmise that it must be spring fed which is the only way it could have avoided all the pollutants released into their current environment.

Courtney and some of the other women collect wild onions and radishes to add flavor and freshness to the stew. They also find some potatoes, turnips, and carrots from abandoned gardens. When they return with their bounty, they begin to make bread out of the flour found in the cellar. Mark manages to find a milk cow and ties her up outside the tavern. He runs in to grab a pale then runs back to milk her while Snootzer keeps the cow calm during milking. The older women take the milk and pour it into a churn and prepare butter for the bread. Laban even manages to find some casks of ale and bottles of wine that are still fit for drinking.

A few hours later they gather together, say a prayer of thanksgiving, and feast upon the food that lay before them. At first, Rachel appears almost offended at the merriment of the people because the time is short and their fates uncertain. Then she remembers what her father told her about seizing these moments and being thankful for them. She then takes a goblet, fills it with wine, and drinks from it like she did on her wedding day. A smile cascades across her face as the wine cascades across her palate. Her body warms in the afterglow of the libation.

Rachel ponders this moment of good fortune and holds on to it as she looks at the faces of her people being full and satisfied. If anyone ever deserved a good meal and drink, it's her people. The night comes quickly at the crossroads, and the sounds are unfamiliar. Laban lights lanterns and lamps. The people huddle together near the fire while Rachel and her friends clear the dirty dishes from the table and hoist them into the kitchen. As Rachel searches cabinets for towels and soap for cleaning, she runs across a jar of clove stick candy. She quickly counts and sees that there is enough for each child to have one.

"Children, look what I found," Rachel announces. The children cheer and run to her with hands outstretched. She places a candy stick in each child's hands including Mark's. They quickly start to chew on the sticks and grin. Each child hugs Rachel and runs back to their parents or adult siblings to show off the treat in hand. Mark lingers by Rachel's side making the most of this opportunity to be childlike. She knows his days are numbered but can see that he needs to impart something to her. He stays by her side the rest of the evening so he doesn't miss his opportunity.

The night wanes on, and the fires have died down to that of glowing embers. It's not cold, so there's no need to keep the fire going through the night. Most everyone has found rooms with mattresses, pillows, and blankets to sleep on. They haven't had the luxury of articles such as these for several months. A small handful of people still have no rooms, but they haven't had a chance to clean up the adjoining buildings yet. These will remain in the main hall of the tavern where cushioned chairs and three large bear rugs cover the floors and will suffice until all can get rooms. All have fallen asleep save Rachel and Mark who quietly watch the others sleep.

"You should be getting to bed," Rachel encourages.

"I needed to talk to you in private first," Mark replies.

"About what?"

"My time is growing short, and when my time comes, I'm going to need you to accompany me to the Plains of Galeed."

"Why are you going there?" Rachel asks. Her heart knows why, but this day had been such a pleasant escape from the horrors around them that she didn't want it to end.

"That is where I will sac…" Mark pauses unable to say the word. "You'll pretend to be my mother. I'll need to get as close as possible before I'm found out. It's this disguise of being a boy that has allowed me to make it this far."

"Okay," Rachel nods warily. "I'll do as you ask. Now provide me some answers to my own nagging questions."

"What do you wish to know?"

"The chronicles and the elders of my village have said that the Redeemer has much power, but all I see when I look at you is a boy, and the cost of your survival has been so high I want to be sure that it wasn't in vain. Before you answer, I said I will see this through to the end, and I will. I just need to know that the cost was worth it," she promises. Mark smiles up at her with such compassion. She is taken aback by the weightiness of his caring look which is far more profound than any child could muster.

"You sweet, obedient child, if you only knew the joy waiting for you. But, you'll see it soon enough. The Most High has granted me one favor in exchange for my sacrifice for all of you. I don't want to tell you what it is because you wouldn't be able to accept it and it would ruin the gift's extraordinary nature. "

"If I don't know what the gift is, how will I know that the gift comes from you?"

"After I'm gone, the gift I send will come with a message," Mark pauses and acquires an impish gleam in his eyes. He wants to tell her so badly, but her present state of mind wouldn't allow her to believe it.

"What's the message?" Rachel presses growing impatient.

"I told you so," he replies. He then jumps down from the chair and finds a spot near Gorham on one of the bear rugs. Rachel looks after him. It's still hard for her to believe that he is the awaited Redeemer because at times he is so impish just like a regular human child, and at others, it's as if he knows her heart and mind so intimately that it unnerves her to her core.

Rachel surveys the room and looks over where her father is lying and sees that he has no blanket. She grabs one from a nearby stack and covers him. This action transports her back in time to when she was caring for Prince Horeb before he remembered who he was. She remembers how he looked at her with such romantic innocence and how her heart skipped a beat when he did. Her time of mourning for her husband is over, but yet she still feels a tinge of guilt for being moved by that memory. If she were honest with herself, she would have to admit that she, too, possessed feelings for him. It was only her engagement to Seth and Horeb's marital status that prevented her from exploring that relationship. She did love Seth very much, but there was something unique with Horeb that even now she can't fully explain.

Rachel remembers the prophecy given by Clairese in which she mentioned something about a future husband and that through him she would become queen. Given the current circumstances and that he has gone to the place of no return, she quickly dismisses the thought that she meant Horeb to protect herself from some future grief. She has suffered enough pain to last a thousand lifetimes and has no desire to add to them. Her mind returns to the present, and she lovingly pulls gently on her father's beard positioning it to lie on top of the blanket.

Now that her father is tucked in, Rachel grabs a nearby blanket and settles into an overstuffed leather upholstered chair. Her eyelids grow heavy, but then a sound catches her ear. It's the sound of a drum beating out a haunting cadence in the distance. She hears voices, moaning and groaning to the rhythm of the drum coming ever closer. The sound is sorrowful, despondent, low, and deep. It grows with each passing moment in substance and volume. Then she hears the sound of footsteps upon the gravel road passing by this dwelling. Woeful echoes bounce off the buildings as something passes by them.

Rachel stands to her feet and walks toward the window. Mark jumps up having heard it staying her hand before she can crack the window open to see what is passing by. Mark motions for her to keep quiet and urges her to stay inside. The boy comes close to her and whispers in her ear.

"Don't make a sound."

"What's outside?" Rachel whispers back.

"The undead made of Fire and Ash. They are marching to the Plains of Galeed to fight against our warriors. Those that once belonged to you will kill you if they discover you are here."

"How can you just sit there and let the Dragon use my family like that?" Rachel asks accusatorily holding back a rising tide of anger. Her patience has run out.

"I promise you that all will be free in the fullness of time."

"How long?" Rachel presses for an answer.

"A few days at best…" he responds gazing at her looking for the perseverance that should be firmly established in her by now. His hopes, however, are dashed quickly.

"Why must we wait until more of us die?"

"The fullness of time must be met, or we'll lose everyone. I know you're angry, but hang on and stay the course with me. You'll see that all the pain that we've endured will be more than worth it once we cross into the joy and hope that lay before us. It's not that much longer, and all will be well again."

Rachel notices her father waking up so she kneels down next to him to inform him of what he missed. Luckily, the rest of their people sleep through the march of the dead. The march continues for several hours. It finally finishes before the first rays of light break the horizon. When Mark declares it safe again, Rachel opens the door and inspects the surrounding area. There is scorched earth where the army of the dead stepped, but there was no destruction beyond their presence.

Her people will be waking soon, so she walks out of the tavern with pail in hand to get some milk for making biscuits and steps on something. She lifts her foot up and notices a woman's hair comb. It seems somehow familiar to her. She picks it up to examine it noticing that it smells of smoke. Rachel studies it carefully, and then it hits her. It's one of the combs she wore on her wedding day that she gave to Hannah.

"Papa!" Rachel screams in terror. Laban runs to his daughter's side. "Look!" she exclaims handing him the comb. Mark also comes to see what had upset her so. "It's the comb I gave Hannah. She was part of the undead that passed by last night. She knows we were here, and she let us live. Don't you see this proves that she remembers our love?" Rachel offers as tears begin to flow.

"Not consciously," Mark informs. "Had you seen her and she you, her orders would have been awakened, and she would have killed you."

Laban just stands there in shock hanging on to the memento. A tear streams down his face falling upon the object washing away some of the soot revealing the mother of pearl underneath.

"My little girl defied the great Dragon to leave us this token."

"It only seems that way. Make no mistake her will belongs to Lucius, but not for much longer. I promise you that."

Rachel continues with her chores trying to stay busy, so she doesn't have time to think about the condition of her little sister.

"I'll hold you to it," Laban informs. "My heart can't take anymore heartbreak."

"Don't lose faith, I can't have both of you doubting me," Mark requests. Laban just nods his head and follows after Rachel. He hugs her and convinces her to return to the tavern and take a nap. She doesn't want to, but her eyes are so heavy from lack of sleep she gives in to her father's request.

CHAPTER 11

Beverly and Beth arrive at the Port of Salt. The port is inhabited by shopkeepers, ship builders, Tavern and Inn owners, travelers, merchants, sailors, and drifters. It's a neutral port that is open to all who can pay the docking and room fees. The left side of the street is lined with stone and wood buildings. Anything one could want from Taverns to an open air market where people can buy exotic goods from across the sea is available. The right side is lined with heavy docks and moored ships. Some of the ships are massive and luxurious while others are well worn from age and use. Further down the street on the southern most edge are a few ships in dry dock for repairs. Right next to them is a fish market with fishermen selling their catches.

The air is full of the sounds of bustling commerce which are accented with the cries of seagulls looking for discarded pieces of shrimp and fish, and the clop of their mule's hoofs on the cobblestone street. The smell of salt, spices, fish, and ale is carried upon a gentle sea breeze. Although it's quite evident that many of the ships have recently gone through a violent storm, this is the closest they've seen of normalcy in weeks. They watch men work at mending ripped sails and decking.

The cloud cover that encased the land of Navarre is not as noticeable here with breaks in the clouds that reaffirm to both women that the blue sky is still there. In the same token, it's equally unnerving that while their loved ones are facing such desperate circumstances that these people seem oblivious to their plight going on about their lives as if all is well with the world.

The women move down the street virtually unnoticed by the crowd of people traveling to and fro focused on their own affairs and tasks. They reach a Tavern with an Inn attached to it. Beverly tips her head indicating to Beth that this is the place that they'll stay until the battle is over. Beth slows the cart to a halt, disembarks the wagon, and secures the mule to a post. Beverly climbs down out of the wagon and follows Beth around the back. They reach into the bed of the wagon to grab the infants still slumbering in their baskets. They walk toward the doors and enter the establishment.

The patrons continue drinking their pints while Beverly and Beth make their way to the bar to speak to the bartender about a room. They set the baskets down on the floor by their feet and remove their hoods to expose their faces. The bartender looks at both of them carefully studying them. Beth's pale skin is in sharp contrast to Beverly's dark skin covered with tattoos, the symbols of her status. The bartender scowls at Beverly unnerved by her foreign appearance. The recent signs displayed so violently in the heavens across the globe have turned even the most accepting individuals into suspicious religious fanatics.

"What do you want witch?" the bartender asks suspiciously.

"She's not a witch!" Beth vehemently defends. She allows her offense to be seen and heard. Her patience is already worn thin by recent events. It's clear to everyone in the room that something isn't right. Everyone stops their drinking. They put their pints on the tables and watch to see how this will play out.

"She's a witch from that cursed land to the north," he states. His pudgy bottom lip scrunches up under his nose. This expression narrows his already beady eyes and crinkles the sides of his bald head. He stands defiant, although short in stature his appearance is one of a tough, unyielding individual that could hold his own even against someone twice his size.

Beth goes to chastise him even more severely, but Beverly raises her hand to silence her. Unmoved by his implications of who she is, Beverly pulls a money pouch from her belt and lets it spill upon the bar top. Twenty gold pieces dump into view sparkling in the light of the oil lamp rolling and spinning until they come to a stop. He reaches out for one of them. Beverly grabs his hand with her boney fingers holding it only inches from the gold.

"It seems that gold makes you forget your fear of witches," she concludes.

"I...I..." he stammers. Beverly, however, intends to correct his presumption.

"To insure we clearly understand one another, know that I'm not a witch and can cast no spells upon you. My gifts are prophetic and as you can clearly see I have more than enough money to pay for a room."

The man withdraws his hand which Beverly reluctantly releases. Her strength surprises him, but after recent events, he's not about to tempt fate or whatever god may now be in charge of the cosmos.

"I was just attempting to check the purity of the coins."

"You can check that when we pay for our room."

"We have no room available, and even if I did, I'll not rent it to the likes of you regardless of how much money you have. I'll not anger the gods any more than they already are by allowing a witch like you to stay here."

"Now wait just a minute..." Beth addresses. Beverly cuts a quick glance over at her indicating for her to back off.

"Very well," Beverly concedes. She can tell that fear has taken possession of an otherwise independent man. She collects the coins and counts them as she puts them back in her pouch. The women pick up their baskets and start to walk out.

"Where to now?" Beth asks disheartened. After this reception, she's not confident that they'll be greeted any differently anywhere else.

"You can stay here, Shamilar will accept your money," comes a robust voice full of authority answering the question that was addressed to Beverly. Beth stops in her tracks as the man's voice sounds very familiar to her. They turn around. To the delight and relief of Beth, it is indeed a very familiar person. He stands slightly taller and is twice as big around as the bartender. This robust individual holds a bejeweled dagger at Shamilar's throat. The bartender's eyes are as big as saucers and display the betrayal he feels from his long time friend turning on him.

"Keevah?" Beth questions just to be sure.

"At your service ma'am," Keevah greets nodding his head. "If I remember correctly, you are the Lady Beth from King Togarmah's court are you not?"

"Yes, sir, I am. It's been a long time. It's good to see a friendly face in such difficult times," Beth confirms. Keevah's smile breaks even bigger across his face.

"Now, Shamilar, my dear friend, you'll rent them a room at no charge. You'll also guarantee their safety while they're here, or

I'll slit your throat with my dagger. Are we clear about the terms of the deal?" Shamilar shakes his head in the affirmative in the presence of all in the bar. "Now apologize to the Grand Oracle of Elim."

"The Grand Oracle of Elim? I...I... I had no idea you were someone of such eminence," Shamilar stutters attempting to curry her forgiveness without actually having to ask for it. He is known to be a very prideful man and not disposed to matters of sentiment.

"Enough of your stammering, I said apologize," Keevah insists.

"That's what I'm doing!" he snaps back at Keevah then turns his attentions to the Oracle. "My apologies, one can't be too careful these days."

"Room key," Keevah insists.

"Yes, of course," Shamilar reaches his hand under the bar to obtain it. "You can have room number twelve. It's the best in the house."

"Thank you," Beverly replies taking the key from him.

Keevah releases the bartender who immediately examines his neck in the reflection of a nearby wine glass. He rubs his neck gently to remove the impression left by the dagger.

"Can I buy you ladies a glass of wine before you get settled?"

Keevah inquires.

"That would be lovely," Beth replies. Beverly nods her agreement. Keevah helps himself to a bottle of wine, one of the best in the house, grabs some glasses and joins them.

They sit down at a nearby table. Keevah pours out the libation, and they drink after toasting their safe arrival and the health of their benefactor. Beth and Keevah quickly catch each other up on what they've been doing since the last time they saw one another. Beverly listens to their conversation smiling while they get reacquainted. He inquires of the boys. Beth is very proud to show off her son to the merchant. The other infant is explained away as an orphan left in their care.

As their conversation progresses, Beverly stares into her wine glass. Images of the coming battle float across its surface. She is drawn into the vision and sees Sasha on the Plains of Galeed surrounded by beings of Fire and Ash with demons tormenting her. She jerks her arm in reaction to the vision knocking over her glass of wine onto the floor. Almost at the same moment of her accident, Keevah mentions his encounter with Prince Javan.

"Beverly, are you all right?" Beth asks.

"It's just the clumsiness of these old bones," she responds as she tries to clean up the mess by using a cloth napkin.

"Here, let me get you another," Keevah offers while snapping his fingers to get a servant to attend to the mess.

"Thank you," she replies kindly while trying to compose herself. Keevah gets up and retrieves another glass for her. While he's gone from the table, Beth inquires more intensely about what just happened.

"What's going on? And don't tell me that you're clumsy because you're old. You're steadier than some knights I've known."

"I saw a vision in my wine. It was Sasha. There's no hope unless Javan comes through with the Army of Light."

"Keevah was just mentioning that he saw Prince Javan in his travels."

"He did?"

"Here you go, a fresh glass of wine," Keevah announces after pouring another glass and places the goblet in front of her.

"Thank you," Beverly responds appreciatively, eagerly waiting to hear news about Prince Javan.

"Don't mention it."

"You were saying that you saw my prince," Beth repeats to be sure she understood him correctly.

"Yes, I saw him. Although he had fallen onto a bit of bad

luck, but our chance meeting turned that around."

"Bad luck?"

"He had been captured as a slave and put to work on a sailing vessel."

"But he's free now?" Beth questions.

"Yes, I insisted he be freed."

"Where did you see him?" Beverly inquires.

"In Sarada, the ship he was on had a run in with the Leviathan. He was on his way to the Island of Vespa when we parted company."

"That's where the Army of Light is said to be," Beverly adds.

"Yes, well, most of us who travel the sea frequently know it as an island of phantoms. No one of sound mind goes there. If it had been anyone but Javan, I'd of thought them mad."

"When did you see him?" Beth pipes in.

"It's been a while several weeks at least."

"Prince Javan was chosen by the Most High to command the Army of Light. It's Navarre's only hope. Even now as we share this wine. Navarre fights for this world's very existence. Yet, the people here go on about their lives oblivious to the precipice that this world finds itself perched upon," Beverly informs.

"They're scared. Even Shamilar, who has seen his share of combat, quakes in his boots. The storms that ravaged the sea nearly took out everything along the coast. I'm told by some of the fisherman that most of the coastal villages were wiped out. My ship barely made it to dock before it hit. I've never seen anything like it."

"And you never will again. It's the Apocalypse, and your fate rests with the fate of Navarre," Beverly expounds.

"I don't know much about prophecy and gods, but I have great faith that Prince Javan will come through. He is his father's son. I've never met a king like Togarmah in all my travels. He was so benevolent and encouraged his people to learn. I was heartbroken when I heard he had succumbed to madness and took his own life."

"My prince has always fulfilled his word. He will bring them, I know he will," Beth professes loudly with an air of pride in her sovereign.

"Time grows short, have you heard anyone else mention anything about the Army of Light in recent days?" Beverly asks.

"No, all conversations have been focused upon the storms."

"Well, if you'll excuse me I need to rest these old bones. They don't travel as well as they used to."

"Of course," Keevah stands to his feet to help Beverly out of her chair.

"I'll be up in a while. I'd like to talk with Keevah some more," Beth informs.

"That's fine, dear. Take a few minutes to enjoy your time with your friend. The boys won't be sleeping much longer, and they'll be hungry. Thanks again for the wine."

"You're welcome."

Beverly takes her leave from their company and heads to their room. The beds are soft and comfortable. She crawls into it drowsy from the wine and dozes off to sleep after muttering a small but sincere prayer.

.

CHAPTER 12

Sasha and Tubal arrive at castle Togarmah to an intriguing and hopeful sight. They see that the valley is filled with dwarfs and human female warriors conducting battle exercises. A sense of relief fills her heart. Suddenly, their presence is noticed. Everyone stops what they're doing and looks up at the ridge where the Dunwoody Road twists and turns through decimated apple orchards. Sasha and Tubal with 500 warriors sporting spears and wagons full of dragon scale shields begin making their way down the ridge. Commander Soba starts to order an alarm, but Connor stops him.

"They're friends coming to join the cause," he informs. "Come, let me introduce you."

They walk up the hill together to greet the newcomers as Sasha and Tubal close the distance between them. Connor smiles up at them breathing a sigh of relief.

"Commander Soba, this is the Oracle of Elim and her

protector, Tubal."

"Commander," Sasha acknowledges.

"The honor is mine Oracle," Soba responds.

"Today we're just Sasha and Tubal. We bring 500 warriors and 3,000 dragon scale shields to share with your fighters. I never dreamed that there would be so many dwarfs, but this is all we have to offer."

"Your gift honors us. We shall make do with what we have," Soba confirms.

"Come and refresh yourselves from your journey," Connor entreats.

"We've come to serve, not be served," Sasha clarifies.

"Your service will be fulfilled when we march to the Plains of Galeed to support what is left of our first wave of warriors."

"First wave? You mean there are more of you?"

"About 350,000 more, but those that are sent to the front lines first will be devoured quickly," Soba informs as his voice trails off. He is taken aback that he uttered a statement that was a direct quote from the Chronicles of Destiny just as if it was a part of natural conversation. A quick glance from Connor confirms his realization as a cold chill makes its way down his spine.

Sasha looks into Soba's deep blue eyes. She can see his inward hope waning away even though outwardly he's as bold as any warrior. It's common knowledge that the next few days will be quick and brutal regardless of what part of the battle one fights in.

"I think you're right. We are tired from our journey and will be more useful to you rested. We accept your gracious and wise offer of rest and refreshment," Sasha finally admits while rubbing the kinks out of her neck.

"It would seem that wisdom belongs to humans as well as dwarfs. Come there is food and drink at the castle to revive you from your journey, but I'll admit it's a humble offering," Connor adds. He motions for Cassandra to take the pair to the castle for food and water.

Sasha and Tubal are escorted into the castle while their warriors are tended to in the shade of the outer courtyard. Cool refreshing water along with a portion of dried beef and bread are quickly distributed to them followed by a pint of ale. The ale will revive them more quickly than anything else, but only one pint will be given. This is not a celebration, but a preparation for battle.

Sasha and Tubal appreciatively take the gifts of food and drink offered them. After partaking of them, Sasha drifts off to sleep in a nearby chair. Tubal doesn't wake her. He knows she needs the rest to deal with the weight of the prophecy she carries inside her.

In her slumber, she enters a dream state and finds herself in the midst of the upcoming battle. The warriors are so engaged with one another it's difficult to distinguish friend from foe. On the opposite side, she sees Princess Sabrina, holding the Dragon's amulet in her hands. Tears are streaming down her face. Sasha sees her lips moving desperately looking for the words to speak. It's evident that she can't remember the incantation. She gazes upon her tears and sees Rainah's image reflected in them as she whispered the magic words to her. Sasha awakes abruptly unsure of which image is the dream. Her arms flail about fending off some imaginary attacker. Her actions startle everyone around her, and Tubal takes notice.

"Sasha!" Tubal calls out to her. Still partially enveloped in her dream, she turns to face who she thinks is the enemy only to find her brother's concerned expression looking back at her, but it doesn't fully register in her mind that she is awake and safe. "Are you alright?" Tubal inquires. She is noticeably shaken but quickly recovers existing in two realms simultaneously.

"Where's Rainah?" Sasha asks. No one responds to her query. She looks around for Rainah, the only female dwarf among the humans, but doesn't find her among them. She frantically begins running to and fro looking into various rooms, but to no avail. In desperation, she looks for Connor.

"Sasha!" Tubal calls running after her, but she doesn't respond remaining intent on her mission. He finally catches up to her and takes hold of her shoulder. "Why are you looking for Rainah?"

"Let me go! I have to find her!" she shouts jerking her shoulder out of his grasp. He again tries to grab her arm to calm her, but her reflexes respond as if in combat. Only her brother's training keeps him from being harmed, but it doesn't stop him from being knocked on his backside.

"You need to calm down!" he demands as he grabs her ankle. This time his words get through as Sasha comes to realize that she's been in a waking dream and finally acknowledges her brother as a friend instead of an enemy.

"I have to find Rainah right now."

"Why?"

"She holds the key to our very survival," Sasha informs.

"You were having a bad dream," Tubal informs slowly and calmly. Connor arrives at their location having been summoned by Cassandra when Sasha started acting strange.

"It wasn't a dream. It was a vision, a glimpse into the immediate future. I know why our troops are being killed."

"No one is being killed yet. The horns haven't sounded. How can our troops be dying?" Connor asks.

"Where's your wife, Rainah?" Sasha asks instead of

answering his question.

"What does Rainah have to do with our troops dying?" Connor repeats.

"Where's your wife!" Sasha demands. Her eyes plead with the dwarf.

"Upstairs recovering from what the Dragon did to her," Connor finally answers.

"Is she conscious?"

"Yes."

"I must see her now!"

"You may want to calm down first."

"Now!" Sasha insists.

"Very well, follow me, just don't upset her," Connor orders.

"I have no intention of upsetting her, but our kin's very survival depends upon the message she gives me."

Connor leads Sasha up the circular staircase to where his wife is recovering. Sasha enters the room while Rainah slowly turns over to face the commotion. She is taken aback by how weak Rainah appears. Sasha reaches into a pouch fastened on a belt at her waist and lifts out a sachet of spices.

"Get a pot of hot water and put this in it. Bring a cup also."

"What is it?"

"Medicinal herbs that will help restore your wife's strength. Now, go. I must speak with her alone."

Connor glances over at his wife, she nods her confirmation. He hesitates, but she winks to let him know that it's okay to leave them alone. He reluctantly leaves them to fetch the kettle of hot water and a cup. After he leaves, Sasha pulls up a chair. She looks deep into Rainah's jade green eyes while Rainah stares deep into hers. It was as if their minds have become one and Rainah can see reflected in Sasha's eyes the images of her waking dream.

"You know that I gave Princess Sabrina the amulet, correct?" Sasha queries testing Rainah's knowledge.

"I know. It was entrusted to the Oracles millennia ago. As I'm sure you're aware it was I that gave her the incantation so she can use it at the proper time."

"That's why I'm here. I had a vision of the upcoming battle. Sabrina is a prisoner of Lucius and our troops are being slaughtered by the warriors of Fire and Ash because she can't remember the incantation."

"Stupid human woman... I made her repeat it so she wouldn't forget," Rainah states with anger.

"It's clear to me that her memory loss is not her fault as she is desperately trying to remember the words. I don't know what happened to make her forget the words, but she's been in the Dragon's presence since she freed you. Her forgetfulness could be due to a magic spell or an injury. Whatever the reason, I have to get those words to her."

"How do you know so much about it, but don't remember that I can't share the words with you?" Rainah quizzes.

"That's really not important right now."

"How do you know that she forgot them?" Rainah inquires. Sasha can tell that she's not going to budge until she answers her.

"I told you, I saw it in a vision downstairs. What's important right now is that you give me the magic words so that I can take them to her. The horns could sound at any moment."

"You know I'm sworn to give them only to the keeper of the amulet. You may not be who you claim to be in order to trick me into giving you the magic words. If anyone should give the princess the words, it should be me."

"I agree, but you are in no shape to go yourself, and I and my mother before me were entrusted with the amulet prior to the princess. I shall prove myself to you." Sasha takes a dagger sheathed on her belt. Rainah pulls away from her, but Sasha takes the dagger and cuts her own hand. Her blood drips onto the alabaster sheets. "Give them to me now! We are out of time."

"You'll be marked for death as penalty for this affront. The Chronicles of Destiny are very clear on this matter. Are you prepared to die to carry the magic words to her?"

"I know my fate and have for some time. Death will be a welcome release from this terrible place and an empty heart."

"Very well, come close."

Sasha leans in and reads the words that Rainah writes with her finger in the dust of the nightstand. She commits them to memory nodding her head that she's got it as Rainah erases them with her hand. At this point, they can't be spoken aloud, or the amulet will release its protection of the princess in favor of its new orders whatever those orders are and by whomever spoken.

Connor arrives with the pot of water which has been steeping the bundle of spices. He pours Rainah a cup and hands it to her. She breathes in the steam erupting from the surface. The aroma seems to bring new energy to his wife even before she takes a sip. Sasha quietly excuses herself allowing them a moment together to rejoin her brother and hopefully soothe his bruised ego. Before heading downstairs, she composes herself, so she doesn't worry him about her apparent sealed fate.

CHAPTER 13

The clouds finally disperse above the Plains of Galeed as the sun breaks the horizon to reveal that the enemy arrived during the night. The human and dwarf guards immediately snap to attention shaking off the feelings of sleep but know they didn't fall asleep. Yet, they failed to alert their leaders of the enemy's arrival during the night. They wake Prince Robert and General Rasmussen first then roust their fellow troops to consciousness. The troops respond quickly jumping to their feet with hands grasping their weapons. They fall into line awaiting their orders while Prince Robert stares with disapproval at his guards.

"Why didn't you wake me when they arrived last night?" Prince Robert demandingly asks. The guards look back at him with a mixture of confusion and unspoken pleas for mercy, but regardless they have no answer to give. "You fell asleep," Robert accuses as he draws his sword.

"Stay your sword, Prince," General Rasmussen requests. "They didn't fall asleep any more than my guards fell asleep."

"I don't understand," Robert admits.

"The Dragon has a sorcerer. I'm sure that he cast some spell upon us all for that many to come in and no one was alerted by their presence. Besides, no dwarf has ever fallen asleep while on guard duty."

"Are you referring to Shaman?"

"We do not know his name. We just know that he is."

"Very well, take your place and await your orders," Robert informs his guards. They swallow the lump in their throats and quickly take their place.

Prince Robert and General Rasmussen turn their attentions to assessing the situation. Rasmussen takes out his spyglass and surveys the enemy lines. Robert reaches for his, but remembers he gave it to Joss to provide long range vision to the troops on the other side of the battlefield. The spyglass reveals that the enemy ranks are filled with thousands of beings of Fire and Ash with trolls and demons securing their flanks. Then he notices that there's a human female tied between two poles high above the battlefield. Rasmussen can tell by her dress that she is of royal blood, but doesn't know who she is.

"Well," Robert begins, "Is it as bad as you thought?"

"It's worse... We're out numbered 3 or 4 to 1, and I already recognize three individuals in the enemy's service among my own dead. I'm troubled by one thing I didn't expect to see, and it's unclear to me how this fits in to the enemy's plans."

"Only one thing?" Robert asks in amazement.

"What do you make of that just above the trees high upon that outcropping of rocks?" he asks as he hands the spyglass to Robert. The prince takes it from the general and looks through it. He swallows hard in an attempt to keep despair at bay as his heart drops to his feet.

"That's my wife, Princess Sabrina," he informs the General.

"I suppose the Dragon didn't take kindly to you aligning yourself with us. I hope that her presence won't have any sway over you..."

"The Dragon's there," Robert interrupts. "He's just come out of a nearby cave. He appears to be giving orders."

"You can't allow yourself to be distracted from the battle because she is his prisoner," Rasmussen insists. The general has yet to see how well the humans will hold up under extreme battle conditions and if they will remain committed regardless of the cost.

"Don't worry, she won't. She's better protected than anyone."

"What do you mean she's better protected?" Rasmussen is noticeably confused by his statement.

"She wears the Dragon's amulet," Robert informs. The astonished look on the general's face is a mixture of surprise and horror.

"Give me the spyglass," Rasmussen demands. He takes it from Robert nearly snatching it out of his hands and looks for himself. "Does she know how to use it?"

"Use it? It protects her from her mother, the Returned One and the Dragon that's all I know."

"The fate of us all hangs around her neck. She can stop the armies of Fire and Ash if she invokes the incantation."

"I don't know anything about that."

"Stupid humans…We should have never left it in your care," Rasmussen mutters under his breath, then continues, "If she doesn't know how to use it, then a lot of us are going to die while she watches."

"For the record, my wife is very intelligent so keep your racist attitudes to yourself. Just because I don't know doesn't mean that she doesn't know," Robert warns.

"I meant no personal disrespect, but your lack of knowledge

about these days is astounding and troublesome," Rasmussen banters back.

"Maybe we would have known more if you dwarfs hadn't tucked tail and hid underground for the past millennia."

"Our hiding had nothing to do with cowardice. Your kind had grown too dependent upon us. We had to withdraw for your own good as well as protect our culture from your less palatable ways," Rasmussen spouts defending the bravery of his kind.

Robert attempts a rebuttal but is cut off by the enemy. They begin to shout a chant using words from an unknown tongue. They chant three words over and over again in loud, fierce anger. Those with spears pound the ground in rhythm with the chant while others shake their swords in the air. Archers simply raise their fist at each crescendo. Robert looks over at Rasmussen who appears to understand the words.

"What are they saying?" Robert asks.

"It's an ancient Dwarf dialect. It means death to our kin."

Robert's countenance drops as the realization starts to take hold that their first lethal battle will be against their own dead who have been reanimated for this purpose. Rasmussen notices the change in Robert's demeanor.

"Control yourself!"

"What?"

"You heard me. You must maintain your outward persona of confidence and determination, or our men will die faster than they need to. Those we are about to fight have already died. No matter how animated they look, they're not the flesh and blood that we knew. They have no will of their own and no choice but to obey the Dragon. They also can't be killed just rendered useless."

"Anymore good news before we start?"

"I think we covered it."

Strengthened and frightened by Rasmussen's words, Robert gathers himself then turns to face the troops with an outward confidence that refuses to give way to doubt. They stand at the ready awaiting his orders to engage. Suddenly, drums begin to sound on the enemy side. They are loud, hypnotic, and keep cadence with the chant. The noise climbs to deafening decibels.

"Warriors of Navarre!" Robert begins, shouting over the rising clamor of the enemy. "We are about to engage our enemy, and he has foolishly used the ashes of our dead kin to sway our resolve and make us weak! No matter what they say to you, do not accept their disguise. These poor creatures are the Dragon's handiwork, and only his will is in them. Do not give quarter or show mercy to any you encounter as they will show none to you. We fight until we die. In death, or in victory will be the only way you'll leave this field. Remember that help will come when your strength has been completely poured out. On that day raise your eyes unto the hills beyond the forest, and you'll see your help come!"

Just as Prince Robert finishes his speech to the human and dwarf fighters, horns blast out a long and haunting sound. It's so loud that it nearly bursts their ear drums as the sound moves with force toward them and spreads out across the land never losing its strength. According to legend, the sound will continue to move across the face of their world until it returns to this battlefield by which time the victor will have been decided. After the blast is complete, the Dragon perches himself upon the outcropping just above them and gives the order.

"Attack!"

The enemy hoards rush onto the battlefield with weapons to bear yelling as they move towards them. Robert sees the fear in his troops' faces and knows he has to one up the enemy or this will be a quick battle. He quickly resolves in his heart to start a chant of his own.

"Victory is ours! Victory is ours!" Robert begins. The men seem stunned at first, but then start repeating the victory cry. Each refrain becomes louder and more confident with each reciting. Rasmussen holds the signal flag waiting for the enemy to advance just a little more. He doesn't want them to spend all their energy running across the battlefield. Then suddenly drops the flag and the men rush forward into the jaws of the enemy. They run headlong into the arms of destruction bringing their courage with them. The battlefield morphs from posturing to engagement. It's anyone's guess who has the initial advantage.

***

In the enemy camp, the Dragon, Lucius, comes to gloat in front of the Princess Sabrina. He glares at her still defiant, resilient attitude and chuckles under his breath musing to himself.

"You find me amusing?" she asks unmoved by his invasive and callous stare.

"Yes, I do. Humans are such arrogant creatures especially when the odds are stacked against you. Your kind should fear me, but you put on this vain pretense of courage."

"Why does this trouble you? Is it because we don't cower in your presence like your minions? Our courage isn't vain. We simply have nothing to lose. Besides, we are nothing more than food to you, but at least we have the satisfaction of knowing we give you indigestion," she counters, with a sadistic grin upon her face.

"Insolent creature," Lucius counters angrily. "Do you not care about your people below being killed by your own dead?"

"They're being killed by your creation. Those creatures may

have the appearance of our kin, but that is where the resemblance stops. We will not lie down and let you take what doesn't belong to you," she informs defiantly.

"You really think you have a chance of beating me," Lucius begins with a touch of wonderment over their resilience. In another place and time, these humans may even be worthy of future study. "Where does this misplaced confidence comes from? Do you have another ally that has yet to show their face?" he questions, goading her to confess any plans she may know about.

Sabrina opens her mouth to defend their strategy and starts to tell him about her brother's coming but stops short of revealing any information. She realizes that anything she shares could potentially undermine their chances of winning. Sabrina purses her lips together and weighs her next words carefully.

"What would I know? I've been isolated for weeks from my kind," she states. Her body language, however, counters her pretend ignorance by a small smirk forming upon her face. The Dragon snorts some flame. She jumps out of instinctual reaction to flames being spat upon her even though they have no effect on her flesh.

"Still jumpy... good. Whatever you're hiding will become apparent soon enough. Besides, there is nothing your kind can conjure that would have any impact upon the forces I have at my command. In the mean time, I hope you enjoy watching your people die," Lucius spouts. In frustration, he takes shelter underneath the shade of a pine tree to monitor the progress of the battle.

Sabrina glances onto the battlefield and tries to find her husband, Robert, but to no avail, the bodies are too entangled below to make out who is down there. Her eyes survey the trees, but can't see the makeshift command towers they've made use of among the massive pines. All she knows is that the fighting is fierce and continues into the heat of the day. As difficult as it is for her to acknowledge, the Dragon is right about one thing. She is watching her people die. The dwarfs that are mingled among the humans are often times too short for her to make out above the dust. She hopes that Connor and Rainah are safe amid this madness.

***

At castle Togarmah, a sound unlike any other fills their ears. Sasha and Tubal are with Soba and Connor discussing battle strategy when the strange sound quiets their words. They clutch their ears with their hands to block out its intensity. It's so hurtful that tears well up in their eyes. Although Sasha doesn't understand what the sound is, it's clear that Soba and Connor know as their countenance drops. After the sound passes, they take a moment to recover before engaging in conversation.

"What's that sound?" Sasha asks breaking the total silence that succeeded the blast of sound.

"The Horns of Hell," Soba informs.

"It's time to march to the Plains of Galeed. Sound the trumpets we move out now," Connor orders to Soba's second.

After the trumpets sound, the dwarfs, the warriors of Elim, and the women warriors quickly gather their weapons, rations, and fall in ranks. They'll march for a day and a night and will reach the plains by mid-day the following day. They move quietly and soberly partly to save their strength and partly out of the realization that they are heading into the last battle. They realize that they'll be finishing the fight that their kin started. This means that those they care about will already be dead by the time they get there.

Rainah, still too weak to join them, looks after them until she can no longer see them. Her hair is considerably shorter now. She gave the braided locks to Connor to keep as a memento and reminder of what he's fighting for. Her mind reflects back upon the mural wall in the great hall that depicted this very thing. She had forgotten until now about the prophetic mural. A cold chill accompanies this remembrance. She knows that there is no more prophecy and that the outcome of this battle was withheld from all Seers and prophets. She doesn't know why, but perhaps it was to galvanize their resolve to not give in to the evil one.

The future now rests with them. To save the world, they must be willing to die for it. Yet, there is a word of hope that springs to her mind to soothe her worry and concern. She speaks it aloud not realizing that anyone was around to hear it.

"Now, within the throws of darkness and despair, an ember of hope rises unnoticed amid the blackness. Sacrifice will give way to freedom and death will give way to life. Like a seed that must die to bring forth life, so this age must pass away to bring forth a destiny of freedom and love."

"That's beautiful. Where is it from?" Mary asks. Rainah is visibly startled.

"It's the last few lines written in the Chronicles of Destiny. My father used to quote them to me when I would have nightmares as a child. It would always calm my fears."

"Are your fears calmed now?"

"Maybe…I don't know, but it's a comfort to know that there is a hope on the other side of this madness even if it costs us everything."

"I've never read them all the way through to the end. I always stopped when it spoke of the horrible things to come. I never dreamed we'd be living through them. Even when King Ophir battled King Togarmah and the treachery he showed when he ripped away our beliefs, I still didn't want to believe that it was prophecy unfolding before our eyes. I've never felt as helpless as I do right now. When I came in to check on you and heard those beautiful words of hope you spoke, it did something for me even if it fell a little short for yourself. Thank you."

"You're welcome."

"Now what do we do?" Mary asks.

"We wait," Rainah responds.

"That's not going to be easy."

"It never is, but that's all we can do right now."

"Do you pray?" Mary asks of Rainah.

"Sometimes," Rainah admits.

"Then I think we should add prayer to our waiting," Mary suggests. Rainah smiles back as she nods her head in the affirmative. The women raise their voices in a unified prayer for victory and safety of those they love. The children in Mary's care seek her out and upon finding her also join in this prayer. Mary opens her eyes to gaze upon these children. She is moved by the simplistic faith displayed upon their faces. There is no doubt amongst them, and her belief is strengthened by theirs.

Glenda C. Finkelstein

CHAPTER 14

The people of the Port of Salt rise early before the sun. Bustling Taverns and bakeries prepare meals for those who'll be leaving at the break of dawn. The noise below awakens Beverly who checks on the slumbering infants that are just beginning to stir to hunger pangs. Beverly fixes a blanket that has become un-tucked around the infant prince. This action brings a fond memory back to her remembrance of tucking in her own son.

"To think my son, Tubal was as small as you once," the baby stretches in response to her words without waking. Beverly smiles upon the living hope entrusted to her care.

The bright orange disk of the sun breaks over the summit of Mount Tiras shining its rays upon the already busy port. The lamp lighters begin to snuff out the lamps along the docks lining the cobblestone streets below. The air is less acrid than it has been in days, and in spite of the terror she knows is coming, her heart is warmed with hope. She breathes in the salt laced sea air until her lungs are filled. She feels at peace, but this feeling doesn't last very long.

The sound of horns explodes through the air descending upon this port town with the same fury as a mighty rushing wind. The sound is strong and painful to the ears. Everyone awake immediately covers their ears, and everyone who was still slumbering is jolted awake. Beth comes to, grabbing her head. The infants start crying incessantly shrieking in pain from the discomfort of the noise. The sound finally passes, and everyone looks at one another wondering what it could be. Before Beth can ask Beverly what's going on, a second blast comes with even more force than the one before.

"What's that sound?" Beth asks anyway, but her voice is drowned out by the horn blast. They both rush to the infants and try to protect them from this harsh sound. Their attempts are futile at best, but they do their best to cover their ears. After the powerful sound subsides, there is a profound silence that hangs in the air.

The silence, peppered only by crying children and infants, which follows the second blast is more unsettling than the first. Even though the silence lasted longer the second time, in mere seconds the silence is broken by sheer panic in the streets below. All crews board their vessels and set sail out of the harbor as fast as they can. It doesn't matter if they are fully loaded or not, they're leaving. Sails unfurl, lines are untied, anchors raised, and the ships set sail full speed ahead. There are a couple of close calls as the harbor master tries to steer ships in an orderly fashion safely out to sea, but calm heads are not in charge today. Fortunately, no ships wreck preventing any from escaping.

The women poke their heads out the window after successfully calming the babies and notice that there is one merchant ship still docked against the backdrop of a harbor full of ships heading to open waters. The crew vainly calls after their Captain who is walking up to the Inn where they're staying. It's Keevah. He commands them to stay put until he returns, but they refuse and set sail without him. He is intent on making sure that Beverly, Beth, and the boys are safe and wanted to evacuate them. His valiant efforts, unfortunately, are for naught.

"What's happening? What was that sound?" Beth asks of Beverly.

"The battle has begun. The sound came from the Dragon's Horns of Hell."

"Why didn't Keevah leave with his ship?"

"I don't know, but I'm going to find out. Stay here and nurse the babies. I'll go downstairs and speak with him."

Beverly grabs a nearby scarf and throws it around her shoulders. The damp air near the sea doesn't treat her old bones very well. Her outward appearance may be younger than her years by a decade, but her bones know different. She slips into a pair of shoes, opens the door, and walks to the main room to meet Keevah.

"Why didn't you leave with your men?" Beverly begins.

"I was coming to offer you safe passage away from here, but my crew has made that impossible," he explains. His anger towards his men is evident in his tone.

"You are a chivalrous man and, we appreciate your concern, but we're just as safe here as on the sea."

"I don't understand. You heard the blasts. Even unbelievers know what that sound means. There is no safety here."

"My dear, Keevah, there is no safety anywhere and nowhere left to run. They only delude themselves by thinking they're safe on the sea."

"The port is abandoned. I've heard the stories of what is to come. We can't stay here," Keevah insists.

"Yes, we can. It'll be too dangerous traveling with the boys. We stand a better chance if we fortify our position here," Beverly submits for consideration.

"Where is the Lady Beth?" Keevah asks looking about the tavern for her.

"She's feeding the babies," Beverly answers.

"Very well, then I'll start fortifying our position."

"Not without me you're not," Shamilar chimed in popping up from where he was hiding behind the bar.

"I thought you left with the others," Keevah states with surprise.

"You think I'm going to let some creature from the bowels of hell mess up my place. I sold my ship to get this place. I'll defend her so long as I'm alive and anyone residing there in."

"There's far more to your character than I have imagined, Shamilar. Beth and I appreciate your noble efforts. You'll receive great honor for your sacrifice."

"My reward will be, not having to rebuild this place. You can keep your medals. I have a trunk load already, not that they ever did me any good," Shamilar admits.

"Where did you acquire them?" Beverly asks curiously.

"I served King Ophir and his father from the time I was sixteen. I built the Frontier Road and all its bridges. It was my ships that provided the marble and the giant timbers from the cedar forests of Ambriel to build his castle."

"Do you still hold respect in your heart for the line of King Ophir?"

"Yes, I do. If I weren't lame, I'd be with his sons now."

"I'm about to entrust you with a sacred trust, and you must promise on oath to your beloved sovereign that you'll fulfill this promise or die trying."

"What is it?"

"One of those infant boys in our keeping is the heir to throne of Navarre and Ophir's grandson," Beverly carefully elaborates. Shamilar drops to his hands and knees before Beverly.

"Woman, I have woefully misjudged you. I vow to the very last drop of my blood that I shall defend him and you."

"You are forgiven, and you needn't bow to me," Beverly informs. Shamilar tries to get back up, but an old injury makes that a little difficult.

"Don't just stand there, Keevah, help me up. I'm stuck."

"Sorry," Keevah apologizes as he provides a sturdy arm for Shamilar to use to pull himself up from the floor.

Suddenly, Beth comes running into the room with a baby still at her breast. She is alarmed and fearful. They look at her with blank stares waiting for her to speak.

"Something is coming!" Beth finally blurts out.

Keevah helps Shamilar back to his feet, and the four of them rush out of the Tavern and look toward the horizon. In the distance, is a massive fleet of ships growing larger by the second. They're heading for the port at full speed. Keevah reaches into his breast pocket and pulls out a spyglass. He peers into it carefully studying the approaching fleet. There is no insignia that he can make out then the wind blows just enough to make out a symbol on a flag hanging from the mast. He swallows hard lowering the glass not quite believing what he's seeing. He returns the glass to his eye to take a second look and studies the armada even harder.

"Is it the enemy?" Beth asks fearfully.

"As I live and breathe, I never thought my eyes would ever behold the Army of Light," Keevah announces to himself as well as to those around him.

"Did you say the Army of Light?" Beverly asks just to be certain.

"My prince was successful. We're saved!" Beth exclaims jumping up and down.

"That remains to be seen. No Seer has ever been granted sight into these days that we are currently living. I'm relieved to know that Javan was successful, but we still have a long road ahead of us," Beverly cautions. Beth's exuberance, however, remains undaunted.

Beverly walks up to Beth standing between her and the men.

She takes the infant from Beth so that she can cover herself and present herself properly to her sovereign. Beverly then goes to check on the other baby left inside his basket. She wants to be extra careful with these babies. Beverly changes their diapers and takes a damp cloth to clean them up. After tucking them neatly back in their baskets, the boys fall back asleep exhausted from the ordeal. Beverly carries them back to the docks with Keevah's help.

***

Prince Javan is looking through a spyglass of his own to determine their location to the Port of Salt. After hearing the horns, he's become anxious about getting to shore. He sees the land with Mount Tiras rising in the background. After a few more miles, he's able to make out the docks. He notices that the harbor is empty. He is relieved that there will be no problem with docking their ships. The waters calm, and the wind dies down as they enter the harbor slowing their speed.

"Lower the sails! Oarsmen, to your stations!" Javan orders. He glances over at Anak to make certain he has his approval.

"Don't look at me, commander. It's no longer I who leads, but you," Anak informs.

"Old habits die hard... The horns have already sounded, and my people have waited long enough for us to arrive. We need to dock as quickly as possible."

"Did it ever occur to you that we're arriving exactly when we're supposed to?" Anak submits for consideration.

"No, it hasn't. Ever since I first laid eyes upon you, I've felt like a slow learner. I never fully understood my destiny until now. I believe this lack has exposed my people to greater harm because of my slowness."

"In the fulfillment of all things in this age, there is a moment when things are meant to be revealed. How many graves did you count before you embarked upon your climb to the summit of Mount Tiras?" Anak asks, testing whether or not Javan fully understands.

"There was a lot at least a hundred maybe more if my recollection is accurate."

"Did you ever wonder why they were there?"

"I assumed it was because they were found to be unworthy."

"Some, perhaps, but not all…Did it ever occur to you that they were trying to bring about the end of the age too soon rather than respond to a calling placed upon them."

"No, that thought never crossed my mind," Javan comments. Anak chuckles at the innocent ignorance of his understanding. "I always manage to amuse you. Don't I?"

"Not so much amuse, but amaze. Your ignorance at virtually every step of your journey enabled you to reside in the moment and allow time to take its natural course to completion. If we had arrived a moment earlier, the full plan would not have been engaged. We also would not have had a place to dock. Those ships we passed were all moored here this morning."

"Full plan?"

"The redemption of man and dwarf kind, of course…" Anak pauses a few seconds to see if Javan can see the full picture yet. "You still don't see the hope on the other side," Anak comments at his friend's short sightedness.

"Hope? There is hope on the other side of this nightmare?"

"Yes, everyone has a purpose, and a place and those that work with the Most High will receive a great reward rather living or dead. Those that live through this battle will see a wondrous new day the likes of which your eyes have never seen before. It'll be a golden age of peace, prosperity, and long life filled with the blessings and the protection of the Most High. Evil will be contained for at least a thousand years or more depending upon what you do with it."

"I like that. All this time I've been focused on the end of things not fully understanding that there is a wondrous new beginning awaiting us on the other side of this darkness."

"Sir!" calls a subordinate from the deck. Anak and Javan look down awaiting the news he has to share. "We've entered the harbor. As you can see all the slips are vacant, we can unload immediately."

"Very good, commence docking!" Javan confirms.

In a few minutes, Anak and Javan's ship docks in the first slip. The troops secure the ship and begin unloading the horses and Firecats. Javan scans the township for any resistance or traps that might be there to slow them down. What he sees are deserted buildings and three familiar friendly faces standing on the seawall. He hurries off the ship to greet them.

"My prince," Beth greets dropping to one knee in his presence before he can greet her.

"Lady Beth, arise and greet me properly," Javan encourages. He throws his arms around her hugging her tightly. It's been a long time since he's seen anyone from the old Southern Kingdom, much less from his father's court.

"My lord," she responds blushing slightly at the lavish attention she receives. She then bends down and pulls the infant prince from his basket and presents him to Prince Javan. "This is your sister's son. She faked the child's death to secure his life and was taken into the Dragon's custody."

"I know about my sister's sacrifice," he admits while holding out his arms to hold his nephew for what he knows will be the only time he'll do so. Holding this little one is so profound that a tear erupts upon his cheek. "Sabrina and I are in your debt. I know he's in good hands, but I must command this army and rescue what remains of our people."

He hands the cooing infant back to Beth. She drops back to one knee to place the baby back in the basket. She then stands to her feet and moves out of the way. Javan moves to Beverly, Sasha's mother, whom he remembers from his time spent in their village.

"It's good to see you again," Javan admits with a smile.

"I just wish my daughter could see you. She has joined the rest in battle."

"I know, and I'll do everything in my power to bring her back to you," Javan informs as a promise, but stops short of confirming it as a promise. In this battle, nothing is for certain, and victory is the only objective. "Beverly, I'd like you to meet my mentor, Anak."

"It's an honor to meet the commander of the Army of Light," Beverly acknowledges with a respectful bow.

"And I you, but Javan is our commander now."

"My prince," Keevah steps up to greet his favorite royal.

"Keevah, my friend, take good care of these in your charge. I'm holding you personally accountable."

"I'll not fail you," Keevah vows.

"I know you won't."

Javan's eyes fall upon Shamilar, who is unfamiliar to him but can see that he is an old Northern Kingdom warrior in need of fresh pastures. This old warhorse salutes Javan, who is surprised by the gesture and returns the salute in respect of his bold move.

"This is Shamilar, an honored warrior from the old Northern Kingdom," Keevah introduces.

"I'm honored, but I must go, our people's…all our peoples' lives depend upon it," Javan expounds and turns immediately to mount his Firecat. He's totally focused on getting his army moved northward.

Beth watches her prince lead the Army of Light toward the Plains of Galeed. The sight of tall warriors on horseback and Firecats so full of noble strength gives them all a renewed sense of hope that they may stand a chance against the Dragon's hoards. Beth remains on the seawall until the last of this marvelous army disappears from view. Beverly permits her this moment of solitude and takes the infants back inside allowing her to return to the Tavern in her own good time.

CHAPTER 15

The battle rages below the bluff unfettered by the passing of time. Sabrina, who is chained in a standing position, has had no rest with little food or water. The amulet's protection only extends to harm inflicted from an outside source but does little to keep her from growing weak from lack of sustenance. She begins to doze off despite her attempts to remain awake. The Dragon entertains himself by watching the slaughter below and throwing his enemy's dismembered body parts to his hounds to sate their ferocious appetites. The only time Lucius spends with his hounds is during times of battle. The rest of the time their care is entrusted to the trolls.

The trolls start gambling over the outcome of certain skirmishes within the battle having grown bored with waiting. They hunger for combat and don't understand why Lucius keeps them from engaging the enemy. Yet, they know when not to push the issue as the current mood of their Master dictates discretion. He doesn't appreciate anyone second guessing or challenging his decisions, so they make the most of their idle time.

Shaman, on the other hand, has been working on ways of corrupting the magic of the amulet so he can prevent Sabrina from taking control of the army of Fire and Ash. So far all of his attempts have resulted in failure. He wrings his hands after his last attempt ends in burning his own fingertips. He begins to pace out of frustration and worry wondering how much longer Lucius will allow him to live. His pacing takes him ever closer to the dozing princess. He soon realizes that she's talking in her sleep. He listens carefully to what she's saying. At first, her words are unintelligible, and he doesn't understand what she's saying. She's speaking a language that he's never heard before with vowels and consonants strung together in random patterns, but then realizes that she's talking to a baby…her baby.

"…My sweet son, you'll never hear my voice again, but know that I love you and you will be well loved and protected…" her voice fades away as she drifts deeper into sleep. Shaman strains to hear more but realizes that his window of opportunity has vanished. He tries to get her talking again, but it doesn't work as smoke wafts under her nose waking her. This peculiar encounter draws the attention of the Dragon, and he comes up behind Shaman to see what he's up to.

"What are you doing?" Lucius asks. Shaman jumps unaware his master is watching him. His reaction causes a brief smile to flash across Sabrina's face, but her smile will be fleeting.

"She was talking in her sleep. I was trying to get her to talk more so I could find out additional information that will be of interest to my Lord," Shaman informs as Sabrina's smile drops quickly from her face.

"Do tell," Lucius requests.

"I overheard her talking to her son," Shaman explains. Sabrina begins to show signs of alarm. She wonders if she could have inadvertently given away the fact that her son is alive.

"Her son is dead. Bog saw the grave," Lucius advises.

"That's right. I buried him myself," Sabrina submits.

"She talked as if he's still alive and being protected by someone. She could have hidden the child and faked the grave. Bog did dig it up to confirm her story, correct?" Shaman asks while casting a suspicious glare at Sabrina. She tries to remain unmoved by the accusation.

"Bring Bog to me now," Lucius insists.

Shaman fetches Bog and brings him to Lucius. Bog drops to one knee to show respect for his master. He's also a little unnerved to be summoned before him. He doesn't fear the enemy or any assignment that Lucius may give, but he does fear Lucius' temper.

"Shaman informs me that the princess has been talking in her sleep as if her son is still alive. You told me that you saw the grave of this infant."

"Yes, master, I saw the grave."

"Did you dig it up to insure the infant was dead?"

"No, master, there was no need. I smelled the child's presence in the dirt. Prince Robert was weeping so uncontrollably over the grave, that I didn't see the need to dig it up. My orders were to bring back the dwarfs, and you wanted them brought to you immediately, so I didn't delay."

"Humans are known to lie even to each other, and a scent can be faked. Isn't that right Princess?" Lucius asks while watching her reaction for anything that would give away her deceit. She looks away from Lucius penetrating gaze unable to maintain her defiance. "Why you sly little vixen, you lied to your own husband," Lucius comments with a combination of admiration and disdain.

"He's an innocent. He can't possibly harm you," Sabrina emphatically defends. She knows she has already given away the truth. She also knows that her pleas will fall on deaf ears. Lucius won't be merciful to the child and is delirious with the thought of killing their only future.

"What are your orders?" Bog inquires.

"Please don't harm him…" Sabrina pleads again this time trying to elicit a favorable response from the troll. Bog doesn't entertain her words. This woman has placed him in a difficult circumstance and refuses to show her mercy snubbing his nose at her.

"Take my hounds, Chaos, and Bedlam, and track this child down. Don't return to me without his bones as proof of his death," Lucius orders paying no heed to Sabrina's continued pleas.

"Yes, my lord," Bog nods his understanding. He reaches into the princess' cage and rips off part of her dress.

"What are you doing?" she demands.

"I'm providing a scent for my master's hounds to track so we can find your accursed offspring and kill him," Bog informs. His words are deliberate and brief.

"Stop! Have you no mercy?" Sabrina asks in a futile struggle against her restraints as Bog tosses the piece of garment to the hounds to sniff.

"Neither the Trolls nor the Dragon has any mercy for the likes of you," Shaman informs. "Neither do the hounds depend on your truthfulness. Living or dead, they will retrieve the child and bring his carcass back to my master."

Tears begin to stream down her face as her helplessness is

reinforced by her circumstance. The only defense her son has rests in the fact that she doesn't know who wound up taking the child or where he is now. Since the Dragon's hounds don't need to know that, she says a silent prayer that those keeping him will be able to defend him. They'll need all the help they can get in order to prepare for what's coming their way and protect him.

Bog allows the hounds time to solidify the scent of the garment in their minds even to the extent of tearing it to pieces in a tug of war between them. He then releases them from their chains. He climbs aboard a nearby mount and commands them to hunt. They growl, snarl, and snap at one another first. Then they sniff the air and bolt forward heading south. Bog goads his mount to follow. The beings of Fire and Ash clear a path through the edge of the battlefield. They run full speed through the human and dwarf lines disappearing into the dense forest.

"Stop them!" Sabrina futilely yells out. No one other than Shaman and Lucius can hear her over the battle raging below. She continues to pray for the safety of her son amid the Dragon's mocking.

"Don't waste your breath princess. If the Most High truly cared about you, do you really think he'd have allowed me out of my prison."

"Prayer is all that's left to me. I can't say why he allowed you to escape, but I do know that you'll be defeated."

"You over estimate your chances. Your forces are no match for my power."

"We would rather die than serve you."

"And die you shall including your accursed offspring. My future will be secure with no one left to challenge me."

Sabrina works a few seconds to collect as much sputum as she can and spits it upon the Dragon's face. He takes his long serpentine tongue and licks it off savoring its flavor. After that, he begins to laugh in her face then turns to continue watching the battle. Sabrina renews her task of remembering the incantation with a vengeance.

CHAPTER 16

In the Canyon of Woes, Prince Horeb and his small band have been working day and night to destroy all the clutches of eggs. They are covered in slime and have begun to stink. Dirt clings to their boots in clods of mud consisting of slime, dirt, and their own sweat. They're tired and in need of sleep, but they dare not rest for a moment. Horeb and Rastus step outside the cave for a breath of fresh air having completed their task inside this particular cave. The prince kneels down and grabs a handful of sand to clean the slime off his sword before sheathing it. He grabs the goatskin hanging from his waste and takes a gulp of water to quench his thirst.

"Do you think we got them all?" Horeb asks.

"It's hard to tell," Oleg responds. "Some of the clutches were pretty advanced while others were not. We're looking at a laying over several weeks, and this place is a maze of tunnels and caves."

"I guess the only way we'll know for sure is if we don't see any dragons," Horeb quips after taking another swig of water.

"Prince Horeb, I found another clutch!" Argo calls out.

"Well that answers your question," Oleg adds.

"It would seem…" Horeb begins to respond but then stops mid-sentence. He hears a strange noise. In the distance a few yards away, peculiar sounds begin to emanate from a cave that has yet to be investigated. Everyone whether inside a cave or not stop their talking and turn slowly around. They see a most detestable sight. Dragons, the size of a full grown war horse, emerge in various flocks and take to the skies.

"It's for sure, we didn't get them all," Oleg offers in disbelief that there could still be more after all that they have already destroyed.

"You think? Everyone follow me!" Horeb yells. His men and the dwarfs follow quickly. Their tiredness is washed away by the flow of adrenaline surging through their bodies. They attempt to fight and kill the dragons before they take flight, but that's easier said than done as they are quickly outnumbered.

Horeb and Rastus arrive at the cave entrance first and begin to combat the dragons. They are very agile and deadly with spiked teeth both in their mouths and on the top of their tails. Horeb lunges for one who maneuvers almost effortlessly out of his sword's path. It quickly turns and slaps Horeb with its tail. The spikes barely miss him knocking him on his backside. The dragon hovers over him and snorts. Horeb instinctively covers his face preparing for fire to be spit at him, but there was none. The animal pauses which allows for Rastus to lop off its head.

"Why didn't it burn me with fire?" Horeb asks amazed his skin isn't charcoal. He returns quickly to his feet to take on another dragon. While he's engaged with one dragon, others are taking to the air. It's painfully evident that there aren't enough of them to stop all the dragons from leaving the canyon.

"According to legend, a baby dragon can't blow fire until a day after emerging from its egg. It would seem that the liquid it floats in is flammable. It doesn't dry and flake off until a full day has elapsed," Rastus finally manages to answer Horeb's question.

"Don't you think you should have shared that information with me sooner since we're drenched in it?"

"Sorry, it's not like we're going to be throwing flames at one another," Rastus apologizes while dodging a snapping jaw. This time it's Horeb that provides the life saving slice.

Young Andrew takes to the fight trying to weed out the dragons numbers, but his efforts have minimal impact. He doesn't let up, however, doing all in his power to thin out the herd. His surge of energy doesn't last for long and calls out to his prince to find out what their next orders will be.

"Too many of them are getting away!" Andrew yells out.

"Cease your attacks, save your strength," Horeb orders. The dwarfs look at Oleg who nods his agreement. Their strength is already spent, and they don't need to die from exhaustion which is where they currently find themselves.

"Do you have a plan?" Oleg questions of Horeb.

"I need to get back to the battlefield and help my brother. We've done all we can here."

"But what about the new clutch I found?" Argo inquires.

"Argo is right, we need to finish the job, but I need to go back and help my brother."

"How do you intend to do that? We are many days travel from the Plains of Galeed. It'll all be over by the time you get there," Rastus adds.

"Not as the dragon flies," Horeb suggests. His eyes light up at the thought of catching a ride on the back of one of these beasts.

"That's a bad idea," Rastus warns.

"Listen to him," Quimby adds having finally joined the conversation. "He has a point. It won't be easy, but I think if we can distract one your window of opportunity will present itself."

"Doubtful it'll be a wide window…" Horeb surmises.

"Well, it's not like we're going to run out of dragons anytime soon."

They continue defending themselves from the dragons as they emerge, and there is no end in sight. Horeb studies with one eye how those that are taking to flight are behaving while keeping his other eye on defending his person.

"My prince, what are you suggesting?" Sebastian asks but knows full well what the prince is suggesting is insanity.

"I'm going to hitch a ride," Horeb responds. Sebastian sees a mischievous gleam alight in his eyes at the thought of jumping on the back of a dragon and flying back to the battlefield. As the heir to the throne of Navarre, it's his place to be with his warriors.

"Are you daft?" Sebastian blurts out without thinking. Horeb cocks an eyebrow and a smirk of a grin.

"Probably, but I have to return and lead my people in their most desperate hour. It's my duty to be there for them."

"But Sire, its suicide," Sebastian reasons, knowing it's not doing any good.

"Maybe, but it's the only way I can get there in time to help them."

"Or you may become dragon food along the way."

"It's a possibility, but I have to try. Rastus, what does your legend say about ridding them?"

"To my knowledge, it's never been done."

"Okay, I have a day before they can blow fire and by that time I should be close enough to the battlefield to rejoin my people and lead them in the last attack."

"We must stay and prevent as many as we can from taking flight. That is our purpose," Oleg informs.

"Understood, to quote my former wife, until next time…" Horeb bids farewell standing to his feet and sheathes his sword.

"May the Most High protect you…" Oleg responds. The goodbyes are short as the dragons are not easing up on the attack.

Horeb breaks through and jumps on the back of the first dragon he comes to. The creature is not happy about having a rider. He twists his head around and snaps at this uninvited guest. Horeb lunges backwards, and into the dirt, he falls with a thud. The wind is knocked out of him, and the dragon takes off for the skies. The others are not interested in him and ignore him. Andrew comes to his side to help him up. Horeb appreciates the assistance.

"I'm going with you," Andrew informs.

"It's not wise to follow me this time."

"My place is with you. I'll not stay unless you stay."

"Well, I'm not staying, but at the moment we're not going anywhere. I have to figure out a way to gain control of the beast like I do my horse. That's it!" Horeb exclaims as an idea comes to him. He still has a small rope hanging from his belt. He grabs it and fashions it into a makeshift lasso. He watches for a moment as several more dragons take to flight looking for the optimum moment to jump onto one of their backs.

The moment arrives, and Horeb takes a running leap. This time he grabs the fins protruding from the sides of its head and tosses the rope over its head. He quickly wraps it around its snout so it can't bite him. The dragon takes to flight and does its best to buck Horeb off its back. It's a wild ride, but the prince manages to stay on the dragon. The dragon makes one final attempt to lose his uninvited guest as he spirals straight up breaking into an upside down barrel role. Horeb wraps his arms around the dragon's neck in a death grip. Finally, the beast tires of trying to rid himself of his passenger and flies toward the Plains of Galeed with his fellow spawn.

Andrew follows his prince's lead and makes another lasso. He waits patiently for his opportunity to come. He doesn't have to wait long for it. He runs, jumps, and quickly secures the dragon's head. He, too, goes for a wild ride before the dragon gives up on dismounting his unwanted rider. Just like Horeb, he disappears from view.

Those left on the ground continue to battle the emerging hoard until their last bit of strength is spent. After what seems like hours, the last of the dragons take to the air. The men and dwarfs collapse in the shade of the cave. The air is still, and quiet save for their breathing. They listen for any signs of other dragons and believe that they have dispatched with all they could. Argo regretfully reminds them that there is still another known clutch that needs to be destroyed. They check a few of the eggs to see how far along they are. Luckily, they're many days from hatching. They release a collective sigh as relief settles over them.

"We have some time. We need to rest, or we'll not be good to anyone," Oleg informs. It wasn't a newsflash as they're all exhausted. They refresh themselves with some water and find shelter inside a shallow cave that is devoid of the smell of rotting dragon eggs.

Sleep deprived, they are quickly overtaken by slumber and sleep through until the next day. After that, they eat to strengthen themselves and then finish off the last known clutch before starting the long journey home. Although none of them know if home will be there when they get back, they still yearn to return.

CHAPTER 17

Rachel is up early and is wandering in the forest near the crossroads. She needs the distraction of doing something familiar so she looks for roots, herbs, and fungus that she can turn into medicines. This familiar task keeps her mind busy. She recognizes that autumn is fast approaching, and she'll need to be ready for the winter, but her heart knows they may never see another autumn or winter again. In an attempt to refocus her wandering thoughts, she continues her search and comes across some fungus at the base of a tree with protruding roots. Rachel hesitates at first, but pushes through her doubt and kneels down to collect them.

After some time spent working on her hands and knees, she leans back to rest and her hand brushes against something familiar. Her mind races back in time to when she found Prince Horeb on a similar scavenging hunt. She closes her eyes and hopes beyond hope that she will find herself back there again in a time before everything was taken away.

When she opens her eyes, she discovers that it's just an exposed tree root sticking out of the ground that was worn smooth. Remnants of children's toys and exploration are still present in this area. Although disappointed that all that came before was not some ludicrous nightmare, she continues to collect the fungus and spies some licorice root not far away. She stops gathering the fungus and starts digging for the treat she knows will delight the children. While digging up the roots, she again allows her mind to wander back in time when she was nursing Horeb back to health. It's only now that she can admit to herself the deep attraction she had for him. It was only her love for Seth that kept her from being beguiled by Horeb's charm. She never knew Horeb prior to his accident. She had a difficult time accepting his explanation of how terrible he was prior to their meeting because she only saw his redeemed heart.

While deep in her own thoughts, she fails to hear Mark following quietly behind her until he steps on a branch snapping it in two. She jumps up ready to face whatever new terror has discovered her. Rachel is relieved when her eyes fall upon Mark. She puts her hand on her heart to calm it from beating so hard. Mark gives her the, 'I didn't mean to startle you look,' but it doesn't save him from her stating the obvious.

"You gave me such a fright."

"I didn't mean to. I didn't want to disturb you. You seemed

to be most enamored with your thoughts just now," Mark comments. Rachel blushes under his observation and then drops her eyes to the ground in shame for being discovered. She feels guilty for entertaining these thoughts of being attracted to another as if she has betrayed her late husband's memory.

"You needn't be ashamed to acknowledge that you love Prince Horeb also."

"How did you know what I was thinking just now?" She asks with grave concern wondering if he could read her mind.

"You were talking aloud as you relived your memories. I didn't mean to eavesdrop."

"I didn't realize I was speaking my thoughts aloud. I'm sorry," Rachel apologizes.

"Why are you sorry?"

"Seth was so jealous of Horeb when we first found him that for me to even be thinking such things offends his memory."

"You don't know do you?" Mark quizzes.

"Know what?"

"Seth gave you to Prince Horeb just before he died."

"He did what?" Rachel questions with disbelief.

"Seth knew that Horeb loves you and you could have no better protector than a warrior who loves you."

"Horeb never mentioned it."

"No, he didn't. He thought it disrespectful of Seth's memory to mention it so soon after his death."

"I don't believe it," Rachel declares.

"Then ask Jonathan. He was there and can bear witness to the truth I speak."

"Why didn't Jonathan tell me?"

"You were grieving the loss of your husband. Do you really think that anyone was going to interfere with that process and tell you that another is waiting in the wings?"

"No, I suppose not."

"The fact that you're allowing yourself to entertain these memories indicates that your time of mourning is coming to an end. You must now turn your focus to life."

"Life, you are amazing to think that life can survive this."

"Then why collect medicinal herbs and roots?"

"Habit and I needed something to keep my mind busy," Rachel states defensively although not convincingly.

"It's a reason, but I've come to you to let you know it's time to fulfill your promise to me. You must escort me to the Plains of Galeed."

Rachel looks at Mark in shock. His violet eyes have never been more serious. It's easy for her to forget that Mark is the self proclaimed Redeemer and no ordinary child. He blends in so well with the other children with one exception. His intellectual maturity rivals many adults. She puts the nearly full basket down taking only the licorice root with her to follow him back to the Tavern.

"Pick up the basket and leave it with your mother-in-law. She can make use of what you've gathered. We'll need cloaks, food, and water rations to bring with us."

"So there will be a winter…"

"I keep my promises. You'll see many more seasons in the coming years," Mark informs. This statement ignites the dying ember of hope within her, and she quickly obeys.

They return to the main building and pack for their journey. Laban watches his daughter as she prepares. He wants to go with her but knows that his place is with their people. He may not be able to fight, but he has wisdom and can keep them together. Rachel feels the weight of her father's stare. She stops her preparation and walks over to him.

"What is it, Papa?"

"You are all I have left in this world, and regardless of the prophecy spoken over you, I still worry. You are going to the battlefield, and you'll see things that you'll never be able to forget. I'm concerned what this will do to you."

"Papa, being left behind while you, Seth, and the others went off to war wasn't a cake walk."

"That may be, but you've never seen the horrors that war brings first hand."

"No, I haven't, but Seth gave his life so that Mark could fulfill his purpose. I can't refuse him."

"I know, but I'm a father first."

"I finished packing your food basket," Agatha informs interrupting their exchange. "Time is short, you need to get going."

Rachel nods her head in agreement. She kisses her father on the cheek goodbye. She kisses her mother-in-law also as she takes the basket from her. She pauses a moment to say farewell to her father-in-law also.

"Father," she begins announcing her presence. He reaches out into the air to take her hand. She grabs his hands cradling them in her own. "I have to go now. I must escort Mark to the Plains of Galeed so that he can fulfill the purpose that our beloved Seth gave his life to insure."

"My daughter," Samuel begins, his voice trembling. "Stay safe and know that no matter what the future holds, you will always be my daughter even when it's time for you to fulfill your purpose."

"My purpose?" Rachel questions.

"The one that Clairese spoke over you before she died…"

A tear wells up in Rachel's eyes and nods her head with humble thankfulness for his unconditional love. She wipes the tear from her face and responds verbally after kissing his forehead.

"I will always love you too, Father."

After saying her goodbyes, Rachel stands up and pulls the hood of her cloak over her head and walks to meet Mark at the door. He takes hold of her hand, and they walk out the door shutting it behind them. The younger children run after them to bid them farewell.

"Stop," Laban instructs the children. They turn around and look back at him. They're confused as this was their custom. To send someone away without a proper farewell was highly unusual. His face is stern but kind. The children look into his crystal blue eyes and respect his instructions returning to the game of marbles they were playing before Rachel and Mark left. Laban walks out alone to fulfill the custom and stands at the edge of the forest until he can no longer see them uttering a quiet prayer under his breath.

CHAPTER 18

Sasha, Soba, and Connor arrive at the Plains of Galeed with their warriors in tow. They've been traveling for a whole day and night and have arrived just two hours after sunrise. Sasha leaves the trio to engage the enemy on her own, but Tubal grabs her arm in response to the alarmed expressions on Soba and Connor's faces.

"What are you doing?" Tubal inquires of his sister.

"I'm going to free Princess Sabrina and perhaps dispatch with a few of the enemy along the way," Sasha explains with urgency.

"You need to rest before engaging," Connor informs even though he is for rescuing the princess that he has served since her birth. "It's suicide to engage in combat after such a long journey."

"He's right," Tubal adds.

"Rest?" Sasha questions defensively. "Are you blind to what is going on out there? They need us to relieve them."

"We wouldn't last long if we engage now. We've been marching for 26 hours straight. The warriors need to rest before they engage the enemy, and so do you. Besides the time isn't right…" Soba informs.

"What do you mean the time isn't right?"

"He means the skies are clear," Connor adds.

Sasha looks at him asking the unspoken question. Her focus is so intent on her specific mission that she temporarily forgot that even her part in this battle must play out within the proper timeframe. After a moment of starring into their shocked faces at her brash attempt to strike out on her own, she answers her own question.

"There are no dragons yet," she responds.

"Exactly, this army's strength is to be reserved for fighting the dragons and trolls," Soba reminds.

"My mission is more important than you realize and time is of the essence. If I wait too long, we'll lose a lot more than the princess," Sasha informs trying to explain her impulse to jump into the thick of it without giving anything away.

"If things don't unfold as they were meant to, you could cost us the war. As much as I would like to see my princess rescued, her life is not as important as our collective mission," Connor soberly cautions.

"Listen to Connor. Our mission could fail if you don't wait," Tubal urges. "I know you're not a patient woman, but please just this once heed their words." Tubal's voice is pleading and lingers in her ears.

"Yes, but I've seen certain things in my visions. Things I must fulfill…" Sasha tries to explain but is cut off by her brother.

"And those visions are incomplete at best. As Oracle, you of all people should respect and know that a fate can't be forced. Nor can you judge the strength needed to reach a particular point within those visions. These are the last days, perhaps the last hours, and everything has already been written," Tubal reminds.

"Brother you don't understand."

"I understand all too well that you're holding something back and not telling us everything."

"I can't tell you..."

"I understand, but in the same token, I can't let you go until the proper time," Tubal sternly informs. Her eyes plead for him to relent, but he remains steadfast. Although he has no prophetic sight, he has always known the proper time to cave and when to hold fast.

"Why do I always lose my arguments with you?" Sasha asks

as she stands down and turns to find a tree to lean upon.

"I've won arguments in the past?" Tubal mutters under his breath not realizing he'd won any of them.

Connor and Soba nod their relief that Tubal was able to talk some sense into his sister. They didn't want to make an enemy of those that have brought so much to the cause. With the impending attack of the dragons, their gift of fireproof shields is worth more than gold. The dwarfs pull away from the pair and begin to assess the lay of the land, so they'll be able to deploy their relief troops to the most badly needed areas.

As they walk around the perimeter of the trenches, they're successful in chasing away the jackals munching on their dead near the fringes of the conflict. They know, however, that the dogs will be back and that not everyone will receive a fit burial. On the contrary, with the dead so numerous, they'll need to dig mass graves. If they should lose, they'll not have that concern.

***

Prince Robert is providing guidance to the troops from the tops of the huge pine tree using signal flags to give directions to the field commanders below. He continues to supply the location of enemy weaknesses to the troops. This tactic yields fruit from time to time, but mostly it's just one mess after another with no clear victor among the skirmishes. His best remaining knights keep a tight perimeter around their sovereign deflecting random spears and arrows. Robert begins to notice that thirst and fatigue are beginning to cause as many casualties as death blows from the enemy. He's uncertain of how much longer they can hold out until relief arrives. The noise coming from the dispatched undead continue their clamoring to deafening decibels so much so that he can barely hear himself speak or think.

He dispatches his remaining knights to remove this hindrance and bring relief supplies to those that are most affected by thirst. They resist at first not wanting to leave their only remaining sovereign unprotected but capitulate to the prince's orders. He's relieved that they finally begin to leave his side. At the end of the day, his life is no more or less precious than those already engaged in the fight.

"Sire, are you sure you don't want us to stay?" Mordecai asks on his and Joss' behalf. He yells the question as loud as he can so that Robert can hear him.

"They need you more on the battlefield. Now go!" the prince responds.

"Yes, Sire," Mordecai nods his understanding and leaves Robert's side to bring water to those who need it with Joss' help.

Suddenly, from the chaos emerges a powerful being of Fire and Ash calling Robert out onto the battlefield by name. This isn't just any being. His skill as a warrior is known far and wide, but in life, Mathias was not his enemy. Now, his most valued warrior and trusted friend is calling him to battle. Mathias moves with smooth, articulate motions and because he's already dead doesn't tire from exhaustion nor thirst for water. The knights recognize Mathias and halt their dispersion to bring relief to their fellow warriors. They quickly return to Robert's side closing their ranks around him as he makes his way down the tree.

"Back away," Robert orders his guards. They look at him as if he's lost his mind. After all, it was he who gave the order to switch with another who's been called out by these creatures.

"Sire, your orders were not to engage with those who knew us in life," Joss reminds Robert.

"This one is different. I will face him myself. Now go relieve your fellow fighters!" Robert is loud and stern so they can hear him over the noise and doesn't have to repeat himself.

Robert continues climbing down from his perch, draws his sword, and faces off against his old ally. They walk circling each other first, taking note of vulnerable areas. Before they begin to fight, Robert attempts to reach out to his old friend.

"Do you know your name?" Robert quizzes. The creature just stares back at him through flickering eye sockets filled with fire never letting his guard down.

"I was called Mathias," the creature states slowly, lacking the emotion of seeing an old friend. Robert wants to know just how much control Lucius has over these beings and whether there is any hope of saving them.

"Do you remember me, your sovereign, Prince Robert? We went searching the forests for my brother, Horeb, together. Do you remember?"

"Yes," the creature finally responds. His voice, lacking the full vibrato of what he possessed in life, carries familiar tones that languish in regret.

"If you remember me, then why fight me? I'm not your enemy."

"I'm compelled to do so by a force I can't control," Mathias responds striking first. Robert is quick to jump to the side out of the way of the attack maneuver.

"You were a logical man. You were also the strongest in will, integrity, and strength of any knight that served our house. You must try to fight against the power of the Dragon."

"You don't understand. I have no choice. I was the sacrifice that allowed Lucius to be released. I'm bound to him in ways you can't possibly understand."

"I don't want to fight you!" Robert insists while he takes

another swing.

"What you want doesn't matter anymore than what I want. Destroy me now! It's your only hope!" Mathias demands as his sword lunges through the air nicking Robert's torso. Robert jumps back to avoid the fatal blade. After this close call, Robert finally begins his attack in earnest.

"Very well," Robert responds. He uses every battle strategy he has ever learned against the former commander of the king's army who always won every engagement. After exhausting every maneuver he knows, Robert finds himself flat on his back against the blood soaked battlefield. He braces for the inevitable death blow, when out of nowhere an ax slicing through the smoke filled air decapitates Mathias' head. His head falls off and rolls into a nearby stream. His body which can't die runs off toward the enemy side of the battlefield useless.

Robert sits up and looks over to where the ax came from to see Rasmussen standing stately at the edge of the battlefield donning a disappointed expression. Robert retrieves his ax and brings it back to the general who walks out the rest of the way to retrieve it. When he hands it over to him, Robert receives a brief, succinct lecture.

"Idiot, stop playing around. Now get back up on that platform and command your army!"

Robert doesn't even muster a defense. He broke his own rule, and it'll never happen again. While climbing back up the ladder to his perch, he notices that reinforcements from the south have arrived. To his surprise, they appear to be sleeping as if on holiday. This angers him a lot and climbs back down to inform Rasmussen.

"Did you know that our reinforcements have arrived?" Robert asks yelling up at the General who was nearly halfway back up to his perch.

"Yes, I saw," he responds halting his climb.

"They're napping, why don't they rise up and fight?"

"You're angry…" Rasmussen surmises.

"You should be angry too. We've been fighting for two days straight. Our troops need rest."

"It'll become apparent soon enough."

"Why must you talk in riddles?"

"I don't talk in riddles," Rasmussen defends.

"Then speak plainly for once."

"Keep your eyes on the horizon. I suspect that dragons will be filling the skies shortly. Once they do, our support will fall in line and take over the fighting from what's left of us. If we waste their resources on this portion of the battle, we'll lose for sure."

Prince Robert nods his understanding and continues on with his task. He returns to his own tree and climbs back to the top. He wipes his sweat soaked light brown hair out of his eyes and surveys the battlefield. His heart drops as he begins to watch human and dwarf alike succumb to the reanimated forms of those they once called their kin. He tilts his head back and forth rubbing his neck to relieve his fatigue. While checking for additional injuries, he may have sustained from Mathias, his eyes catch a glimpse of something in the sky growing larger with each passing moment. It looks like more vultures at first, but then in the glow of the setting sun, he catches a glimpse of shiny scales reflecting the sun's light.

"Sound the trumpets and raise the alarm flags!" Robert yells. No one can hear him over the clamor of the battlefield. He then drops the appropriate colored flag to the ground. This catches Angus's eye, and he alerts the trumpeters.

The trumpeters' sound the alarm while those who remain near the trenches tend to the wounded that could be retrieved. They raise red warning flags. All eyes on the battlefield that are able look toward Prince Robert to find out what the alarm is for understand the meaning of the red flags. Even the enemy pauses to see if their reinforcements have come. They are redirected to look towards the northern horizon. All of them including Rasmussen look in the direction the prince is pointing. As the sun gives its last rays of light, the full moon rises above the mountains casting an eerie glow upon the creatures heading straight for them.

"Dragons!" Rasmussen yells at the top of his lungs. He quickly drops another flag. This time the dwarf trumpeters sound a second volley of alarms announcing the dragons' arrival. This was the sound that Soba and Connor have been waiting for. Now it's time for the secondary troops to enter the fight. The dwarfs, women warriors, and the warriors of Elim form their ranks and move into position. The Warriors of Elim form a defensive line of interlocking shields and march across the field pushing back the enemy step by step.

The commotion catches Lucius' ear. He sees the dragon scale shields and knows that there is only one reason the humans would deploy those. He takes off into the sky to get a better view. Lucius flies upward so that he can see over the mountain tops. He catches the first glimpses of his progeny heading straight for him. With great delight and pride, he shrieks and bellows in rhythmic calls deep from inside his throat to his young that are fast approaching. They respond back in like manner. A satisfactory grin fills his face to the full exposing every razor sharp, jagged tooth in his mouth. He circles back for a precise landing near the princess to gloat.

"Now princess, you'll witness the end of your people. My

children will be here in minutes, and they're hungry."

All of a sudden the new troops make their full presence known. The women warriors ride atop armor laden horses storming the battlefield with maces and javelins. Rested and ready, the second wave of dwarf troops rushes onto the field to take over for the exhausted infantry. The survivors attempt to make their way back to the safety of the trenches but must fight for every inch of their retreat.

"I wouldn't be too sure," Sabrina counters. She looks on with pride at the fierceness of her women warriors, the steadfastness of the next wave of dwarfs, and Sasha's kin.

"Don't take too much comfort in this secondary line of warriors. They eat just as well as any other human or dwarf."

"You're over confidence will be your downfall."

"Mine? You amuse me. It's you who are overconfident. You are my prisoner and will never see your family again. Not even your God raises a finger to save you."

"You say that as if I should be shocked," Sabrina whispers, her throat dry and cracking. She swallows what little bit of saliva she can muster and continues, "Leave God out of this! He didn't leave us, we left him. We'll never serve you and will go down fighting. Besides, I already knew I'd never see my loved ones again when you took me prisoner..."

"So be it," Lucius comments, cocking the dragon equivalent of an eyebrow at her. He was curious about her foreknowledge, but the reason was too inconsequential to warrant further study. He leaves his troops to continue the fight while he flies to greet his children and lead the first raid with them. The young have now acquired the ability to blow fire, and they approach the battlefield with flame on and strafe the enemy below. The troops take shelter under their shields. They join them together to protect more warriors than the number of shields that were issued.

A spearman standing atop one of the trenches manages to take out one of the young on its first approach. Unfortunately, it was the one that Prince Horeb was riding. He and the dragon come in low spiraling out of control toward the human and dwarf side of the field landing with a thud among the growing pile of dead bodies. The humans rush toward them to finish off the dragon when Mordecai sees Horeb. He hurries to help his prince.

"Are you alright my prince?"

"The wind was knocked out of me is all…" He's cut off mid-sentence by Andrew's attempted landing.

The young knight hopes he can land near his prince. His plan quickly fails as the dragon he's riding attempts to take out Prince Horeb and Mordecai. Andrew pulls back hard as if pulling back on a horse thwarting its attempt.

"Get out of the way! Run!" Andrew yells.

Horeb looks up at the growing fireball in Andrew's dragon's mouth. He grabs Mordecai's arm and dives under the wing of his downed dragon. Andrew's dragon fights his attempt to pull its head to the side. The fireball the dragon spews, glances the ground below missing its intended target.

Horeb and Mordecai attempt to get make a dash for their side of the battlefield, when a second dragon trailing the one Andrew is riding attempts to burn them. It misses as they dart back under the dead dragon's wing. A warrior of Elim tosses them a shield which Mordecai uses to quickly escort Prince Horeb to the safety of the trenches.

"I'm glad to see you and Andrew made it. I hope he can find a way to get off that beast," Mordecai greets.

"We're glad to be here. Andrew's young and inventive. He'll find a way. Where's Robert?"

"Up there in the tree."

Horeb runs toward his brother and climbs the tree with enthusiastic relief. Robert turns sword in hand to defend himself and is quickly relieved to see his brother. They hug slapping each other on the back.

"Damn, you stink," Robert comments.

"You don't smell like a rose yourself," Horeb counters back.

"I don't care I'm glad you're here and safe. I take it I can assume from the sky filled with dragons that you were unsuccessful."

"Well, it wasn't a total success, but we did manage to destroy over 500,000 eggs before they could hatch."

"Okay, I take that back. Well done!" Robert congratulates.

"What's the plan?"

"Kill the enemy and live."

"Good survival plan, but I meant strategy," Horeb comments

Robert nods his head to the affirmative and takes the next few minutes to explain their strategy. All, however, depends on the Army of Light showing up and the slimmest of chances that the Redeemer will arrive to seal the deal.

***

While the brothers get caught up on the progress of the battle and the plan for victory, Sasha starts to weave her way through the chaos taking the enemy out along the way. Tubal notices that she is moving deeper into enemy territory and follows behind her to protect her blind spot.

"What are you doing?" Tubal asks as he finishes off a

reanimated warrior that was about to take out his sister.

"I have to reach the princess before more people die."

"What does freeing her have to do with fewer casualties?"

"To give her the incantation," she confesses.

"You're not supposed to have the incantation," Tubal confronts in a panic. Although he would never be an Oracle, he is well versed in the prophecies and the penalties for violating fate.

"You think, but something's happened, and she can't remember it."

"It's a suicide mission!" he yells over the noise of the battlefield. They duck under their shields as a low flying dragon comes whizzing by with flames at full intensity. Luckily it had its sights set on another group, or they could have easily lost their shields in its talons.

"I know that, but it's necessary. We have to stop the beings of Fire and Ash. They don't tire, thirst, grow hungry, or die."

"Alright, but I'm going with you every step of the way," Tubal insists.

"I wouldn't have it any other way."

"Then why did you start without me?"

"You always said I was impulsive, and you always follow me.

I assumed you were already doing what you normally do."

Tubal just cocks an eyebrow at her then yells, "Duck!" Sasha obeys ducking down toward the ground while Tubal sways to the side then comes back around sending the head of their attacker flying into the chaos.

"Nice," Sasha comments on her brother's battle skills.

They continue weaving their way through the enemy. Progress is slow between the attacks coming from the skies and from the ground moving two steps forward and one step back. The howls of jackals fighting over human and dwarf remains are equaled only by the screeches of vultures demanding their own prizes. Her impulse is to run them off so they can be buried with honor and dignity, but the living is of greater concern at this moment. Victory depends upon her getting the magic words to the princess, and that task isn't going to be easy.

Glenda C. Finkelstein

CHAPTER 19

Rachel and Mark make it as far as Indra arriving just after moonrise. Most of the buildings of this once great city are burnt out shells. Some of the disheveled piles of blocks boast the finishes of a more elegant building while others are nothing more than pulverized rubble. The stone blocks made from marble and quartz reflects the moon's light glowing in subdued hues upon random heaps of debris. Statues that once stood proudly in the various squares litter the ground in dismembered chunks clustered near their pedestals. The remaining walls that still stand erect are peppered with broken windows. Signs identifying merchant shops hang in disarray by a single chain or lay broken on the ground. The closer they come to the ruins the more their presence disrupts the foraging of opossums, mice, rats, and the occasional feral cat as they scamper away in search of quieter spaces.

Rachel jumps when she accidentally startles a cat on the hunt for a mouse. She grabs her chest as she simultaneously jumps backward. The cat runs headlong into her ankles, and Rachel loses her balance and steps on the end of its tail. The cat screeches. Rachel lifts her foot, and the cat makes its getaway unharmed save for its own nerves hissing and meowing as it goes.

"Startle easy?" Mark asks.

"Really? That didn't startle you?"

"I saw him stalking the mouse, I thought you did too."

"No, I didn't see him. I was looking around at what's left of what was a beautiful city. Seth didn't exaggerate about its beauty. Even in ruin, it bespeaks of beauty."

"Yes, it was lovely, and it will be again," Mark comments as he gazes about.

"You speak so confidently that there will be a future. How can you be so sure?"

"Because I'm not a boy...I'm much more than that. I was hoping you'd be able see that by now."

"You're asking me to see things that aren't there. How can you rescue us from this present evil?"

"How is not your concern I'm asking you to trust me and have faith so that you can maintain your hope."

"Hope and faith, you sound like my father," Rachel counters rolling her eyes.

"At least one of us does. Don't you understand that faith is being sure of what we hope for and certain of those things we can't yet see?"

"You make it sound so easy to believe."

"There's the rub, it's simple, but not easy," he explains. Rachel looks at him with wonderment in her eyes. She wants to believe, but her reality screams the opposite of anything hopeful. They continue walking through the abandoned streets in silence with Mark taking the lead allowing Rachel to reflect upon their conversation in private.

They continue on for a few more minutes traversing the debris carefully in order to avoid injury. The full moon is of great assistance in allowing them to discern the safest path through the mess. As they near the far end of the city a lone building stands erect and intact. The roof also appears to be whole. The sign which has accumulated several layers of dirt and dust hangs intact by the door. Rachel takes her hand and wipes away the dirt so she can see what it says.

"The Royalty Inn," Rachel reads aloud.

"This is where we'll spend the night," Mark informs as they enter the building amazed at how unscathed it is.

"It's so dark inside," Rachel comments.

"Not for long, I have my flint and knife. I'll just light this oil lamp."

"Isn't the oil gone by now?"

"There's enough to keep the wick lit until we can start a fire in the fireplace. We'll want to be indoors tonight. The forest is thick on the other side. There's no road to the Plains of Galeed, so we'll have to find our own way."

"Very well," Rachel acknowledges her agreement with his plan and takes to heart his cautionary statement.

In no time at all, they have a fire going in the fireplace. The light it gives off fills the room with a golden warm glow. It's enough light to be able to find more intact oil lamps and explore the Inn for food, pillows, and blankets. Rachel finds a hidden freshwater well in the kitchen, and after sampling the water which is cool and refreshing, she fills their water skins to the full for the next day's journey.

"Look what I found!" Mark announces with the glee of a child.

"What?" Rachel asks poking her head out of the cellar which is full of food.

"Licorice..." he announces already having started chewing on a stick.

"I think we need more than just candy. I found some dried beef, fruit, nuts, and oats. I can make us a bowl of porridge."

"Excellent."

Rachel obtains a small pot and places the oats, fruit, and water over the fireplace. Soon the kettle is cooking nicely. They munch on some dried beef and nuts while they wait for the oats and fruit to cook. They sit quietly in front of the warm fire wrapped in some blankets that Mark found in an upstairs linen closet. They stare into the fire watching the flames dance along the timbers. Rachel finally breaks the silence and asks the question that she's been dying to know the answer to ever since she found out he was the Redeemer.

"How will you defeat the dragon? I know you say that you are more than you appear and that it's none of my concern, but all I see is a boy that my husband died to save. What can you do that no one else can?"

"You want to be certain that Seth's sacrifice was not in vain."

"Yes, I do."

"Then you can rest in the fact that I can," Mark offers. He then picks up a poker to stoke the fire. Rachel can tell from his manner that he intends to leave the matter at that, but she can't accept that simple of an answer.

"You didn't answer my question. How...?"

"Can I defeat the Dragon?" Mark cuts her off, finishing her question then continues, "That's not your concern."

"But..."

"No buts. Clear your mind of questions. You'll see for yourself soon enough. Besides, if I told you now, you'd never believe me."

"Alright then, what's going to happen after you defeat the Dragon?"

"Something wonderful..." Mark responds beaming a great smile.

"Let me guess, I wouldn't believe you if you told me," she offers.

"Your understanding is improving," he comments with a mischievous grin on his face. Rachel goes to sound a rebuttal, but Mark points out that the oats have finished cooking. She expels a heavy sigh glaring at him in pretend anger. He continues grinning un-phased by her frustrated response. She flashes a sarcastic smile back at him as she fills each cup to the full. They let it cool for a little while before eating it, but their conversation is over until the next morning.

***

Several miles away Bog, trailing behind Lucius' hounds, reaches an area where the scent has become diffused. Bedlam and Chaos pace in circles keeping their noses to the ground searching for the right scent to follow. The dogs are panting heavily, but are entranced by finding the scent which has almost grown cold. Bog pulls back on his mount allowing the dogs to pick up the scent again in their own time. He doesn't want to hurry them and waste time on a trail that's no good.

Suddenly, Bedlam lifts his head and sniffs the air blowing in from the south. He barks alerting Chaos to do the same. He sniffs and barks also then both hounds take off at full speed across the low plains. Bog goads his mount forward to follow. The hounds are quick and stop only long enough to catch their breath and take a drink from one of the tiny brooks that trickle through the lowland areas. Bog realizes that their heading will take them to the Port of Salt. He begins to worry if their quarry has boarded a vessel. If that is the case, then they'll never find the young prince. Bog does his best not to concern himself with things he doesn't yet know and maintains his focus on keeping up with the hounds.

The moon shines brightly illuminating the terrain as if it were noonday. This allows them to travel through the night being limited only to the endurance of both the hounds and his mount. The crisp night air keeps them invigorated and sharp which is excellent for their purpose but spells doom for their intended target.

Glenda C. Finkelstein

CHAPTER 20

On the Plains of Galeed, the new warriors take their places on the battlefield relieving the battered first wave. The fighting continues fiercely. No ground is lost in the process, but none is gained either. The sun breaks the horizon like it has done thousands of times before and goes unnoticed by the fighters. Yet, this daybreak will bring with it something unprecedented. Prince Robert continuously monitors the progress of the enemy and notices that they're attempting to out flank them. He instinctively signals the troops that are taking a respite to create a welcoming committee for the intruders. If it works as intended, the enemy will think twice before trying that again.

Robert's attention is captured by Rasmussen leaning over a branch pointing frantically to the south of them. Robert pulls out his spyglass and looks first at ground level. All he sees is a huge cloud of dust with movement inside the cloud. He then raises his sightline above the trees and sees creatures coming towards them above the huge cloud of dust. Their speed is exceptional. At first, he believes that the dragons have slipped around them with goodness knows what racing towards them on the ground. He begins to think that what was happening on the battlefield was a rouse to catch them off guard and soon they'll have a war on two fronts.

"Horeb!" Robert calls down with alarm.

"What is it?"

"Get up here! I need you to take a look at something and give me your opinion on what is coming towards us."

Horeb quickly climbs the tree. He positions himself onto an adjoining branch, reaches out to take the spyglass from Robert and nearly drops it being glanced by a passing arrow. He immediately grabs his arm with his hand.

"Are you alright?" Robert asks.

"I'll live," Horeb responds after examining it to discover it's just a cut not even deep enough to require stitches. He repositions himself, so he doesn't fall out of the tree and holds the spyglass up to his eye. He peers intently into it looking for what Robert couldn't articulate. He searches the sky, and then he sees them.

"It's more dragons, isn't it?" Robert asks in a panic, his tone displaying the discouragement in his heart.

"No, brother, they're not dragons. I'm not sure what they are, but I do recognize who's leading them."

"Who?"

"Javan, your wife's brother. He's got an army on the ground and in the air!"

"The Army of Light!" Robert exclaims in relief.

"Yes!" Horeb confirms with such enthusiasm that he nearly loses his balance, but catches himself just before falling out of the tree. Another volley of arrows whiz by his ear but misses him this time.

"Take it easy. You better get down before those archers hit their target. Go and tell Rasmussen."

Horeb agrees and quickly descends down the trunk. Once on the ground, he looks up to make sure Robert is still okay then runs over to the General to inform him of what's coming. An expression of relief fills the General's face as Horeb explains what's approaching from the South. No sooner does he finish his explanation than Javan's troops arrive upon the battlefield with explosive force.

Horse and rider weave meticulously through the camp but maintain a heady speed. The horses leap over the trenches where their wounded lay and engage the beings of Fire and Ash. The Firecats, divide into two squads and assume both defensive and attack positions against the dragons.

In the heart of the enemy camp, Lucius looks on in horror when he sees the Army of Light enter the field. Sabrina, however, dons a great smile recognizing her brother in the lead. He accomplished what he set out to do and his force is more massive than she ever imagined. Even in her weakened state, her chest puffs up with pride which is solidified when she sees weakness flash across Lucius' face.

"What's the matter Lucius feeling scared?" She questions, but Lucius ignores her.

"Trolls Engage! Demons destroy!" Lucius yells out giving the attack order to his reserve troops. His expression of shock is fleeting as thousands of trolls come rushing out of the caves while demons begin to do their hideous work. Now it's Sabrina that expresses a flashing moment of concern.

"What's the matter? You wouldn't be feeling scared would you?" Lucius asks. His question gives birth to an insidious grin.

"My brother shouldn't be underestimated," Sabrina finally responds with unwavering determination in her voice.

"When are you going to accept that this is my victory? You have failed to stop me or even slow my progress. Even the weapon that hangs around your neck is impotent because you don't know how to use it," Lucius taunts. His words prick her heart like a thorn, but she maintains an outward stoic facade.

Those on the battlefield unaware of the cavalry's arrival, feel the shift of the tides and realize that things are about to get worse and quick as trolls and demons descend upon them. Yet, at the same moment the enemy forces reach their position, the Army of Light bursts upon the scene. They clash like mighty Titans nearly crushing the humans and dwarfs. The human and dwarf warriors quickly respond to this change and reposition themselves so that they're not accidentally crushed by those sent to help them while remaining engaged in the battle.

Sasha and Tubal are in the thick of it and are presently attempting to avoid a fiery attack from above. They quickly dive under their shields at the last minute bracing for the force of a dragon's fiery breath, but it never comes. The sound of a roaring lion breaks the dragon's concentration as a Firecat jumps on its back and digs its claws in pulling it off them. The dragon shrieks from the intense pain of the razor sharp claws digging deep into its back. It tries to knock the Firecat off with its tail. When that doesn't work, it whips its head around snapping at the beast but fails to free itself.

Tubal peers out from behind his shield first then Sasha. Her eyes light up when she sees who rescued them. Tubal salutes his friend, Javan, who nods a quick acknowledgement. He can't allow himself to be distracted if he's going to finish off the dragon.

"You're boyfriend's back," Tubal comments with a huge grin.

"Yes, he is…Hurry Tubal we don't have much time left."

"I agree, but now we have trolls and demons to contend with. It's not going to be easy…Look out!" Tubal shouts grabbing Sasha's arm pulling her to himself out of the way of a falling dragon's head.

"Thanks!" Sasha acknowledges her brother's quick response. She looks up at Javan, who relieved the dragon of his head. He circles close to their position providing needed cover for their continued infiltration of the enemy camp.

***

Sasha and Tubal are making good headway inside the enemy lines. Javan surmises that they're attempting to reach his sister. He flies a little higher to find a safer route for them when he finds himself suddenly surrounded by three dragons. He quickly dives straight down onto the battle field pulling up only three feet from the ground and levels off to behead a row of trolls with his sword. Anak blades are much sharper than the human's blades and can pierce the troll's thick skin easily. The dragons are newly hatched and aren't experienced tacticians and follow after him. Two of them are dispatched by Javan's ground forces with a barrage of spears. They crash land amid the piles of dead bodies.

The third dragon is unscathed and engages Javan and his

Firecat. The animals lock jaws with fire gurgling in each of their mouths. They spiral towards the heavens locked in mortal combat like a monster tornado. Fire explodes from their mouths. Javan does his best to avoid being burned, but can't escape the heat. He finally manages to break the death lock, and they continue fighting high above the battlefield.

The row of dead trolls below provides an opening in the enemy lines for Sasha and Tubal. They take quick advantage of the opening to reach the other side where they can wind their way through the crags. In no time at all, they are within reach of Sabrina. Suddenly, they find themselves surrounded by demons. The demons first attempt to possess them, but their faith is too strong for that, so they fall back to another well known tactic, discouragement and oppression.

"Little Sasha..." they call to her in raspy droning whispers.

"Go away!" Sasha orders.

"You don't have the authority to order us..." the demons respond creating a whirlwind of sorts from the dust and blood of the battlefield. It's getting harder for her to breathe. Tubal can't reach her.

"You have no authority over me either," Sasha informs while gasping for every breath.

"We can still block your path."

"Leave us!" Tubal orders.

"We choose to stay here."

"In the name of the Redeemer of the Most High I command you to go!" Sasha orders with her last breath.

"She invokes the name of the Most High we must go," the leader amongst them orders and they withdraw. The demons dispersal disrupts the whirlwind, and she drops to her knees gasping for air. Tubal kneels down to help her.

"I'm alright," she informs as she begins to replenish the air in her lungs.

"No you're not, but you're alive," Tubal corrects. She smiles at his distinction. "Can you stand?"

"Yes."

"We must keep moving. No place will be safe for long."

After she catches her breath, Sasha and Tubal notice that they have reached their destination. Now it's just a matter of climbing up the wall. All of Lucius' troops are engaged with the enemy, and no one will even notice their infiltration of his camp. The only one not in the battle is Shaman, and his eyes are locked upon the violence below. He doesn't notice the two intruders sneaking into the camp. Lucius, too, is preoccupied with providing attack maneuvers to his progeny.

Luckily, they are downwind, so their human scent won't give away their presence. Sasha reaches for an outcropping of rocks and pulls herself up. Tubal follows closely after her. They scale the rock face with ease and pull themselves up and onto the plateau. They are careful to be as stealthy as possible so as not to give away their presence before they complete their mission. After they survey the area, Sasha makes her way to the princess while Tubal remains hidden behind the rocks.

Sasha quietly and gently makes her presence known to the princess. Sabrina recognizes her and realizes she's there to help. Sasha positions herself behind the princess kneels down and writes the magic words on the sand with her finger. Sabrina looks down near her feet. Her eyes light up as the words resonate in her memory. The princess nods her head, and Sasha quickly erases them with her hand and retreats back behind some rocks. Although Sabrina's voice is nearly gone, she finds new strength in receiving the magic words and begins to recite them.

"Batu, Ramah, Gleemah! I command the beings of Fire and Ash to return to their rest!"

Lucius and Shaman hear her speak the incantation and are stunned. The beings of Fire and Ash stop their attack, and their form blows away like dust in the wind. Now only the trolls and demons remain on the battlefield. With the arrival of Javan's forces, the advantage has turned slightly to the humans and dwarfs favor. Shouts of victory resonate through the battlefield as the last of the undead dissolve before their eyes. Now that the incantation has been invoked, the power of the amulet is released. The protection it previously afforded the princess is gone.

In a seething rage, Lucius inhales filling his lungs to the full as he prepares to expel his fiery fury upon her. Young Andrew, who followed Horeb on the back of a young dragon, has been making his way to the princess' position to fulfill his vow to protect her. He comes out of nowhere and jumps in front of the princess at the last second. He doesn't have a dragon scale shield. Andrew's bronze shield holds up for only a little bit then becomes red hot. It's form folds and buckles under the powerful breath of the Dragon. Lucius burns both Andrew and the princess alive reducing them to cinders. Lucius quickly returns to watch his victory unfold after dispatching with the princess while Shaman stands there staring at the aftermath contemplating his own mortality.

Sasha, safely tucked behind a rock and her dragon scale shield manages to remain safe. She is close enough to feel the intense heat released by the Dragon. It was so severe that perspiration breaks out upon her skin. Her brother Tubal is close by but remains hidden behind some rocks. He hopes that Shaman won't notice her, but with the princess and the surrounding brush gone her position doesn't shield her from Shaman's prying eyes. His worst fears are quickly realized as Shaman walks around the cage.

He catches Sasha by surprise. Tubal isn't close enough to prevent Shaman from overpowering his sister. Shaman sees Tubal rushing toward him to protect her and pushes her off the cliff's edge to defend himself. Tubal dives after her narrowly missing her tunic.

"Sasha!" he yells.

Shaman hovers close by. It's apparent that Tubal will be more difficult to deal with now, but expresses some satisfaction with getting his hands dirty again.

Javan has been keeping a close eye on his love's progress. The moment he sees her falling to her death, he leaps into action taking his Firecat into a steep, rapid descent. He swoops in just in time to grab Sasha by the shoulders preventing her from being dashed upon the rocks below. He carries her to the human side of the battlefield gently depositing her onto the meadow grasses.

"You have to go back and save Tubal!" Sasha pleads. Javan nods his head and begins his return trip to help Tubal. He is unfortunately ambushed by more dragons. Sasha says a quick prayer for her brother.

***

Tubal quickly turns and engages Shaman with a vengeance not knowing that his sister is alive. The sword fight attracts the Dragon's attention. Oddly, Lucius chooses not to defend his right hand minion leaving Shaman to defend himself. Shaman squares off against Tubal, and they fight ferociously. Tubal's grief and anger drives him forward. He attacks the physically stronger Shaman until he is backed against the rocks.

"You killed my sister!"

"That's my job puny human," Shaman responds. He manages to slip out of the corner that Tubal had boxed him in to. They pace around each other for a few seconds, then Shaman takes another jab at disarming Tubal. Their swords clank and clash sparking under the power of their swings.

"You have no honor," Tubal informs as he retaliates. His rage gives him the power to finally disarm Shaman and pin him against the rocks with no escape.

"No, I don't. Kill me and get it over with if you can," Shaman taunts. It's been a while since a human provided him any sport. It's only now that he realizes he underestimated his opponent and resolves to himself not to do it again.

"With pleasure," Tubal informs as he pulls back for the death blow. Shaman wriggles out of his grasp again and manages to re-arm himself. They fight and fight, until Shaman disarms Tubal, or so he thinks. Shaman doesn't know that Tubal has a dagger. This time Tubal doesn't waste his efforts talking and finishes Shaman off spilling his guts upon the rocky ground. Shaman's surprise fades quickly as his body drains of blood and organs.

Lucius gazes over to see Shaman face down on the ground amid his own innards. He looks briefly over at Tubal who wonders if he'll be eaten or burned alive. The Dragon surprises Tubal by turning his head back around to watch the battle. Tubal wastes no time in escaping down the rock face to retrieve his sister's body. To his surprise, he can't find her. He doesn't understand what happened to her, and fears that she became food for the dragons. All he finds is her shield. He grabs it and heads back to rejoin his people. His face is stained with the tears of personal loss. The salty rivulets mingle with the blood of the enemy that killed her.

***

Prince Robert watches helplessly through the spyglass the demise of his wife. His heart breaks and tears stream down his face. Out of the blue, an arrow comes whistling through the air and hits him center mass. An Anak warrior sitting atop a Firecat sees the attack and rushes in to kill the troll that did it, but it's too late for Robert. The force of the arrow causes irreparable damage to his vital organs as its poison tip disperses its venom. He falls out of the tree landing with a thud on the ground below. The force of his fall is broken only by a pile of dead warriors. Horeb runs to him pushing away anyone who gets in his way.

"Robert, talk to me," Horeb pleads as he arrives at his brother's position. He gently picks him up off the dead and cradles him in his arms. Robert looks into his brother's eyes.

"Andrew sacrificed himself to save her, but it wasn't enough…" Robert mutters. His last few words are punctuated by coughs as blood fills his lungs. In a matter of seconds, Robert is gone. Horeb squats down. He sits there a few seconds more holding his brother close to his chest. Horeb knows he has to continue to lead the people and can't allow himself the luxury of grief. He carefully lays his beloved brother down in the grass. He then climbs the tree to take his place. His clothes stained by his own and his brother's blood is a visual reminder of his heartache, but his resolve is strengthened. He gives the signal for the final push, and the battle continues with even more ferocity than it previously saw.

Today there is no Southern or Northern Kingdom warrior, just warriors of Navarre. All those that know what had just transpired say a silent prayer for Prince Horeb and continue to fight in the memory of Prince Robert. The touching moment between brothers reminds all of them of what they're fighting for. This war isn't about land, power, or resources. It's about life, family, and freedom.

Deep inside enemy lines, Connor and Soba fight back-to-back slicing out a path across the battlefield. Their preferred weapon, the ax, is lethal in their hands. Trolls fall to their right and to their left. The disappearance of the beings of Fire and Ash provide one advantage, their weapons were left behind to be used by anyone who can wield them. They notice that the trolls that are about to engage them suddenly do an about face. They look up to discover a dragon on approach. It spews its fire onto the ground slicing it like a knife. Connor and Soba jump out of the way.

The dragon rises high enough off the battlefield to turn and come back for a second strike. Connor goes to grab his ax, but it's currently residing in a troll's chest. He glances around and grabs one off the field lying near a slain comrade in arms. He pauses only briefly to mutter a 'thank you' under his breath. He grabs it by the leather strap swinging it like you would a mace, but faster and with a practiced hand lets it fly. The ax quickly finds its mark piercing the heart of the young dragon.

A horrifying and deafening screech erupts from its innermost being as it crashes onto the battle field. Soba tries to jump out of its way, but only manages to jump into its path. He is tangled in the creature's wing grunting and groaning as he tumbles head over heels. Friend and foe alike run to avoid being hit by this crashing reptile. Connor follows after his friend to make sure he's alright. The dragon finally stops, falling limp he pins Soba under his massive tail.

"You're not supposed to run into danger," Connor quips seeing that Soba is alive.

"It was out of control. Besides I didn't expect you to hit it the first time."

"I'm hurt," Connor admits.

"No, you're not. Are you going to help me up?" Soba asks.

"Of course," Connor replies extending his arm to help him back to his feet.

These comrades make their way back into the battle and meet up with another group of dwarfs. They gaze over at the signal trees to make sure they are where they're supposed to be. Their respite is brief as another squad of trolls head for their position.

CHAPTER 21

Rachel and Mark near the Plains of Galeed. Rachel's attention is captured by strange creatures flying above the trees engaged in combat. Her mind reflects back upon what her father told her in that she would see things she's never seen before. The tops of the trees are on fire here and there, but the ground is too saturated by the preceding storms to allow the fires to travel far. She has never seen a dragon or a Firecat and wasn't sure which, if either, was on their side.

"Mark, what are those creatures?"

"The scaly ones are the dragons, and the furry ones are Firecats."

"Which one is fighting on our side?"

"The Firecats are on our side."

"They're both so ferocious…Look out!" she shouts pushing Mark out of the way of a mortally wounded dragon falling from the sky. After the creature lands with a huge thud that shakes the ground beneath her feet, she picks up a stick and pokes it to insure the creature is dead. Satisfied that it's dead, she looks about for Mark. She doesn't see him and becomes panicked. "Mark, where are you?"

"I'm here," he announces popping up out of the bushes behind her. Rachel jumps six feet in the air.

"Don't do that," she insists.

"I'm sorry. I thought you saw me moving around in the bushes. I, too, was curious if it was really dead, but I wasn't stupid enough to poke it."

"Sorry, it's my first dragon. Besides if I saw you, would I be calling out to you?" Rachel questions in frustration. He just cocks his head and shrugs his shoulders. Rachel rolls her eyes unsatisfied with his non-verbal response.

"My apologies, I forget that you only have one lifetime to learn about your world."

"It's okay. I've never seen sights such as these before, and I'm scared of what else awaits us beyond the trees."

"You'll be physically fine. Come on, we need to go this way, or we'll wind up on the enemy side of the battle," Mark informs. Rachel nods her head in agreement and follows close behind.

As they walk forward, the air becomes increasingly acrid with the aroma of rotting corpses on the battlefield. They see some jackals and vultures feasting upon a dead troll nearby only to discover that this was where the most pungent of odors was coming from.

"I'm not sure what smells worse, a live troll or a dead one," Mark comments.

"I vote for the dead one, nothing could be worse than..." Rachel suddenly stops speaking and bends over holding her hair back to vomit into the bushes. Now the taste of bile in her mouth mingles with the putrid smells in the air to the point that she can't breathe. She tries to catch her breath after holding it a moment, but it doesn't last for long. She even tries sniffing a licorice stick, but it's no match for the smells permeating the air all around her.

"You'll get accustom to the smell in a little while. Besides the battle is winding down, and you won't have to endure it for long even if you don't," Mark points out.

"How comforting..." Rachel states. She is dissatisfied with his remarks but this is war, and Mark has more important things to do than to concern himself with her comfort.

They continue walking only a short distance more. They

can see the battlefield for the first time unobstructed by the forest and note that there are, but a few pockets of fighters left facing off against one another. The rest of the battleground is piled high with the dead, but the sky is still full of dragons and Firecats facing off against one another. They walk near the trenches to find hundreds upon hundreds of wounded and dying warriors. Dwarf and human alike are piled together with the nearly dead lying next to the already dead. Their wounds are covered in flies and gnats, and their clothes are soaked in perspiration, urine, fecal matter, and blood.

Her purpose as a healer is so overwhelmed by the egregious slaughter of living beings that she can scarcely even stop to offer comfort to any of them. Her eyes fill with tears of sorrow so great that she can't hold them back. Her voice, however, is mute. Her emotional display is composed only of silent tears of both grief and helplessness in the face of such overwhelming sights. Then inside her heart grows a righteous rage. Her tears stop, and she turns to confront Mark.

"When do you step in to save them? When they're all dead?" she questions accusatorily.

"I knew this would be difficult for you, but I promise you in a matter of hours all of this sorrow, pain, and death will be wiped away. Everything will be new again as if the battle never took place. All who have died will find rest and peace and those who survive will understand this and will possess a peace that passes all understanding and be filled with unrestrained joy."

Rachel stares into Mark's eyes. His demeanor is no longer that of a child, but of a divine being with a purpose and mercy, she has yet to fully understand. His violet eyes disarm her anger without condemnation for her reaction. She is lost in his gaze as if staring into a peaceful pool of water. Rachel turns away and begins to watch the final battle come to an end.

Dragons and Firecats although fewer now than when they first arrived still fight overhead, but the ground battle is over. The Trolls are dead, and the demons have no one left to frighten and have withdrawn to the caves behind Lucius' position. Prince Horeb realizes that the battle is nearly done and there are few that remain. When the battle is finished, there will still be Lucius to contend with, and that isn't going to be easy. Should they win, the survivors will begin the arduous task of extracting the remaining injured from among the dead and digging mass graves for the fallen.

Horeb climbs down and sends Mordecai up to keep watch just to be certain that the enemy doesn't have any other surprises in its arsenal so he can make preparations. On the way down he spots Rachel walking along the trenches with Mark. He blinks thinking he may be hallucinating. He hasn't slept or eaten in days.

"Rachel?" he calls questioningly.

"Horeb?" she responds.

His heart leaps inside his chest when he hears her voice call his name. He runs to her and embraces her in his arms. The moment he touches her, Rachel's heart beats so fast that she can barely contain it in her chest. She melts in his strong arms while he caresses her head allowing his fingers to intertwine in her long black hair. Rachel pulls her head away so that she can look upon his face. Her hazel eyes gaze deeply into his. His face is unshaven sporting a scraggly beard of several weeks. His hair is longer than she remembers. Horeb leans in, and Rachel does not pull away even though he stinks as bad as the rest of them. He kisses her with the sweetest expression of love he could muster. Their lips linger pressed together before he finally pulls away to inquire why she is here.

"What are you doing here? This is no place for you."

"Mark requested that I escort him to this place," she responds, her voice still reflective of their very private moment.

Before Horeb can comment on that, a long mournful and angry howl pierces the air. When they turn around, they discover that the air is free of dragons and Firecats alike. They lay littered upon the ground like refuse. The cry comes from Lucius, the Dragon. His anger seethes inside him. Fire streams from his mouth lashing out in all directions as he takes to flight. Horeb pushes Rachel to the ground so that the trenches can protect her from this attack. She doesn't resist his instinctual response and stays put.

"Stay down!" Horeb insists. She nods her head yes.

Lucius strafes the battlefield. Those still out on the field dive under the Dragon's dead young to keep from being burnt alive. After circling the battlefield, Lucius then takes up a position in the middle of the field. At one time the place on which he currently stands was an alter not unlike the one found in the town square near Ophir's castle. He refuses to surrender even though a few thousand human, Anak, and dwarf warriors remain vs. none of his forces. He stands defiant, taunting, and vengeful.

"You have slaughtered my children. I shall kill all of you for that crime myself."

The humans and dwarfs attempt no response. They meet his decree with silence.

"I demand that you fight me! Send me a champion," Lucius declares. Again he is met with silence, but none of them move. Then all of a sudden Mark appears upon the battlefield. He is unarmed and walks slowly towards the great Dragon.

"Have you run out of warriors that you send your children to sate my appetite for vengeance?"

"Your fight is with me Dragon. I'm their champion," Mark

calls out his voice still maintains that childlike resonance.

"You offend me, little one. Although a tasty-treat to be sure, you are no challenge to defeat."

"Are you so heartbroken that you can't even fight a child?" Mark counters.

"Run home to your mother, so I can eat her too."

"No need, she's right over there. I've come here to find my father, and she brought me here to do so," Mark informs. Rachel goes to stand, but Horeb shakes his head no. She whispers in his ear that it'll be okay, so he allows her to stand.

"Did you find your father little one?"

"No, it would appear that he's dead after all. I have, therefore, come in summons to your challenge to avenge his honor."

"You? You are unarmed."

"There are weapons all around me, but I'll not need them."

"Why not?"

"I'm a boy. I only have a rock and a sling. The swords and axes are too heavy for me."

Lucius breaks out into a hideous laugh filled with ridicule and indignation. Mark ignores his laughing and puts a stone in the sling, twirls it above his head and lets it fly. It hits Lucius in the chest. He is not moved, damaged, or harmed. He's amused by the boy's attack and laughs all the harder at this valiant, but stupid attempt to take him down. Mark ignores the Dragon's reaction and loads another stone. This, too, hits the mark and inflicts no harm upon this mighty beast.

"I admire your spirit, but I'm tired of this nonsense," Lucius comments as he walks stately forward until his head towers above Mark. He then bends his head down and snaps his jaw shut eating Mark where he stands. The sling he held in his hand drops to the ground. A horrified gasp is heard amongst the humans and dwarfs. At about the same time Lucius goes to munch on his snack he hears a pop. Those on the ground believe it's the sound of the boy's bones breaking, but it isn't. It's the releasing of a divine omnipotent power. In a matter of seconds, the Dragon realizes only too late that he has been tricked again. Light begins to pour forth from his mouth in powerful rays of light overpowering the sun at noonday.

This light is pure and white growing in intensity with every passing second. Those on the ground raise their hands to shield their eyes from this very bright, piercing light. Then after building to a level of brilliance that their flesh can't withstand, it explodes in all directions penetrating every last cell of every living thing. It bursts forth consuming the Dragon first decimating the beast at a cellular level. The light continues to travel forth covering and consuming everything in its path transforming everything it touches. Even the vegetation is changed.

The light goes forth covering the land of Navarre. Where there is sickness, the light brings healing. Where the earth was dead, the light brings life. Any living thing that was touched by the evil the Dragon brought forth in this final battle is restored to its former glory. Fruit trees fill with sweet ripe fruit. Various grains sprout from abandoned fields and ripen to full heads awaiting the threshing floor.   Trees that were scorched are renewed like springtime. The red grass of the Plains of Galeed transforms into a green meadow. The carcasses of the trolls and dragons are vaporized into nothingness, and the demons are sucked back in to the dark abyss which seals behind them.

Those that gave their lives in battle are spiritually raised from their failed flesh. Their corpses dissolve into a fine dust that is swept away by a gentle breeze leaving behind a sparkling image of themselves composed of colored lights. Those who were injured are healed without even a scar to testify of the infliction of pain and misery thrust upon them. The survivors witness the transformation of their fallen companions and realize that they're no longer dead, but alive. They marvel as the transformed are lifted up into the heavens where they can't be harmed ever again.

Those remaining on the planet are filled with amazement in this moment of revelation and are renewed in strength as cool refreshing water springs forth from the earth to revive them. The air is purified. The smells of wild jasmine and lavender fill the atmosphere wiping away the stench.

***

In the Port of Salt, Beth and Beverly face off against the Dragon's hounds having been cornered in the hallway. They snarl and growl moving ever closer. Keevah and Shamilar are busy with the Troll. Neither man is in fit shape, so they tire easily, but will themselves to endure so they can take down this hideous creature and help the women protect the babies. Beth holds a chair poking it at the dogs to keep them at bay while Beverly thrusts a trident at them to try and push them back.

The hounds, however, are very strong. The women are pushed so far back into the corner that they can't get enough room to inflict any injury upon the hounds. Chaos bites the chair leg and tries to pull it out of Beth's grasp. She hangs on for dear life while Bedlam snaps at the trident. Beth is starting to let fear get the better of her. Beverly senses that and starts to speak in an ancient tongue. She calls out for the helper of the Most High to come to their aid. The chant has the added benefit of slowing the hounds down. They understand that she is a woman of faith and is not easily swayed by fear.

Sensing this power within Beverly, the dogs change their tactic and focus on Beth who becomes increasingly more fearful by the second. They each have a chair leg in their powerful jaws while drool is slung back and forth as they try to shake the chair out of her grasp. The infants are crying, and her instinct is to run to them, but Beverly grabs her arm to keep her steady. Beverly's touch renews her courage, and she changes her stance, so she'll not be easily moved. Beth begins to repeat the words Beverly is chanting even though she has no idea what they mean.

The hounds still sense that Beth is the weakest. They focus their energies with a renewed determination. They glance over at each other and work together to pull the chair out of her hands. They tug and pull finally freeing it from her grasp. Beth screams out in terror and instinctively covers her face as Chaos leaps towards her. Beverly tries to defend them both with her trident but is unable. In a millisecond, the light that was released on the Plains of Galeed moves through destroying the hounds and the Troll only a hair's breadth from harming the women or the men.

Beth falls back against the floor and braces herself for the inevitable ripping bites of the hounds, but they never come. Beth opens her eyes, and all she sees is Beverly who helps Beth to her feet. The women rush into the room and find the infants safe and cooing at a butterfly that flew into the open window. Keevah and Shamilar make a mad dash inside to check on the safety of everyone.

"Beverly! Beth! Are you okay?" Keevah shouts.

"Yes! We're all safe," Beverly responds.

"What just happened?" Shamilar inquires.

"The Redeemer has sacrificed himself to destroy the evil," Beverly informs coming out of the room with a child in her arms. Beth follows soon after with her own son. They make their way down the stairs.

"I never believed in the Redeemer," Shamilar admits.

"The Redeemer offered himself for everyone regardless of whether you believe in him or not. Do you doubt your eyes as to what transpired before them?"

"No."

"Then know that belief is not vain or empty but has everlasting consequences."

"What's going to happen now?" Beth asks.

"Peace is what is going to happen now. We have crossed over from darkness into light and are entering a time of rebirth. The world has been transformed and a time of unity, prosperity, and love has come to us."

"What do we do now?"

"We bring the young prince to the new king and queen of Navarre, and we rebuild our world," Beverly informs with a great big beaming smile. The men are happy with this news. They help the women prepare for the journey and will accompany them back to Navarre.

CHAPTER 22

On the Plains of Galeed, the dwarfs and humans look about in astonished silence. No one really knows what to say in this moment. They are awestruck and at peace with an undertone of joy that starts to percolate beneath the surface of their stunned faces. Finally, it's Rachel that squeals for joy first breaking the silence. This startles those around her, but instead of being upset with her they join in the revelry. All that is, except Tubal. He alone seems to maintain a glum expression. He didn't see his sister in those that were lifted up. He asks every individual he comes across, but no one has seen her. He knows he can't go to his mother without knowing for sure what happened to her. He slowly makes his way through the camp but notices that the warriors are beginning to disperse.

"Excuse me, did you see my sister get lifted up, she's short, was wearing a red tunic, and goes by the name of Sasha?" he asks as he approaches a small crowd of men. They shrug their shoulders in response.

"I'm afraid I didn't either," responds a familiar voice.

"Javan?" Tubal inquires.

"Indeed," Javan answers with a beaming smile. Tubal looks around Javan to see Sasha with her arms wrapped around her beloved's waist. She is snuggled up against him like a small child clutches a stuffed animal. He can't believe his eyes. He stands there speechless with his mouth agape.

"She didn't get lifted up because she's alive," Javan informs as if Tubal is blind.

"But I saw her go over the cliff," Tubal explains in bewilderment.

"Javan caught me before I hit the rocks," Sasha elaborates. Tubal begins to shed tears of joy as it sets in that she is alive and safe. "Brother, don't cry. I'm fine," she requests leaving her love to comfort her brother. She wraps her arms around her muscle bound brother as far as they will go. Tubal responds by wrapping his huge arms around her enveloping her small frame.

"I'm just so relieved. I don't think I could bear to bring our mother the news of your loss," Tubal informs, then addresses Javan. "I'm thankful to you for rescuing my sister when I could not."

"I love her, too, you know. It was no small sacrifice to leave her behind to acquire the Army of Light."

"I'm glad you acquired them," Tubal expresses. Suddenly, a tall being unlike any he has set eyes on before comes up to them. He releases Sasha to look into the eyes of this legendary being not seen in the flesh for millennia or more.

"Anak," Javan begins. "Let me introduce you to Tubal, Sasha's brother and protector."

"It's a pleasure to finally meet you. I've heard lots of good things about the both of you," Anak greets. His taller, but less muscular frame is covered in olive colored skin. He has shoulder length dark brown wavy hair pulled back out of his face by an elaborate headband. His eyes, his most unique feature, glow like opals which gaze beyond the surface and directly into your soul. His gaze, as intrusive as it is, contains no condemnation but is full of forgiveness and grace imparting an inner peace unlike anything he has ever known.

"I'm very glad to make your acquaintance. I'm also thankful that you came. If you hadn't, we wouldn't have lasted until the Redeemer could rescue us all," Tubal responds.

While they're talking, Sasha goes back to her love, Javan. She is quite content being held in his arms. Her smile beams a great joy, but Tubal is concerned that her joy will be short lived and his sister will find herself alone again.

"So what happens now? Do you stay among us, or must you return to your domain?"
Tubal asks. Sasha cuts him a quick disapproving look because she doesn't want this moment to end.

"We must decrease so that you and the dwarfs can increase. We will return to our domain until we are needed again."

"And Javan?" Sasha inquires as tears begin to well up in her eyes.

"He has become one with us, there is no undoing it. He must, therefore, come back with us. Our existence and our deeds will fade into legend."

"When must you go?" Sasha asks her voice full of panic. This time her tears overflow their boundaries. Javan gives her a reassuring squeeze as sorrow begins to cast its shadow upon his own face.

"Don't cry," Javan requests. He takes his finger to wipe the tears from her beautiful dark face composed of high cheekbones and graceful lines. Her beauty is unmatched among all the women Javan has ever seen. "We knew what we were getting into."

"Why these tears and downcast faces?" Anak asks.

"Our love was never meant to be," Sasha mutters aloud to herself.

"Nonsense, Javan was first man before he became Anak. It's not good for man to be alone. Although he can't remain here, it doesn't prevent you from coming with him."

"I can?" Sasha asks with relieved astonishment. This surprises Javan also but is a welcomed one.

"There is only one thing that you must know. If you go with him, you'll never see your family again. This must be your decision alone. We must decrease so that your people will increase in peace and unity. The only evil that can befall you now will be at your own hands."

Sasha's expression turns from sad to glad and back to sad again. As much as she loves Javan, she loves her brother and mother also. Although Tubal and their mother will miss Sasha terribly, Tubal knows that she'll never be happy staying behind. Her heart belongs to Javan, and it's only right that they be together. She looks over at her bother then at Javan and back to her brother. She leaves Javan's side to go to her brother looking for his approval. At first, Javan appears alarmed but knows that this is not an easy decision to make and doesn't interfere.

"Tubal, you know I love you very much, but my heart belongs to Javan. Can you forgive me?"

"There is nothing to forgive. Mother and I will be fine so long as we know that you're safe and happy."

"Going with Javan will make me very happy," she explains, then turns and addresses Anak. "Will I be allowed to say goodbye to my mother before we leave?"

"Yes, of course. We saw her in the Port of Salt where we docked our ships. I'm sure we will pass her and Lady Beth on the road back."

"They made it safely with the infants," Sasha states aloud expelling a sigh of relief.

"Tubal, you are welcome to ride with us to the port," Javan offers.

"I'd like that very much. I can then escort my mother and Lady Beth to the new King and Queen of Navarre and present them with the heir to the land."

"Thank you brother," Sasha acknowledges. Tubal's only response is a quick wink and happy grin.

Anak offers a mount to Tubal to ride upon. He goes to offer one to Sasha but notices that she has already subdued a Firecat when he wasn't paying attention. He smiles as she mounts the back of the Firecat and it accepts her as if she were one of them. Anak approves of this woman even more now. Not only is she an honorable human who is pure enough that a Firecat will allow her atop its back, she harbors no regret. Her joy leads her heart. Although he has no doubt that she will miss her kin, her heart will not be heavy because she has accepted the joy in her destiny.

***

Rachel and Horeb come out of their embrace and gaze into one another's eyes. Horeb realizes that he'll now be king, but will not rule unless Rachel will become his queen. He whispers the proposal in her ear, and she nods her agreement. They embrace again but notice that the human warriors have gathered around them and are kneeling in their presence. The couple looks around. They are taken aback at the solidarity displayed regardless of their former allegiances. Rachel even recognizes a man from her own village. The dwarfs respond in a similar fashion around General Rasmussen. They await his next orders with bowed heads. He, too, has no words to address them as he's still processing the events they've just experienced.

"Please rise," Horeb entreats.

"What are your orders?" Mordecai inquires on behalf of the group. Horeb starts to respond but notices that the dwarfs are starting to leave the battlefield.

"One moment," he informs his people and follows quickly after the Dwarf General. Connor and Soba stand nearby. "General!" Horeb calls closing the distance between them. The General halts his progress and waits for Horeb to catch up. Horeb slows as he approaches and salutes him in the dwarf style.

"What do you wish to say to me?" Rasmussen inquires. He appreciates the respect that Horeb gives him by using their traditional military greeting.

"Where are you going?"

"Home."

"I wanted to thank you on behalf of my late brother, Prince Robert, and all the humans for joining our fight against the Dragon. We couldn't have done it without you," Horeb expresses after he drops to one knee. Connor is saddened that the prince, whose wife he served, did not survive. Rachel overhears Horeb's words as she approaches their position and adds to them.

"General," Rachel begins. "We've lived for centuries without knowing of your existence. We would be honored if your kind would consider living on the surface amongst us and help us build a new Navarre on the foundation of unity and a renewed relationship with the Most High who redeemed us all."

"I can't speak for the Dwarf Council, but I shall propose this to them. If they accept this invitation, our trades and commerce will require a lot of water."

"The coastline is a blank canvas. All of the villages that lived along the coast were wiped off the face of our world by a tidal wave called up by the Dragon. It would provide all the water you require."

"What of your people?" Rasmussen inquires remembering passing through on the way to Galeed.

"They're safe, but our numbers are too few to maintain a coastal existence. Anyway, they'll follow where I go which is to be with Prince Horeb."

Rasmussen looks curiously at the couple and wonders what is meant by this statement. Horeb picks up on his confusion as he stands to his feet.

"Rachel and I will be getting married. She will become my queen."

"Congratulations! When will these nuptials take place?"

"In thirty days," Horeb explains.

"In the city of Indra outside the old Royalty Inn, this is where our new home will be constructed. It's in the middle of Navarre. We would be honored if you could attend," Rachel adds.

"Alas, our journey home and the Council's deliberations will take longer than that, but I wish you well."

"My wife, Rainah and I will attend as representatives of our people," Connor offers, then continues. "If the council chooses to remain underground, we shall return together after the wedding celebration."

"Your presence would do me great honor," Horeb expresses to

the dwarf, who he once considered an enemy. Connor's eyes well up with water, but they never overflowed their boundaries.

"General," Soba addresses, "With your permission, I'd like to escort Connor and Rainah to the wedding of the new King and Queen of Navarre."

"Permission granted. The rest will return home with me," Rasmussen answers.

Connor and Soba take their leave, but to Castle Togarmah to check on Connor's wife and deliver the wedding announcement news to those abiding in the castle. Rachel and Horeb linger there a few moments until the dwarfs are nearly out of sight. They then return to their own people to advise them of the coming nuptials.

All of the surviving commanders including Cassandra kneel at the approach of their new King and Queen. Horeb again bids them rise. He wants to address them as fellow humans first.

"My people, we have endured a long dark season. My first command as your king will be to send you home to your families and for the next thirty days take time to remember the loved ones you've lost. Honor them however they should be honored. Then I want you to take stock of what you have and what you still need to rebuild our land. At the end of the thirty days, you and your loved ones are invited to attend mine and Rachel's wedding. She will become your new queen. After the wedding, we shall work with you to help you rebuild this great land."

A jubilant voice bursts upon the crowd, "Hip, hip!" The crowd responds, "Hooray!" The cheer is repeated three times. Horeb asks Mordecai to step forward. As the only remaining prophet of the Most High, it is his honor to anoint Prince Horeb, King of Navarre. Horeb kneels down before him. Mordecai bends down, scoops up some of the water from one of the newly formed fresh water springs, and pours it upon Horeb's head.

"I, Mordecai, a servant of the Most High anoint you, Prince Horeb, King of Navarre. Rise my king."

Horeb rises to his feet. His first command is to have Mordecai pronounce a blessing upon the people before they depart for their homes. Mordecai complies with great joy and enthusiasm.

"Most High, who has redeemed this people and this world, we give you praise this day. I ask that you bless every family represented here and that you sharpen our minds and hearts to reflect the mercy and compassion you showed us this day as we rebuild our world. Let us never forget this day and remember that we are all part of a larger family. Keep us from sickness and calamity. Prosper us in love and mercy."

The crowd disperses after the blessing is given leaving only Horeb and Rachel. They stand in silence looking into one another's eyes for a long while. The sound of birdsong fills the air with joy. They relish this moment of peace and life with an appreciation unlike any before the darkness.

"Rachel," Horeb begins. "Where is your family staying?"

"At the abandoned Inn and Taverns of the Crossroads," she answers.

"We better get going then. The sun only has a few hours left before it sets."

"Can we linger here this night?" she asks.

"Why?"

"I wish to build an alter in remembrance of Mark, our Redeemer. I had gotten rather callous in my attitudes towards him not understanding that he could actually redeem us. I want this place to be remembered in ages to come when we have slipped into the realm of myth and legends. Let it testify to the truth of it. It may keep future generations of our people from stumbling again."

"You are truly a queen even before coronation."

"I'm a Chieftain's daughter first. My father taught me that the people come before our own needs and that the most important thing we can do for them is secure and maintain a hope for the future."

"The best day of my life was when I awoke and saw your face for the first time. It was the day that I discovered the meaning of love."

"That seems like such a long time ago, but I too am glad that I found you," Rachel comments kissing him gently upon the lips. She lingers in his arms a moment longer.

"We better get started if we want to get this built before sunset."

The two of them begin to collect rocks and pile them up to be a witness for all time of the remarkable things that happened this day. It's a witness that there is a God in the land of Navarre and that he rescued the people from their own darkness reversing judgment and releasing freedom and unity to the masses.

CHAPTER 23

Mary awakes from a sound slumber to find her son, Andrew, hovering close to her bed. His sudden ethereal appearance startles her at first, but his expression of bliss and affection for her dispel any fear she may have experienced when she first opened her eyes.

"Andrew? Is it really you?" she timidly asks while she reaches out to touch him. Her hand passes through him. She withdraws her hand and pulls away from him slightly.

"Don't be afraid, mother, it really is me. I didn't want to leave without telling you goodbye. I want you to know that I gave my life in an attempt to rescue Princess Sabrina although it did little good."

"You're dead?"

"My flesh perished, but I still live. I won't be able to be with you until the day you can join me on this side of the horizon."

"What side?" She asks. She reaches out a second time to

touch him, and again her hand passes through him like a mist. His form, however, is undisturbed.

"You know the place of which I speak. It's the one you always told me about when I would wake from a nightmare. I've come back to you so that you'll know that it's real and so you'll not grieve my passing."

"But how can I go on by myself. You're all I have left."

"You'll not be alone. You're well loved by so many, and you have a lot of love to give. There'll be many orphans that will need your love and care as many parents perished in the fight. I know your heart is large enough to care for them just as you have cared for me," Andrew explains and begins to fade away.

"Andrew, wait!"

"What is it?"

"I love you. I know I was upset with you when you went and enlisted serving under your uncle, but I want you to know that I'm very proud of what you've done in the time you spent here."

"I know, mother. I'm proud of you, too. I have to go now, but I promise we will see each other again."

"Goodbye son, I love you," Mary bids farewell as she tries to touch his image again, but her fingers pass through his fading image like nothing is there, but air. A substance, like stardust, accumulates on her fingertips and sparkles in the morning sun.

"Mary!" Rainah cries out from her chambers. Her cry startles Mary as her son's image dissipates completely. She immediately jumps out of her bed. She grabs a robe and throws it over her arms as she hurries to Rainah's room.

"What's wrong?" Mary asks as she bursts through the door thinking that Rainah may be hurt. She's been so slow to heal that Mary has wondered if she ever will. The sight that greets her eyes is one she refuses to believe at first.

Rainah is jumping up and down on top of the mattress like a little girl. She has a smile a mile wide across her face. Her short red tresses jerk with every bounce. They stand out straight suspended in mid air just before she lands only to jump again. Rainah starts to laugh like she hasn't laughed in months. Mary stands there in amazement watching her bob up and down.

"You're well," Mary concludes finally addressing the giddy dwarf.

"Yes, I'm well. I haven't felt this good in so long...Do you know what this means?" Rainah inquires jumping in between sentences.

"That something good has finally happened," Mary offers.

"Not just something good, something wonderful! The

Redeemer has sacrificed himself and saved us all. Evil has been vanquished!" She declares.

Mary just stands there shaking her head back and forth while the truth of Rainah's words sink into her mind. A smile slowly grows upon her face. Between encountering her departed son, and witnessing the immediate and complete healing of a woman whom only the day before needed help just to sit up, a joy unlike she has never known grows quickly inside her. Suddenly, she is hit with a pillow. Rainah cocks her eyebrows in mischief. Mary picks up the pillow that landed on the floor next to her. Instead of placing it back on the bed as her mature age would dictate, she throws it back at Rainah who ducks. Mary then climbs up on the bed and starts jumping with her.

"I haven't done this since I was a little girl," Mary admits.

"I know, isn't it great?"

The women continue squealing like children until their raucous laughter catches the ears of the children living on the first floor who inquisitively climb the stairs. The children are in shock and quickly run to join them on the oversized bed before anyone can come to their senses. Squeals of unrestrained joy erupt amongst the children. They continue jumping gleefully until they're all exhausted.

"Oh…I can't remember the last time I've done that," Mary

admits.

"I can't either, we have to do this more often," Rainah adds trying to catch her breath.

The children just pile atop them both as they each tire of jumping. They start grabbing pillows and tossing them at each other.

"I'm hungry," informs one of the children popping up from underneath a pile of pillows.

"Me too," Rainah chimes in.

"Well, all we have left in the pantry is barley," Mary adds.

"I don't care," Rainah admits.

Their conversation is interrupted by the elder women downstairs calling out, "Apples! We have apples!" There haven't been any apples since the Dragon's forces invaded. One of the women carrying an apron full of the red ripe fruit bursts through the door.

"The orchard is full of apples. Look!" The old woman exclaims picking one up to show them. Rainah, Mary, and the children rush over and grab a juicy treat. They bite into them immediately. Apple juice runs down their chin as they gleefully consume the fruit.

"What happened?" Mary asks with a mouthful of fruit.

"Everything has been restored. The orchard is full of apples and the groves full of nuts. The royal vegetable garden is full of squash, beans, carrots, turnips, and potatoes. It's like they've been hiding behind a veil of darkness."

They all run downstairs to see for themselves all that has happened. The sun shines bright but is not too hot. The sky is sapphire blue with lacey white clouds dotting the horizon. The rolling hills about the castle are covered in lush green grass, the orchards and groves hold a bounty the likes they've never seen. The vegetable garden behind the castle is full of mature plants ready to be harvested and eaten. They immediately start picking what they can and begin to prepare a feast for all of them. The stream that runs along the outer edge of the apple orchard is clean, clear, and full of fish jumping onto the banks.

In no time at all, the smell of fruit pies, grilled fish, and roasted vegetables waft through the air. There is a joy overflowing amongst them the likes of which they have never experienced before even in the happiest of times. Perhaps it's because evil has truly been vanquished and they can start fresh, their past swept clean of their mistakes and shortcomings leading to a new beginning.

***

Oleg, Rastus, Quimby, Sebastian, and the other humans that accompanied the group to the Canyon of Woes are making their way back. The wilderness they passed through to get to the canyon has been transformed. The foreboding nature of the area has been removed, and the group is filled with a sense of peace and serenity. They hear noises coming from the bushes and trees. They jump at each sound only to realize there was no monsters just harmless wildlife foraging for food. This forest hasn't seen game such as this in centuries.

"I don't believe it. Look at how this place has changed," Rastus blurts.

"I, too, see it, but I'm having a hard time believing it. The forest went from a desolate place to one filled with abundance. Can you imagine the banquet we could have in the Grand Hall?" Quimby asks.

"Do you always think with your stomach?" Oleg asks.

"Well, I'm hungry."

"I've never seen so many deer, rabbits, quail, and ducks!" Sebastian adds.

"You're as bad as he is," Oleg quips.

"There are berries too!" Sebastian shouts with the gleefulness of a small boy. He goes to retrieve a clump of the sweet ripened fruit when he notices how filthy he is. His own stench overwhelms the fragrance of the wild roses growing nearby.

"Well, what are you waiting for?" Oleg asks of Sebastian.

"I'm filthy. I can't even smell the roses over my own stench. We're probably covered in poison from those eggs. We need to clean up."

"Look, there's a lake, and it's crystal clear," Quimby announces to the group. Rastus wastes no time and takes a running leap into the crystal cool waters. He lands with a splash. He erupts from the surface able to put his feet on the bottom and stand up above it with the water level standing just at his chest. He thrusts his head back in and drinks in a huge gulp tossing his head back as if downing a pint of ale. "It's sweet too!" he announces after swallowing. He then continues to frolic about like a child.

"You didn't take your clothes off," Quimby chastises.

"But they're dirty too," Rastus replies.

"He has a point," Argo adds as he takes a running start. He lands in the water with a huge splash. The water douses the remaining dwarfs standing on the bank. The rest of the group follows Rastus' lead and jumps in. They wash and refresh themselves in the purity of the water. When they emerge from the waters, they discover that they're not emerging alone.

"Something's on me!" Oleg cries out climbing onto the bank of the lake. He twists and turns dancing about. The rest of them start laughing hysterically as they see fish wriggling in his pockets with their tails hanging out.

"It's only fish, you idiot!" Quimby yells.

"That was quite a jig you did, is that a Dwarf dance?" Argo asks.

"Ha Ha, like you wouldn't do a jig if something you didn't know was getting familiar."

They laugh and leave the water for the shore. They, too, discover that they have scaly hitchhikers. They pile the fish up on the shore and start gathering wood for a fire so they can cook the fish and renew their strength. Sebastian, now clean, takes the liberty to gather the ripened berries he spied earlier.

In no time at all, they have a good size campfire burning brightly. They find enough sticks to skewer and cook their fish while munching on the berries. The sunset lights up the clouds and sky in brilliant orange, pink, and gold. As the sun's light disappears below the horizon, fireflies begin to glow in the forest that surrounds them. Their jubilation of finding life and purity where once there was desolation and malevolence convinces them of the outcome of the battle which they realize is over now.

"How many of our friends do you think survived?" Oleg asks somberly, leaning back against a tree with a full belly.

"I don't know, but we had to have won, or this place would be fouler than what it was before," Quimby responds.

"There's no sense in worrying yourselves about it now," Sebastian adds, then continues. "There's no doubt that it was a hard won battle. I can't remember the last time I could just enjoy a peaceful moment. We shouldn't deprive ourselves of the joy of victory because of worry that we may have lost someone in that battle. They sacrificed for us and did no more or less than we did."

"He's right," Rastus jumps in.

"Well, I don't know about you, but I'm exhausted, and I plan to sleep like I haven't slept in months," Sebastian informs. In unison, the group responds, "Here, here," in agreement with the suggestion.

The group settles into the thick, soft grass leaning against the trees. They fall into a peaceful slumber that renews their tired bodies and spirits. The warmth of the fire dries their soaked clothes and its crackling lulls them to sleep. The next morning they awake renewed and full of optimism about the future and continue to make their way home.

***

Upon reaching the Sentinel Mountain Range the Dwarfs and humans part company. They embrace like brothers hoping that they'll have an opportunity to see one another again. Their eyes well up with tears, but none allow them to overflow their boundaries. Friends forged through battle become brothers for life. They'll never forget this time, nor will any future request go ungranted by the other. It's a bond that death can't break and life will never diminish. Now they turn their focus on being reunited with the family and friends they left behind. When they make their final turn to start the final leg of their journey home, there are no last looks keeping their faces pointed in the direction of their destination.

Glenda C. Finkelstein

CHAPTER 24

At the crossroads, the remainder of the village of Tierney sleeps peacefully in the knowledge that the Dragon was defeated. Unlike at the epicenter of the Redeemer's sacrifice where everyone was instantly healed, the evidence of the victory was seen only in the light passing through and the transformation of the nature surrounding them. Unbeknown to them there are more surprises in store as a new day dawns.

The sun rises over the horizon. Its golden rays cascade upon the renewed land of Navarre bringing light, life, and warmth. The people begin to stir from their slumber and breathe in the sweetness of freedom. They open their windows wide to let the air in and fill their rooms with freshness. The acrid scents of sulfur, rotting flesh and foliage are gone. They have been replaced by clean, fresh air laced with the scents of wild roses and lavender. This invigorates them and imparts a feeling of serenity and security.

Suddenly, a commotion is heard emanating from Samuel and Agatha's room. The noise startles Laban who doesn't know what to make of the shouting and bouncing around. He runs as fast as his legs will carry him past other villagers who are peering out of various rooms to see what all the raucous is about. Laban bursts through his brother-in-law's door to see him standing and dancing about like a fool in a king's court.

"What's going on?" Laban asks. His confusion is evident in his tone.

"I can see! I can see!" Samuel shouts. He then takes Laban's hands and begins to dance around in a circle leading the bewildered Laban about the room as the truth of his words resonates within him. Agatha stands there beaming a great smile approving of her husband's antics. She claps her hands keeping rhythm with his dance steps as laughter bubbles forth from deep inside her heart.

"You can see? How many fingers am I holding up?" Laban asks testing his vision.

"Three!" he announces with pride.

"You can see!" Laban jubilantly shouts.

In the middle of all this jumping about, Laban realizes that he isn't tender in certain areas anymore. He suddenly pulls his hands away from Samuel and runs to a washroom shutting the door behind him. He looks at himself in the mirror, breathes in a lung full of courage, and lifts his robe. To his amazement, the scars on his torso and other more tender areas are gone. His skin is fresh as a newborn's save a few wrinkles. He rubs his hand across where the scars used to be and not even a lump underneath the skin remains. He cuts loose with a shout.

"Woo Hoo!" he exclaims. He then drops his robe back down and emerges from the washroom leaping and jumping and praising the Most High. "I'm healed too!" He exclaims to his bemused village, which quickly joins in the celebration. The men begin to share and record all the miracles happening in their midst.

The women of the village send the children out to collect eggs and fresh berries for a celebratory breakfast while they prepare pancakes to go with the honey they found the day before. Agatha finds a bag of tea leaves and begins to brew a pot of this rare but favored drink. Everyone is assigned a task and in no time at all the breakfast feast is ready for consumption. Everyone's face is full of joy. Courtney and Jonathan join in the revelry of the celebration with special news of their own.

"Everyone, Courtney and I have an announcement to make," Jonathan begins. The room falls silent. "We're going to have a baby!" Jonathan exclaims. The villagers rejoice in this news, but not just the fact that there is a new life on the way, but that this new life will be born into the light of this new world.

Scenes like this unfold everywhere amongst the surviving population of Navarre. The land went from desolation and hopelessness to abundance and hope in an instant. The returning warriors only add to the celebrations of families and friends popping up all over. These celebrations, although rooted in old traditions imparts a familiar comfort to them, and they include those that the war left as widows or orphans.

***

A day's travel from the crossroads, Rachel and Horeb walk through the forest with a wary sense of hope for the future. They've won the day, and although they're happy about that, the cost was dear. Their concern is not driven by grief over what they've lost for they know that those who perished are still alive in another realm, but in the great task that lay before them. Rebuilding and securing a nation will be difficult with their depleted numbers.

Their personal loses have been equally great, and they'll have to find new ways of being strong for themselves and their people. As the leaders of this newly united nation, their burden and responsibility is greater than the rest. Even in this moment of victory, their response equates more to relief that it's over and that the human race survived rather than the unrestrained joy of those they serve. They long to feel that release and hope that in the next month before their wedding they can revive themselves among Rachel's people.

They walk quietly amongst the trees adrift in their own thoughts holding hands as a show of both affection and comfort for having endured so much. Rachel's mind is lost in the cost of the victory and the need for rest, whereas Horeb's mind is lost in the rebuilding of a nation. As they walk along each in their own world, Rachel begins to hear familiar laughter amongst the trees. At first, she dismisses it believing it's her imagination playing tricks on her, but then she catches a glimpse of someone hiding amongst the foliage. She pulls her hand away from Horeb to pursue this individual.

"Where are you going?" Horeb asks oblivious to what Rachel has seen and heard.

"Do you hear that?" Rachel asks as she begins to run after the sound.

"Hear what?"

"Laughter, familiar laughter," Rachel responds then darts after the sound. This time Horeb hears it too. It's very familiar, but he knows that it can't be what they think it is. It would be impossible, but he chases after it also.

Suddenly, the forest falls silent save for the sound of birds.

Rachel becomes frantic looking about trying to find the person she thinks she saw. She goes from tree to tree looking for this person. Horeb, too, helps her search. He's in no mood for games. Then without warning, a young maiden jumps out from behind a tree.

"Boo!" the girl shouts. Rachel jumps back as her eyes fall upon the maiden in disbelief. She is astounded at what her eyes behold. Horeb joins Rachel catching a quick glimpse of the woman who disappears back into the forest before he can confirm what Rachel already knows.

"Wait!" Rachel calls chasing after her. Horeb is quick to follow after Rachel. He's afraid she may wind up getting lost in the thick forest chasing this sprite, but is far slower that his betrothed. His body is fatigued by the extended stress placed upon it by the conflict.

"I win!" the familiar voice calls out. The maiden plops down on a patch of soft grass to catch her breath.

"Hannah?" Rachel inquires finally being brave enough to call out the name of her sister.

"Who else would it be, silly?" Hanna questions back.

"But how? You died…" Rachel sputters as she closes the distance between them.

"Yes, I died, but Mark sent me back. Although I missed you,

coming back here even now pales in comparison to where I was. Spending time with mom was so…"

"You were with mom?" Rachel asks cutting her off.

"Yes, and she's proud of you."

"What about Mark?" Rachel asks circling back to the first statement she made.

"I could answer your questions if you'd stop cutting me off, but Mark said you'd be like this."

"Like what?"

"Doubting…and he told me to give you a message…"

"What's the message?" Rachel asks impatiently wanting her to spit it out.

"I told you so!" Hannah blurts out with impish delight.

All of a sudden Rachel is reminded of a conversation she had with Mark about a singular gift he was allowed to give and that she would know that it came from him with that message attached. Upon this realization, Rachel throws her arms around her sister returned to her from the other side. Hannah's energy is as vigorous as ever. Rachel had forgotten just how full of life and vitality she is. Horeb stands amazed at what his eyes witness.

"Hannah?" he questions not sure whether to believe his own

eyes or not.

"You too? Didn't Rachel tell you about Mark's promised gift?"

"No, it must have slipped her mind."

"To be honest, Mark refused to tell me what the gift was because he said I'd never believe it. After everything that's happened, I forgot about it. Nor would I have guessed in a million years that it'd be you," Rachel admits.

"He was right about that," Horeb adds pinching Hannah to be sure that she's real. She winces slightly then retaliates with a slap. He looks stunned but erupts into a deep belly laugh.

"It's her!" he exclaims with confirmation.

"Hannah, I'd like to present my fiancée."

"I knew you'd two would get together someday. Oh, and Seth sends his blessing."

"Okay, this is getting weird. How did you know that Seth gave me his blessing to marry Rachel?" Horeb asks. He becomes outwardly uncomfortable under Rachel's stunned scrutinizing gaze.

"Because I was where he was and he wasn't sure you'd tell her."

"Seth gave you his blessing to marry me..." Rachel states aloud. The doubt and surprise is thick in her tone, but not fully convincing. "When were you going to tell me?"

"When the time seemed right," Horeb offers.

"Don't blame him. Mark told me he told you so don't act so surprised," Hannah chastises.

"I thought that he was just trying to make me feel better about how I've always felt about Horeb. Please don't take this the wrong way as I'm very glad to have you back, but how are people going to react to the fact that my loss was restored and not theirs?"

"Don't panic about that. It's true that I'm back, but not just for you my doubting sister. I was sent back to help all the people of Navarre. I'll be taking the place that Clairese left vacant when she passed away and the Oracle of Elim when she decided to go with Prince Javan back to Vespa. I will assume the role of Prophetess of Navarre, a servant of the Most High."

"Has father seen you?"

"Not yet. Mark and I thought it best that we do that together."

"Let's not make him wait any longer than necessary, but I have to prepare you our father has been through a lot. He was captured and tortured, and he isn't as strong as he used to be," Rachel explains. Hannah's enthusiasm remains intact as if she has knowledge no one else does. A flood of memories cascades through her mind, but Rachel just shakes her head. "It really is you," she admits with complete certainty this time.

"I'll race you to the crossroads. On your mark, get set, go…" Hannah fires off then sprints ahead at full speed.

Rachel releases a sigh and comments under her breath, "you little sprite," and lifts her skirt up to follow after her as fast as she can run.

"Wait for me!" Horeb yells after them as he tries to keep up. The race back to the crossroads cures any lingering doubts that she is who she claims to be.

The threesome keep a brisk pace continuing toward the crossroads even after their little race leaves them slightly out of breath. Now that Hannah has been returned to her, Rachel is finally able to embrace the fullness of joy that all of Navarre has been reveling in these past two days. Horeb is grateful for this, but the revelry and celebrations will soon come to a close as the work of rebuilding their society upon a new set of laws with respect for one another begins.

***

At sunset, Rachel, Horeb, and Hannah arrive at the crossroads. Rachel notices how even here the earth has been renewed. The garden which was just a shambles with the occasional vegetable hanging from a less than lush plant was full and producing like it would at peak harvest. The livestock no longer looks gaunt, but healthy. She takes a look at Hannah one more time before she knocks on the door and sees that familiar gleam in her beautiful green eyes. Her long brown hair is in need of combing as usual, but she is as beautiful as ever. Horeb tires of waiting for Rachel and knocks on the door.

They hear a myriad of footsteps rushing to and fro in the room as they discern the sound of one of them heading towards the door. Rachel grabs Hannah by the arm moving her behind herself and Horeb. She doesn't want to frighten anyone. The door opens, and it's her father, Laban. His face lights up. He seems stronger and livelier than she has seen him in weeks.

"Rachel, Horeb, you're alive!" He greets with outstretched arms. Rachel goes to hug her father and kiss him on the cheek when her sister announces herself.

"Surprise!" Hannah squeals jumping out from behind them. Laban is startled at first and pulls away, but soon tosses any doubts that arise out of his mind and rushes forward to hug his youngest daughter.

"Rachel, Horeb, Hannah!" Samuel yells out. "I'm so glad to see you," he quantifies with heavy emphasis on the word, 'see'.

"Father…You can see?" Rachel questions in amazement.

287

"Yes, child, I can see!" Samuel responds. Rachel runs over and hugs her father-in-law.

"Come and eat, you must be famished," Agatha chimes in. She then gives additional orders. "Lara, draw a bath for them."

"Yes, Ma'am," Lara complies. She enlists the aid of her friends as they begin to heat water for the baths.

Hannah makes her way to the table hugging people along the way. No one has asked the obvious question on everyone's mind. Jonathan hovers close to discern for himself as he plops down beside Hannah at the table.

"It really is you, isn't it?" Jonathan questions, poking her arm with his finger. She slaps him.

"That's not polite," she informs.

"It's her," he confirms.

As the warmness of the initial greetings subsides, Hannah who is usually full of energy sits still and quiet eating the food brought to her. She gazes about the unfamiliar room filled with familiar faces. They're so much fewer than when she departed. Her face begins to turn sullen with a sadness that was profound even to those around her. Gorham sees her expression and squeezes in beside her and gives her a hug. Her sad expression melts in the simplistic love of Jonathan's little brother.

"Perhaps everyone should allow us to explain what happened and what's going to happen in the coming days," Rachel begins. Everyone gives her their full undivided attention gathering around the table. While Rachel speaks, Horeb and Hannah eat their fill of the food Agatha brought.

"Go on, daughter, continue..." Laban coaxes.

"As you can see, Hannah has been restored to us. Her life is a gift from Mark, the Redeemer. She will be assuming the position of Prophetess of Navarre. In twenty-eight days, I'll be married to King Horeb officially becoming his Queen."

She is interrupted by cheers. Rachel holds up her hands to quiet the crowd so that she can continue.

"Please allow me to finish. The ceremony will be taking place in Indra where we will construct our new home. I would like for all of you to move to Indra and help us build a new kingdom of unity, peace, and freedom."

"What about rebuilding Tierney?" Jonathan asks.

"At this time that is not a viable consideration..." Rachel informs with a downcast face. Horeb can see giving up those lands was not an easy decision.

"Perhaps, I can explain the reasons," Horeb begins with a mouth full, and then continues after swallowing the rest of the food in his mouth, "We have invited the Dwarfs to live with us on the surface. We have both lost so many fighting this war that we need to come together as one people to give us all the best chance of survival. Their industry requires the use of a lot of water. We felt that the coastal areas would be best for them."

"You said you invited them. They haven't accepted?" Jonathan queries further.

"Not yet. That decision must be made by their council. They will have an answer for us after our wedding. I know it's a lot to ask, but will you be willing to help us build a unified nation at its heart?"

"You have our full support," Laban responds on behalf of the village. He then turns to address them. "For too long Tierney has insulated itself against the political struggles of the country we are citizens of. In addition, there are so few of us left, we don't have the numbers to create a sustainable village amongst ourselves. We shall, therefore, contribute to the building of the new Navarre and be actively involved in its construction."

"Thank you, Laban," Horeb acknowledges.

"I know we'll miss the sea, but our skills are transferable to other industry and will do what's best for all the people not just ourselves," Rachel adds.

"I suppose it was foolish to wish for something familiar,"

Jonathan admits.

"No, it's not foolish. It's just not possible. We'll make new memories and establish new traditions that will take on familiarity over time." Rachel concludes.

After her explanation, Rachel, who is still in disbelief that her sister sits among them, watches her sister interact with the others while she finishes her own meal. Although Hannah seems very familiar and normal in her behavior with herself and Horeb, she notices that she is maintaining a discrete distance with the others. This is out of character for her. After thinking about it for a moment, she surmises it's just her trying to acclimate back to a human existence. She can't imagine what it was like to exist as the pure energy of soul and spirit and then to be thrust back to the limitations of flesh. For now, Rachel will give her the benefit of the doubt and give her time to adjust.

After some discussion, the people agree and support Laban and Rachel's decision to move their remaining numbers to Indra. The excitement of the return of Hannah, Rachel, and Horeb makes it difficult for them to fall asleep, but there is much work that lay ahead of them. Each person has a responsibility to contribute to this new world. The old world has been swept away, and a new life must be built in a way that doesn't allow the old prejudicial attitudes from shaping a new society. For this endeavor to be successful, they must establish a firm foundation built upon mercy, love, and forgiveness.

CHAPTER 25

Beth, Beverly, and their odd male protectors make their way
to Castle Togarmah. Shamilar rides in the back of the wagon with
the infants while Keevah walks along side. They marvel at the
transformation that has taken place across the landscape and stop
periodically to collect handfuls of ripe berries growing along the
roadside. Mount Tiras rises stately into the clouds along the
distant horizon. The snow capped mountain is a symbol of the
power of the Most High. This singular peak rising above the
grassy plains makes the Sentinel Mountains look like foothills by
comparison.

They round the bend and see a huge military contingent
heading in their direction. They're alarmed at first, but then realize
that it's the Army of Light returning to the Port of Salt. Beverly
notices that there are others traveling with them and recognizes her
children. She halts the wagon and climbs down with Keevah's

assistance. He walks with her providing an arm for her to lean upon. Her gate is sprier than most even with her limp. She wastes no time in closing the distance between them nearly dragging Keevah along. His portly body, although strong, is not built for speed.

Sasha sees her mother heading towards them and slides off the back of the Firecat. She runs to greet her with Tubal keeping pace beside her. They collide in a loving family embrace relieved to see the other alive. Javan dismounts and follows behind them to greet Sasha's mother. Beth sees her prince bowing her head in respect, but keeps her place in the wagon. Beth's expression reveals to all her relief that Prince Javan survived. This gives her hope that Princess Sabrina may have also survived.

"Sasha, I'm so glad to see that you're alive. I was so worried about you," Beverly begins hugging her daughter a second time.

"I love you too, mother," Tubal submits with a hurt expression.

"Oh son, you know I love you too, but it was Sasha that I saw in my terrible vision, not you," she explains as she moves over to hug him. His expression brightens the moment her hands touch him. Her head only comes up to his chest, and he bends down to kiss her atop her head.

"You can thank your future son-in-law, Prince Javan, for my

safe return," Sasha announces.

"Did you say future son-in-law?" Beverly asks then sees the young prince hovering close by. She leaves Tubal, walks over to Javan, and hugs him with all her might.

"I love you, too, mother-in-law to be. We're glad that you made it through safely," Javan responds with a big beaming smile wincing slightly. This elder woman is stronger than he imagined.

"You can thank Keevah and Shamilar for our safety. Without them, both us, and the future king would be dead."

Keevah walks up to Javan and begins to kneel before him. Javan stops him and embraces Keevah as a brother burying his head into his thick neck. "Thank you, my friend. I'm in your debt," Javan whispers in his ear. Javan is glad that he is able to see and speak with Keevah one more time before he departs for Vespa.

"No my prince, it is I who am in yours. I don't believe victory would have been secured without your sacrifice," Keevah responds dropping to one knee before Javan can stop him again.

"Save your homage for Horeb, the new king of Navarre," Javan instructs.

"But what of you? Surely your service is equal or greater than his. Why can't you assume the throne? Your line has always had more honor than Ophir's," Keevah shares.

"My friend, you honor me, but don't discount Horeb. I've seen what he has done and what he has sacrificed for this peace. He'll make a fine king. Promise me you'll give him that chance."

"I promise, but where will you go?"

"My daughter is getting married!" Beverly exclaims aloud as the news sinks in interrupting Javan and Keevah's conversation. "I can't wait for the ceremony. There is so much to do," she continues in a flurry already making plans for the big day.

"Hold on mother, there's a catch, one that we can't ignore or change, but we still want your blessing," Sasha interjects.

"I don't understand, you just told me you're getting married," Beverly admits as her countenance begins to fall.

"Because Javan had to become Anak to lead the Army of Light, he can't go back to being just a man. They can't remain among mankind as their powers would be too much of a temptation for humans and thrust us toward an even more terrible fate than what we just survived. They must fade into legend. It is, however, permissible for me to join him."

"You're going to the Island of Vespa," Beverly concludes.

"Yes, and once I leave, I can never return home as I, too, will change in time."

"I will never see you again or any children you may have,"

Beverly states with disappointment. Her painful heartbreak is so profound that sorrow overwhelms her and tears stream freely down her face.

"Mama, please don't cry," Sasha pleads looking over at Javan. Tubal steps up and places his hand on his mother's shoulder to give her comfort.

"You'll still have me. You know releasing her to be with the love of her life is the right thing to do," Tubal submits for her consideration.

"I know, but not to be able to touch her or hold her again is too hard for this mother's heart."

"Perhaps, I can ease your burden," Anak informs making his presence known. Beverly looks up into his face through tear blurred vision. Javan, too, is attentive to what Anak may offer as his heart has been rent by her profound sorrow.

"What are you offering?" Beverly inquires.

"I'm offering that once a year on the summer solstice a boat will be sent to the Port of Salt to ferry you to the Island of Vespa to spend 30 days with your daughter and family. The only thing is that you must not tell anyone where you go to and you must come alone."

"I can live with that so long as my son can bring me to the

port," Beverly informs.

"I think we can manage that," Anak agrees.

"Sasha, I want you to know that even if that wasn't offered to me, I would have released you with a full heart. My pain would have mended in time being comforted in the knowledge that you are with your soul mate."

"Thank you, mama," Sasha hugs her mother again.

"I can see that you're happy and that Javan loves you as much as you love him. This knowledge will allow me to sleep at night between visits."

"Don't forget you both still have your vision," Tubal suggests.

"Of course, my son, thank you."

"We must go now, we can't linger if these people are to rebuild a society," Anak informs urging them to keep moving forward.

Sasha hugs her mother and Tubal one last time. Tubal joins his mother, and they wait until they can no longer see them before continuing on to Castle Togarmah. After they have disappeared out of sight, Tubal helps his mother back up on the wagon, and they continue their journey.

"How many of our warriors survived?" Beverly inquires as her position as matriarch dictates.

"Not many. Our victory was costly. I didn't take a full count wanting to accompany Sasha as far as I could, but I would estimate that only 50 to a 100 survived," Tubal answers with an undertow of sadness in his voice. "I've seen their stardust images, so they are well. They just won't be returning to us."

"I understand. Even though the land has healed, it'll not be easy for our people to move on."

"What of the Princess Sabrina and Prince Robert?" Beth inquires then quickly holds her breath. She doesn't want to hear but wants to hear the answer at the same time.

"They were both killed and are together again. I'm sure that King Horeb will honor their sacrifice and raise the child as his own."

Beth cries silent tears. In many ways, she was closer to Sabrina than her own family. She'll miss her so very much. Being the first Lady in Waiting is a sacred trust, and she'll honor that trust by continuing to take care of her Lady's son and present herself to serve whoever will become his adoptive mother.

"Take heart, Lady Beth. My vision is very clear. This child will be loved, and you will serve the new queen and this young prince for many years to come," Beverly enlightens.

"Will the new queen be kind?"

"I think you'll approve..." Beverly adds with a sprite like glint in her eyes. She refuses to elaborate any further to Beth's aggravation but knows she won't say until she's ready. They continue on to Castle Togarmah hoping to reach the castle by nightfall.

***

At the Castle Togarmah, Rainah stands on her bedroom balcony gazing northward hoping to see her beloved coming over the hillside. She continues to stand for hours on end since the victory was won. In spite of Mary's attempts to involve her in the work of repairing the castle and making it presentable for the warriors, she remains steadfast at her post. Nevertheless, Mary pours herself into making the palace ready clearing away the debris, sweeping, and washing with the helping hands of the children. Although the land and the people were transformed, the buildings were not. They'll need major repairs, or simply torn down the rest of the way and rebuilt from their foundations.

The absence of their warriors hasn't deterred their enthusiasm in getting this ready. Most of the people who lost close family members in the war had the same experience as Mary. They believe that if they didn't see them in these stardust visions that they'll return to them. The sun rises to noonday, and in the distance, Rainah can make out horse and riders coming over the ridge.

"Mary! Mary!" Rainah calls repeatedly. Her voice is full of excitement.

Mary is working on the other side of the castle and finally hears Rainah calling to her. She hands the towels she's holding to another woman and rushes up the stairs in response to Rainah's summons.

"What is it?" Mary asks as she enters the room.

"The women warriors along with some of the men are returning. They're just coming over the rise," Rainah informs. She's happy but is disappointed that she doesn't see her Connor yet.

"Really?" Mary questions with anticipation. She hurries to the balcony to look for herself. "It's Cassandra with the women and the men. I have to tell the others."

All of a sudden the gleeful shouts of women and children fill the air as they rush out of the castle and surrounding huts to greet them.

"I think they already know," Rainah comments.

"Indeed, do you see your Connor yet?"

"No, I don't…wait…is that…it is!" Rainah exclaims in spastic sputters. Her eyes behold for the first time since he left, her beloved walking along side his best friend. She takes off running out the door, down the stairs, and out the large doors. Connor sees her as she runs around the castle wall and he begins running towards her as well. Racing full speed ahead, they collide into one another's arms. They hit the ground landing on the soft, lush grass covering the hill. They kiss like they were trying to resuscitate each other oblivious to all the other reunions going on around them. Soba just stands there giggling like a school boy at the pair.

This same scene repeats itself over and over again as spouses and families are reunited. They're home and the women and children that were not able to fight gleefully welcome everyone back. No one has a sad face this day, not even over those who didn't return because they know that they're safe and sound where nothing can ever harm them again. With great delight, they begin to prepare a banquet fit for a king to celebrate their homecoming. The castle will be quite full until their homes can be rebuilt, but the halls are again filled with laughter and joy.

Mary looks out over the masses, however underwhelming they may be, and notices that even the orphans are elated that so many have returned safe and sound. Some still have extended families that she is sure will take them in, but others are alone in this new world. Mary resolves that they'll not be alone for long.

Connor and Rainah finally come up for a breath and make their way back to the castle arm in arm. Mary greets Connor, Rainah, and Soba.

"We're very glad you're safe. I'm aware that we lost the Princess, but please tell me when Prince Robert will return?" Mary inquires. Connor looks at Mary with a downcast expression. Even though he knows he is now safe and very much alive on the other side of this realm, his loss here will be felt very deeply along with Sabrina's.

"Your prince will not be returning. He, like Sabrina, gave his life to protect us all."

"Then who will reign?"

"Prince Horeb will be your new king, and he'll be marrying Rachel, the Healer in twenty-five days. They plan on making Indra the place where they'll rule from. Everyone is invited to the wedding."

"What will happen to this place?" Mary asks, but her expression doesn't match her question.

"Something tells me you already know," Connor surmises.

"My son, Andrew, he…"

"Yes, he, too, died bravely trying to save the Princess. He was truly the bravest knight I have ever known," Connor informs as he drops to one knee to honor Andrew's mother.

"I know. He came to me in a stardust vision to bid me farewell and told me to look after the orphans. I shall petition the new king and queen to see if they'll allow me to make the castle a home for them."

"That sounds like an excellent plan. I'm sure it'll be approved," Connor adds.

"Did we lose all of our fighters?" Rainah interrupts looking about for her fellow dwarfs.

"No, they went to the council to present a wedding invitation and a proposal to migrate our people to the surface," Connor informs.

"To answer the actual question presented, our survivors are few having lost two thirds of our troops. We'll need each other more than we ever have before," Soba explains.

"I'm glad to see that you're safe Soba," Rainah acknowledges.

"It's nice to see you up and about," he adds, smiling.

"Yes, well, when we won the battle everything transformed. I was completely healed. You can't even see the scar that…the enemy left," Rainah stops short of mentioning the Dragon's name as it's sound should never be given form in this new world.

"The same thing happened to our wounded fighters as well."

"Come and rest, I know you must be tired. I'll fetch some wine from the cellar," Rainah encourages.

They follow her to a sitting room not far from her chambers. Mary walks with them escorting them to the sitting room. She then excuses herself and returns to her cleaning. When Rainah passes by on her way to get the wine, Mary stops her.

"Why don't you stay and enjoy the company of your husband and friend. I'll fetch the wine and some glasses."

"Thank you Mary," Rainah says appreciatively as she rushes back to the sitting room.

***

By nightfall, Beverly and company arrive at Castle Togarmah. They find blissful chaos surrounding the castle. Mary greets them upon arriving at the castle doors. She rushes to hug Beth first having become good friends before they were separated to protect the infant prince. She reaches out her arms to hold Beth's son while Beverly hovers close by awaiting an introduction. After a few awkward looks and prompting by Mary, they receive a formal introduction.

"This is Beverly, the Matron of Elim and Sasha's mother. Sasha entrusted her to look after the prince," Beth explains.

"It's a pleasure to meet you. I'm Mary, and you gentlemen are?"

"I'm Keevah, and this is Shamilar. We protected them while

they protected the infants."

"Who is this?" Rainah asks having followed after Mary to see why she left their table.

"You remember Beth."

"Yes, but I don't believe I've ever met you," Rainah interjects referring to Beverly. "I must say you bear a striking resemblance to Sasha."

"She's my daughter," Beverly confirms.

"And these gentlemen with you?" Rainah asks.

"Keevah and Shamilar. They protected us from the Dragon's assassin sent to kill Sabrina's son," Beverly introduces.

"And this is Rainah, Connor's wife, who has served the house of Togarmah for many years. Gentlemen, your presence honors us, and you are welcome among us," Mary interjects with a warm smile. The men simply nod their heads acknowledging the greeting.

"Who will be the young prince's mother?" Beth asks interrupting the introductions. She hopes that with so many people listening she'll get an answer this time.

"I would imagine it'll be King Horeb's new bride, Rachel the Healer. They are due to be married in twenty-five days. The whole land has been invited to Indra for the ceremony," Rainah jumps in to bring them up to speed on the latest information. Beverly just smiles at Beth. Her beautiful white teeth beam between her ebony lips.

"She'll make a good mother," Beth adds. Having met the woman, she is relieved that it will be her. She has become quite attached to the young prince and loves him as much as she does her own son.

"We shall arrive two days early to speak with his majesty about the child. Until then, we shall continue to care for him and rest from our own journey," Beverly informs.

"Come and eat, we have plenty for all," Mary entreats.

"Thank you."

CHAPTER 26

General Rasmussen and his remaining troops arrive at the catacombs and march down into the earth. They are greeted by the joyous faces of their kin. There are tears of joy and sadness as some families are reunited, and others are faced with the reality of their loss. The General, along with his surviving officers, head towards the Council Chambers to file a report. The news of their warriors return prompts the council members and their spouses to assemble in the Council Chambers to await their arrival.

Although the General's wife is grateful that he has returned, he must dispense with his duty first. She waits impatiently, but her outward appearance is that of a proper general's wife, stoic and strong. All are eager to learn about the outcome of the war as they've not witnessed the transformation on the surface. They gather outside the Council Chambers pressing in to learn what happened. It's apparent to all, however, that their numbers have been dramatically reduced as the full extent of their sacrifice begins to sink in.

"Most honorable Council, I bring you good news. We have won the battle against the Dragon and his minions, but I regret to inform you that I return with only a third of the dwarfs I left with. They fought bravely and sacrificially so that the rest of us can be free."

The Council collectively releases a sigh of relief and reverent sorrow for the high price paid for this victory. The catacombs require a great deal of maintenance to preserve the integrity of their structures and insure proper air flow and fresh water. There are several communities that live inside these structures. Their depleted numbers threaten their ability to continue living here.

"How can we maintain our existence with so few workmen left?" Wilhelm inquires.

"The Redeemer transformed the people and the surface world into a paradise. His sacrifice even restored our own injured. To that end, the new king, Horeb, has extended an invitation to his wedding to his future bride, Rachel, and has offered us the coastal lands of Navarre to build a community that will live in unity with the humans. We no longer have to live underground as our adversary will never return. The surface is lush, green, and bountiful both in game and produce."

"It's a generous offer, but does King Horeb expect us to submit to human leadership?" Wilhelm asks.

"That was not discussed. I told the new king that I would deliver this offer to the council and send a messenger with your ruling…" Rasmussen stops speaking when he notices that he has lost Wilhelm's attention. Wilhelm the Great, the council leader, keeps looking behind him as if looking for someone. In addition, Leopold the Honorable is doing the same thing as if they haven't heard a single word he's said.

"May inquire what your Excellencies are looking for?"

"Forgive me General for my selfish inquiry, I was in hopes that Connor would have returned with you. Unless you didn't find him alive…" Wilhelm admits with a tinge of fear in his voice.

"And, Rainah, did she survive?" Leopold adds before the general could respond.

"They're both alive. Connor returned to Castle Togarmah to be re-united with his wife, Rainah. Before anyone asks about Soba, he accompanied Connor. They plan on attending the king's wedding on your behalf knowing that we would never make it back in time. After that, they'll abide by any ruling the council makes in regards to the offer of the coastal lands. I have had the scribes record the names of the fallen, so we have an exact accounting of all the lives in my charge," the General motions for the roll of the fallen to be handed over to Leopold.

Both councilmen and their wives seated in the gallery breathe a sigh of relief and return their attentions to the General's report. Rasmussen continues giving his report in the required detail when he is cut off by another member of the council.

"What about the scouting party we sent ahead? Is there any word on their status?" Thornton inquires.

Before Rasmussen can respond, the three scouts in question enter the council chambers and present themselves to the council and the general. Relief fills the faces of all in the room. All are now accounted for both alive and dead.

"General," Quimby begins. "Forgive our intrusion, but we have come to report that we destroyed every egg we could find. We also apologize that there was a clutch that we missed allowing some to hatch and escape."

"How many do you estimate you destroyed?"

"At least 500,000 thousand," Quimby answers.

"Then you'll be pleased to know that only 200 made it to the Plains of Galeed. By the time they arrived, the Army of Light arrived shortly after with Firecats, and all were destroyed."

"We apologize for not getting all of them in time and submit ourselves for disciplinary action for our failure."

"Failure?" The general asks.

"Our failure resulted in the deaths of our brothers. We deserve whatever punishment you decree."

"There is nothing to discipline," Rasmussen informs.

"But we failed to complete our mission," Quimby submits.

"You reduced their numbers to the point that they could be defeated. On the contrary, you deserve medals, not discipline," the general corrects.

"Which will be awarded later," Wilhelm interrupts. "Please, general, finish your report."

The three scouts step back in stunned realization that they're to be awarded and not punished. They stand at attention while the general completes his report.

"Yes, of course," Rasmussen replies and continues, "As I was saying, the cost of winning the battle was dear. I would like to submit for consideration that we commence immediately with the reading of the names to commemorate their sacrifice followed by the banquet to honor the survivors, and then you can deliberate on the land grant. How do you wish us to proceed?"

"The council will need to deliberate on both the land grant and how much autonomy we need to keep in governing ourselves. Are the humans as weak as we are in number?"

"I would estimate weaker than us. The risk of another nation taking advantage of the situation is greater without our number added to theirs to provide security."

"We'll have an answer for you, but it'll have to wait until well after the Warrior's Banquet tomorrow evening. We'll commence with the Roll Call immediately after your report is concluded."

"Excuse me," Rastus addresses the council.

"The Council recognizes Rastus. What do you wish to say?"

"I want the Council to know that the new king of Navarre risked his life to save mine from the clutches of a terrible monster. The humans are trustworthy. We found them to be different than what we thought them to be."

"How so?"

"We found them to be honorable," Rastus submits.

"We'll consider this when making our decision," Wilhelm responds. Rastus nods his appreciation and returns to his ranks behind the general. "General do you have anything else to report?"

"No Sir, I was finished."

Rasmussen, the officers, and scouts give the customary salute as they're dismissed from the Council's presence. He, in kind, releases his officers to be with their families while he takes some time to be with his wife. She maintains her report as a good

General's wife should just outside the chambers, but the moment he passes the threshold into the hallway, she leaps into his arms embracing him with all her strength. He breathes in her scent and is comforted from his long journey.

The scribes that went with the warriors recorded the names of the dead on special scrolls that will be entered into their archives. A special herald will stand outside the Great Hall and call each name on the scroll. A bell will toll after each name is read. Only after this is complete will the preparations begin in the Warriors Banquet Hall for the celebration. After the standard period of mourning, a mural will be commissioned to honor those that fell in combat and will contain each and every name within its artistic beauty.

The Warrior's Banquet is a full day and night of feasting, drinking, and dancing until they drop from exhaustion. It's a bold celebration for a bold Dwarf class that is worthy of this extended revelry. This will be followed by a day of rest. After that, the council will begin its deliberations and establish what stipulations will need to be met should they accept the land grant. They'll have to weigh the future of their people against the possible loss of self governance on the surface world. They still have a numerical edge over the humans and rest in the knowledge that they can't be forced into a decision that they're uncomfortable with, but shudder to think that the humans would do anything so despicable after all that they've been through together.

Glenda C. Finkelstein

CHAPTER 27

As survivors return to their towns, they begin the arduous task
of rebuilding their families, their homes, and their livelihoods.
Amid this overwhelming task hovers the glad news that their new
king will soon be married and all of Navarre has been invited to
attend. In the past, such an event would have placed a burden
upon the people to bring tribute to the king in celebration, but in
this instance, it's the king that will be providing gifts to the people.
Horeb is insistent that no one who comes regardless of station will
be turned away empty handed. Although Horeb knows that not all
will be able to attend for a variety of reasons, he's setting the tone
for the type of ruler he'll be by placing the needs of the people
above his own.

In the city of Indra, there is an excitement as they clear away
the rubble and debris, not only to make their dwellings more
livable but to prepare for the wedding of their new king and his
future home. Mordecai has taken it upon himself to organize the
preparations for the upcoming nuptials and gives Joss the task of

preparing the Royalty Inn to be temporary housing for the King and his council which he has not yet selected. The Prophet wants everything to be ready, so King Horeb doesn't have to concern himself with such ordinary details. Mordecai also enlists the aid of Argo, who recently returned from the wilderness, to act as a messenger between King Horeb, who is currently staying at the crossroads, and himself.

"Shouldn't we wait until the king arrives before we start pestering him about how he wants his temporary residence to be set up?" Joss inquires of Mordecai after he dispatches Argo to inquire of Horeb about any additional preparations.

"The king gave me strict orders to make sure we had enough rooms prepared for his council, their spouses, and children. He wants to get this nation rebuilt as soon as possible."

"Did he mention who he was going to place on the council?"

"No, we'll know when he wants us to know, but right now I need to confirm how many rooms he anticipates on needing. It's not like we can build anything in less than thirty days. This Inn is the only structure large enough and intact enough to be used," Mordecai informs. Joss looks around him with a more discerning eye and realizes that Mordecai is correct.

"Yes, Sir," Joss concedes. He then finds a couple of young maidens to assist him in getting all the existing rooms clean. At least then all he has to do is acquire whatever things will be needed for the King, future queen, and each council member.

"Joss, when you're done with that Argo mentioned that the King wants to provide for the people some gift whether its land, a job, blankets, or a tent. He said you would know where the closest stashes of supplies are at because you helped hide them during the war."

"Yes, I know of several nearby."

"Good. Get some help and bring those supplies here for distribution."

"Yes, Sir."

After finishing his conversation with Joss, Mordecai continues with the wedding preparations. He selects the most beautiful of places in the city for the ceremony. In the heart of Indra is a flower garden in full bloom like the rest of the land. It also contains beautiful statuary. Many of the statues are broken beyond repair, so he is having those removed. Others, however, although scarred are good enough to be placed back upon their pedestals. It'll be a reminder that no matter what the difficulty beauty can still survive.

While Mordecai works to prepare the flower garden, he notices that the people come here often to rest from their labors and drink from the water fountains dispersed throughout the garden. When they leave they appear invigorated and inspired. They seem to work all the harder on their own pieces of property to bring that same beauty to the rest of the city. It occurs to him that they have an opportunity to make the whole of Indra something beautiful and inspirational. This excites him like nothing else in a very long time.

***

As the wedding date draws near the population of Indra steadily increases. The new arrivals put up makeshift tents along the perimeter of the city or simply make do amongst unclaimed ruins. Any family that is able invites those with no tent to share their home until the wedding ceremony is over. There is a sense of community, no, a sense of family where there is unity. Each shares what they have with those who do not. Possessions or region of birth is no longer important to them. Social status has been nearly wiped from their consciousness as knights and dukes remember marveling at farmers and fisherman holding their own against the enemy.

In appreciation and acknowledgement of their acts of bravery, these former nobles who had accumulated wealth and political status prior to the war, focus on relieving any potential suffering that they can. They actively offer opportunities to their fellow citizens to be equally successful by partnering with them to help repair their lands, buildings, and vineyards, rather than taking advantage of them or providing a simple act of charity. It's important to all of them that the people obtain a level of respect and position in society based upon their talents, not their bloodlines.

This spirit of unity and hospitality continues to bind the people together in ways they never dreamed possible before the war. Reports of these acts of love and kindness that King Horeb set in motion are sent to the king every few days. He is both pleased and wary knowing that what they feel so keenly in these days after the Great War will lose their edge over time. He is careful to provide specific instructions to Mordecai to insure that things continue along this vein.

Among those that are arriving for the wedding are Beverly and Beth along with many of the survivors who live in the old Southern Kingdom. They are greeted with open arms, and there is no hint of the old prejudice that used to be so prevalent. Beverly hopes to meet with Horeb and Rachel prior to the wedding only to discover that they've still not arrived. Disappointed that she may not be able to meet with them until after they are wed, she asks Cassandra to prepare a place for herself, Beth, and the infants to stay while they wait. She remains positive that they'll accept the child. In the meantime, Cassandra insures that the future prince and his guardians are well taken care of while they await the festivities.

Shamilar didn't come with them. After dispatching his duties seeing them safely to Castle Togarmah, he longed to return to his tavern and repair the damages. He has no desire to be awarded any medals or fame. He considers himself a cripple with his glory days far behind him. His medals never gave him an advantage in the marketplace and sometimes became a disadvantage if he was dealing with someone from the Southern Kingdom. He sees profit in this new unity and wants to cash in as soon as he can.

Keevah, the merchant without a ship, doubts his mutinous crew will return to the Port of Salt. He'll remain with the women until the prince is handed over to the new king and queen. Keevah is curious about what kind of ruler Horeb will be. The news of him providing gifts to the people to celebrate his wedding instead of the other way around intrigues him. He has clear memories of Horeb prior to the invasion and counted him no better than his father, King Ophir.

At the moment, Keevah has no immediate plans to embark on any ventures, but he still has relationships with high profile contacts both economically and politically that owe him, so it's not out of the realm of possibility for him to return to the life he loves. Before he makes any decisions, he wants to determine if King Horeb has truly changed or if this is some kind of cruel rouse to perpetuate the evil inclinations of his father. If something doesn't sit right with him, he'll have no part of Navarre. But, if there is any truth to this new nature, he may find opportunity here to turn his fortunes around.

***

Horeb has spent the last twenty-two days under the council of his future father-in-law and Samuel. If the king has known anyone in his life with wisdom, it would be these two. His heart is warmed by the reports of the selflessness of the people but realizes that this harmony of putting others before themselves will eventually fade as time goes by. There is a keenness of purpose and discernment of what's important that will eventually dull as the people return to their daily lives of buying and selling goods, farming, raising children, etc. Horeb desires to provide a just standard that all can live by as well as a proportional discipline when the standard is violated.

The harshness of his own father didn't deliver justice, only cruelty depriving the offender of their dignity and hope. Even though evil has been evicted from this world each one of them is still all too human. Horeb recognizes that none of them are perfect nor will they always make the right decision. Sometimes even the most well intentioned actions can result in terrible consequences. Horeb knows that some actions will demand punishment while others will carry their own punishment. He is committed to making sure that mercy will always have a prominent place in the judgment seat.

"I want to thank you for your kindness and your words of wisdom these many days, but we must get ready to go to Indra.

We have much work to do. I want you all to know that although I am firstly your King, in my heart you have become my family."

"You honor us," Laban responds on behalf of everyone in the room.

"You have done more for me than I could ever repay and we have become quite familiar with one another over the past few days. For the sake of the rest of the nation, I must ask you to address me by my formal title once we arrive at Indra. I can't allow for any display of favoritism to create a rift amongst the people."

"Of course, we understand and are not offended by your request," Laban confirms. The people nod their heads in agreement.

Horeb and Rachel prepare to leave for Indra with the entire village of Tierney in tow. It doesn't take them long having lost all their belongings in the tidal wave. They make quite a procession leaving the Crossroads taking the main highway to the city giving him the honor that he is due as their sovereign. It's a fuss that Horeb didn't need so soon wanting to revel in just being one of them for a little while longer, but keeps his objections to himself as he doesn't want to dampen their spirits.

The one thing that Horeb desires to do is to array his bride in the finest of silk befitting the queen she is about to become but is doubtful he can provide that much for her. The war stripped the country of any such finery. Although he knows that such finery may still remain in Ophir's castle, he refuses to step foot back into the granite castle to retrieve anything for himself. He doesn't want the spirit of what occupied his former home to contaminate her purity with the vanity that so permeated his ancestral home. Besides, after looking at her, he realizes that there is nothing that is worthy of her beauty anyway. It will be her that makes the garment beautiful and not the garment that will make her beautiful.

The weight of Horeb's burden is beginning to show on Rachel as well. Their expressions become somber, and thoughts inward focused until Snootzer bursts forth with one of Gorham's licorice sticks in his mouth. The dog weaves in and out of the walking villagers with Gorham hot on his heels. The boy leaps trying to catch this fur covered thief only to miss and land face first into the dusty road. Horeb and Rachel start to laugh. Horeb pauses to pick up the youngster by his belt loops out of the dirt.

"I think Snootzer wants you to share," Horeb adds as he places Gorham back on his feet.

"Here is one for you," Rachel offers having kept a small stash of these treats secret.

"Thanks!" Gorham exclaims and runs back to his older brother Jonathan. Now that the boy has stopped chasing after Snootzer, the dog turns around and runs after the boy.

Inspired by this bit of laughter and entertainment, Hannah, who has been aloof over these many days, collects flowers and fashions a crown of color and fragrance. She places it upon her sister's head. Rachel beams a great smile and blushes under Horeb's approving gaze. Laban looks on with fatherly pride and relief that his beloved daughter has finally found the joy that has eluded her these many months. Samuel, too, is pleased. He knows that Rachel will never forget his Seth or the sacrifice he made for the Redeemer.

Laban keeps a watchful eye on Hannah. Although in many ways she is the same girl he knew before he was sent off to war, in many others she is quite different. He shouldn't be surprised by this since she died, was used by the enemy, and then restored to them by the Most High. It has to be an adjustment for her which he recognizes can't be easy.

"Your highness," Laban begins.

"Yes?" Horeb inquires back. He's alert and open to whatever nuggets of wisdom Laban may have for him as Laban is not a man of casual conversation.

"It has occurred to me that the deeds and attitudes of the past are dead and gone. We need to insure that these old ways are actively replaced by love, mercy, and hope. Everything we do must be focused on the future of Navarre."

"The reports that my knights have been sending me has relayed just that, but I perceive there is something more to your statement than the obvious."

"Yes, what's happening now is a natural outpouring of the bonding that took place during these difficult times. As life returns to normal, these attitudes will slowly fade as it often does when the toil of rebuilding begins to wear on them. The destruction was so severe in some places that it'll be difficult to tell which properties belonged to whom. Those that had none have nothing to claim, but will see an opportunity to claim those that have been left vacant. Disputes will arise as various parties see the same opportunity and attempt to claim the same property."

"This has occurred to me also, which is why I want Samuel to be judge and settle any property disputes that arise among the people. I've fought by his son's side, and have never met a fairer more compassionate man as Seth. If the son is that wise, then his father must be even wiser."

"I would be honored, but it'll take more than a judge to resolve disputes. You'll need to set the tone of how the society will move forward," Samuel acknowledges while Laban looks on with pride. "But I'm sure you realize it'll take more than that. Actions need to be taken to prevent disputes from happening."

"Yes, which is why I intend to take the abandoned property and give land grants to those that were not land owners prior to the war. As soon as we reach Indra, I'll be summoning the balance of my council and will assign a helper for you. I'll make the formal announcement after our wedding so that the people understand that there will be enough for everyone to have something that they can build a future on," Horeb explains.

"Excellent idea, your majesty," Samuel adds.

"Don't forget that traditional family structures have changed as the people try to accommodate the large number of orphans and widows. If these are not dealt with also in a way that doesn't overburden the people, we could find ourselves with hundreds of starving homeless beggars, or worse yet, become embroiled in an internal conflict of civil unrest."

"I realize that there will be many orphans with no family left to care for them. And I know that something needs to be done, but I'm not sure what at this time. I will bring this up at our council meeting to entertain suggestions of the proper course of action. We owe these children, widows, and the aged our love, provision, and support to honor the sacrifices of their loved ones."

They continue walking toward Indra discussing the affairs of state. It's helpful for Horeb to bounce ideas and to glean from others' wisdom. One thing is painfully evident to him is that there must be moments of laughter, joy, and celebration. These things ease burdens by focusing on the blessings of life rather than the difficulties. Towards that end, Horeb resigns himself to establishing a day of rest. Every eighth day he'll encourage games, dancing, music, and feasting.

***

Soba, Connor, and Rainah enter the city of Indra like so many other pilgrims. They waited a day after the humans left Castle Togarmah to travel in order to spend some time alone. Connor looks upon the city through the eyes of the past. His heart is moved by the condition of this once beautiful city which contained alabaster and marble facades, cedar window frames, shutters, and doors. Soba and Rainah have no such comparisons and are taken aback by its size and although tarnished, the beauty of what was is still evident. The humans look upon the trio with favor and offer cool water and food to revive them from their journey. The humans know that they owe their existence to the dwarfs and will never look on them the same ever again.

"I had no idea that all humans were so friendly. We were taught to be cautious and untrusting of them," Rainah comments believing that those she met in the south were an exception to this long held attitude.

"That's because you weren't here prior to the Great War. The last time I was in this city I was bringing word to Princess Sabrina that her father had jumped to his death," Connor shares. The memory is still a painful one for him. It wasn't easy seeing such a great leader deteriorate into madness and suicide. Now Connor takes comfort in the fact that his beloved daughter is forever with him.

"I'm sorry, my love. I didn't realize what your life was like being alone amongst them. Nor did I know the depth of feeling you hold for the royal family of the old Southern Kingdom."

"Of all the humans, the Togarmahs' treated me as if I was part of their family. I was keeper of the royal seal and trusted confidant to both the prince and princess. It was the Northern humans that didn't treat me so well. Now, the people are one and the mistrust from the long civil war a forgotten relic of the past."

"Well, I don't know about the two of you," Soba interjects. "But I like the surface. I love feeling the sun on my face and tasting the rain on my tongue. You can't get that in the catacombs. Also, the forests are alive with game and vegetation. It's so different than the tunnels. Do you think that if the Council decides not to come to the surface that they'll let those of us that want to stay do so?"

"I don't know my friend. The Council can be very strict when it wants to be."

"I sense some trepidation in you when I mention the Council. Do you think your father has forgiven you?" Soba inquires. Connor's eyes drop to the ground avoiding Soba's inquiring gaze. He is visibly uncomfortable. "Maybe the proper question is have you forgiven your father for exiling you?"

Connor stands there silent pondering the question. He has spent fifty years exiled to the surface by his own father. He's carried the guilt of his mistake for just as long. His anger has always been focused on himself. His feelings towards his father have always been one of deep hurt. It has never occurred to him to consider forgiving him.

"We should find us some shelter. The nights can get a little chilly," Rainah reminds attempting to change the subject. She can see how uncomfortable her husband has become.

"In a moment," Soba responds. "Connor hasn't answered my question. Have you forgiven him?"

"It's never been a matter of forgiving him, but forgiving myself. I've blamed myself for setting things in motion that made the Great War possible."

"Hold on, my friend. I've always known you to be a bit arrogant, but this takes the cake. How can you possibly believe that everything we went through is your fault?"

"It's partly my fault because I disobeyed my father."

"And how many people surrounding us right now could make that same claim. Get over yourself, Connor. You're not perfect."

"Now where have I heard that before?" Rainah asks.

"So I'm not the only one. Good, maybe you should listen to the rest of us," Soba adds.

"Perhaps we should calm down. People are beginning to stare at us," Rainah suggests.

"You're right," Soba relents. He ceases his line of questioning as Connor's silence and expression provide its own response.

"Since we are the envoys representing the dwarfs, we should see if there are any preparations made for us at the Royalty Inn or something close to it. The King did invite us in front of all of the people," Connor suggests hoping to segue into a different conversation.

"Sounds like a sound plan, husband," Rainah concurs. She reaches out her hand and squeezes his tightly to reassure him that no matter what she'll never leave his side again. He smiles back in loving appreciation while Soba rolls his eyes at the cheesy display of affection between them.

CHAPTER 28

King Horeb arrives at Indra. The greeting he receives is unparalleled to any he has received before. All the people are genuinely glad to see him. He is appreciative and beams a great smile shaking hands with the men and patting small children and babes in arms gently on top of their heads. Women throw flowers upon the ground as they make their way to the old Royalty Inn. Although Horeb is pleased, he knows he needs to get to work right away. His first order of business is to form his Advisory Council so they can meet the immediate needs of the people and develop long term plans for their continued growth and success.

Laban has already agreed to be his Chief Advisor, and Samuel his Chief Justice. He wants to enlist the aid of Joss, Sebastian, Argo, Jonathan, Mordecai, Hannah, as well as have some representation from the village of Elim and the Dwarfs. As he nears the city center, he sees and greets a friend.

"Sebastian, I'm so glad to see you made it safely to Indra.

Have you had a chance to survey your family farm?" Horeb greets with a personal inquiry acknowledging in advance any personal sacrifice he may have made to be here at this auspicious occasion.

"Yes, your majesty, I was able to survey the damage. It'll take a lot of work to get the farm back in working condition. I'm hoping to hire some workers who may have lost their own homes to help us both. I'm glad to see that you're looking well and survived your ride on the back of a dragon."

"I'm glad you made it safely back through the Wilderness of Desolation. You are in an elite group to have succeeded in that venture."

"You may want to consider renaming the Wilderness of Desolation as it has been transformed into a paradise of beautiful forests filled with game and crystal clear lakes and streams. There are no monsters left," Sebastian informs with a beaming smile.

"It would seem that every inch of our land has been renewed with great abundance," Horeb adds with restrained joy.

Although this abundance is of benefit to the people and will keep hunger at bay, it'll make Navarre a tempting target of conquest by neighboring nations. Securing the borders especially of long abandoned areas will be important and difficult with their depleted numbers.

"I'm sorry to hear about the death of Prince Robert. You have my deepest sympathy on his loss."

"Thank you, but the time of mourning is almost over. It's time to look forward and honor what they sacrificed for rather than lamenting their loss. I have a spot that I'd like you to fill on my Advisory Council if you're willing. I've given instruction to Mordecai to prepare rooms for my council and their families inside the old Royalty Inn until the peoples' needs can be met."

"I'd be honored to serve in any capacity you need me to, and if I may be so bold, I'm proud of your decision to focus on the peoples' needs first."

"Have you seen Joss or Argo since you've arrived?" Horeb inquires.

"Yes, I have."

"I'm not sure what errand Mordecai may have sent them on, but if you could find them and bring them to me at the Royalty Inn I'd be most appreciative. I wish to offer them posts on the council as well. They've served me well during the war and these past thirty days and wish to reward them with this honor."

"Sure, I'd be happy to."

"One more thing before you go, do you know if the dwarfs or anyone from Elim has arrived?"

"I'm not sure, but I can certainly find out and get back to

you."

"Thank you, I want to speak with them as soon as possible."

"Of course, your majesty," Sebastian responds. He bows respectfully before leaving and quickly goes about the king's business.

As they continue on their way to the Royalty Inn, Horeb greets all who have waited for him. He is pleased with what he sees. The people are standing arm in arm with each other. There is no discernible difference between the Northern and Southern people as existed before the war. He is encouraged by this confirmation of the reports he received. He was hesitant to get too enthusiastic in case the reports were exaggerated but is overjoyed to see that they were not.

His first order of business will be to lay the groundwork of his kingdom and secure the safety of their borders. Upon entering the Royalty Inn, he allows Rachel the time she needs to prepare for their upcoming nuptials while he focuses on a special task that he wants to be completed as soon as the wedding is over. Her coronation as the queen is paramount to him and meets up with Mordecai to provide specific instructions.

***

A few hours later, Horeb holds his first court inside the main room of the Inn. Around the table are Joss, Argo, Mordecai,

Laban, Sebastian, and Hannah. He has thought many times about what he is going to share with them. He knows it'll make him appear vulnerable perhaps even to them, but it must be done. He's also still missing some key members but hasn't come across the proper fit for those positions yet and must move forward with what he has. As he begins to speak his heart, his hopeful countenance drops to one of deep concern.

"I've called you together to discuss a matter of grave importance. As you know Rachel and I have decided to move the throne here to Indra. This leaves my previous home Castle Ophir vacant. Although the land has been renewed the structures that we've built were not. That said I'm sending a special group that you, Joss, will manage and lead. You'll retrieve from the castle anything of use, dishes, linens, pots, etc. a tenth will remain in my ownership the balance will be distributed to the people as they have need.'

"Before these articles are to be divided between myself and the people, they must be brought before Hannah to judge whether they are usable or if they must be utterly destroyed. My father's castle housed many evil secrets even before the Dragon occupied it. Some I knew about, others I'm sure I didn't. I'm not proud to admit to that, but I don't want anything of my father's legacy to remain. He ruled by fear. He was selfish and disposed to cruelty. I want the people to clearly understand that I will be a just King that is disposed to mercy. After its contents are removed, you'll begin to tear down the structure stone by stone this too will be judged by Hannah."

"Begging your pardon, your Majesty, but why Hannah to judge?" Joss asks.

"Hannah is the only one amongst our people who has been in the presence of the Most High and returned to us by Mark the Redeemer. Only she has the keen discernment to know what still contains a remnant of evil and what is innocuous."

All eyes fall upon Hannah. Her response is one of disarming charm. This both answers the question and puts them all at ease that it's her ability to discern good from evil, rather than her relation to the king, which gives her this position of authority.

"I want the castle leveled and the tunnels that run under its foundations filled in and sealed. If the bricks are deemed usable, they'll be brought here to build homes and shops. If they're not, they are to be pulverized and used to fill and seal the dungeons."

"That could take years," Joss informs.

"Probably, but it must be done. Put a plea out while people are here. They'll be paid well for their labors. See to it that there is enough housing to protect them and focus on their dwelling first before you begin your task," Horeb insists. Joss nods his head to confirm he understands his orders.

"What about Castle Togarmah?" Argo asks.

"I've not made a decision regarding that castle. It never saw the evil my own home did and will not be destroyed. What it should be used for is another matter entirely. I'll not have it sitting derelict nor remain as a symbol of division. I know for a fact that the South saw their share of destruction. The people can use it for shelter until their own is repaired without fear of being evicted."

"I believe that is a wise decision," Argo commends.

Suddenly, the meeting is interrupted by one of the guards. He enters their presence with a woman in tow. Horeb recognizes her and stands up to greet her. She immediately drops to her knees before the new king.

"Your highness, this woman claims to be the mother of Sir Andrew and requests an audience with you. I know you would want to see her in light of his sacrifice."

"Yes, she is always welcome. She is also the sister to Mathias, your former commander. Rise, Mary, mother of Sir Andrew, what can I do for you?"

"Thank you for seeing me, your highness. I have come to you with a petition about how to use Castle Togarmah in light of you moving the throne to Indra."

There is a collective gasp among the council as to the timing of this woman's entrance. It's as if fate orchestrated the previous discussion.

"Did I say something wrong?" Mary asks in response to the council's reaction.

"No, on the contrary, please continue," Horeb entreats.

"Since you'll be building your residence here in Indra, I would like to turn Castle Togarmah into an orphanage. The war has left many children with no family to care for them, and I with no family left to care for me. The old castle is the only structure large enough to house their numbers. I would be honored to create a new family with them."

After submitting her idea, she looks about the room. Their expressions are difficult to read being as there is a mixture of approval and shock. Horeb smiles a great smile. He knows that his former wife and sister-in-law would approve of this use of her ancestral home.

"That's a marvelous idea. We shall make sure that all are aware of this so that every child can be taken care of. Please remain a few days after the wedding to formalize your request and plans so that any additional needs you may have will be managed."

"Of course, but I would ask one further petition of you."

"What is that?"

"Permission to rename the castle to, Sir Andrew's Home for Children."

"Granted," Horeb approves with great pride. "Please kneel before me and allow me to bestow the highest honor I can upon a woman."

Mary kneels before him. He draws out his sword and gently taps her shoulders and head and pronounces a title upon her.

"Arise, Dame Mary honored mother and sister of the armies of Navarre."

"Thank you, King Horeb," she responds. She rises with profound gratitude and a heartfelt smile upon her face and turns to leave. "Oh, before I leave, I ran into the Matron of Elim who requests an audience with you and your bride prior to your wedding ceremony. If that is possible, of course," Mary requests.

"Have her come back after sunset, and she'll have her private audience."

"Thank you, Sire."

"Is Connor with you perchance?"

"I've seen him. He arrived today with his wife and Commander Soba. We've found them suitable shelter."

"Send Connor to me at once. I wish to speak with him on an urgent matter."

"Of course," Mary responds. She kneels briefly before departing. After she departs, Horeb leaves word with the guards that they are to immediately escort Connor into their presence the moment he arrives.

Horeb and his council continue their deliberations of how to proceed with the reconstruction of Indra. After the wedding, Horeb knows that a large portion of the workforce currently represented to prepare for the wedding will leave to attend their own homes. He knows it's important that many of them return so the nation can heal. He suggests offering land or remaining foundations to those parcels that are unclaimed here in Indra to any family that lost their home as an incentive to keep more workers here. Since this will be the epicenter of Navarre, it's important to make sure that the city gets up-to-speed as quickly as possible. The ruling seat of the land should be the most secure and operational as he doesn't want to show a weak front to any visiting envoys from neighboring lands should they come.

Clearing away the rubble and reusing building materials is paramount on his list. They need to see what they have to work with before they start dipping into the natural resources around them. Horeb has given orders to close the borders at key entry points until they have reached a certain level of strength. After the terror this land brought to this world, it's not going to be easy to re-establish trade relations. In the meantime, Horeb orders the remaining knights to distribute the tents that Joss retrieved prior to his arrival to provide shelter for those that will require them when they leave for the perspective villages or during their stay here.

"Forgive the intrusion, my king, but you requested I bring Connor to you as soon as he arrived," a guard announces.

"Yes, thank you, you're dismissed. Welcome, Connor. I'm forming my new council and would like you to be a part of it if you're willing," Horeb offers. Connor looks at him in surprise. Their personal history is a rocky one at best, but Connor can see the sincerity in his face.

"I'm honored of course, but I've been away from my people for a very long time and have longed to return to them."

"I know, but both our peoples suffered such heavy losses we'll need each other to overcome those losses and become prosperous again."

"Knowing the Dwarf Council as well as I do, it's doubtful that they'll submit to your authority, no offense."

"None taken, I don't expect them to, but we can still be of benefit to one another. Mutual protection, trade of goods and services, your peoples' skills with iron and our farming abilities, are but a few things that we can offer each other. Now that your presence is known although, at peace with each other, there could be other nations that may take advantage of our vulnerability."

"Are you that suspicious of others?"

"Not suspicious, just realistic. Until we know for sure their intentions, can we assume that all will be peaceful ones? After all, it's Navarre that took this world to the brink of oblivion so it's they who may be suspicious of us."

"You have a valid point. It's not like other lands came to our aid."

"After all the signs that went forth across the skies, the seas, and lands, they may be afraid of us even though we mean them no harm. Even if you choose not to stay, it's important that we each have a representative in the other's council meetings to represent both dwarf and human affairs. I would not presume to rule over dwarfs, but issues that concern us both we should come together in unity for the benefit of both peoples."

"You make a lot of sense and it'll put any fears to rest about our ability to maintain our own government. I shall participate until such time that I know the council's decision to remain in the catacombs or come to the surface. Regardless of their decision, I do agree it's beneficial to have an ambassador that will reside with each group for a specified term. I have no issue with being the first to serve in that role and represent dwarf interests in the rebuilding of Navarre until such time another can be appointed."

"Thank you, Connor. I'll try not to detain you any longer than necessary."

Connor takes one of the open seats at the large table, and they continue to discuss the feasibility of Horeb's plans. The king demonstrates unusual flexibility if any of the Council members perceive a problem with the plan. This first session lasts until sunset when they dismiss for a well disserved meal.

Glenda C. Finkelstein

CHAPTER 29

The sun is setting in the west. Horeb and Rachel are reclining in private in front of the fireplace sharing a glass of port. The fire provides a warm embrace from the crisp cool air. They quietly await the arrival of the Matron of Elim enjoying this quiet moment together. Neither one of them understands the significance of the pending meeting nor how it will change their lives. A knock on the door invades their quiet contemplation. The guards answer and escort Beverly, Tubal, Lady Beth and an infant into their presence. Rachel recognizes Tubal, Lady Beth, and the infant as does Horeb.

"Tubal, Lady Beth," Rachel greets.

"Queen Elect, Your Highness," Tubal begins, "allow me to introduce you to my mother, Beverly, the Matron of Elim."

"The honor is ours," Rachel responds on behalf of them both.

"What can we do for you?" Horeb inquires gazing beyond Tubal at the infant held gingerly in the old woman's hands. His mind begins to reel with what this could mean.

"Your highness, Lady Beth and myself were entrusted with the life of your brother's son."

"He lives," Horeb announces as he stands to his feet. He extends his hands out to receive the young prince. Beverly hands him the baby boy. Horeb cradles the child in his huge arms while tears of joy fall unrestrained upon his tiny head. Rachel's face displays relief over his safety.

"This child is the heir to the throne of Navarre. My visions are clear that he must lead when he becomes a man or Navarre's future will be short lived," Beverly warns.

"I'm happy that my brother's son lives, but what about the children that Rachel will bear for me? I was the throne prince and my children would be the legal heir to the throne."

"Your bride is unable to carry a baby to full term. She has already lost Seth's son."

"Forgive me," Horeb pleads. "So much has happened that I forgot you lost Seth's baby."

"I believed that the loss of my child was due to the stress of the situation and that perhaps someday I would be able to have a child of my own. Clairese our Prophetess had foreseen my marriage to Horeb, and I assumed that the joy she spoke of after the dark times she referred to would be related to the children I would have."

"Alas, this is not the case. My visions have been very clear in this matter," Beverly delicately reinforces the facts to her.

"If you need to choose another bride to bear you an heir, I understand," Rachel offers in concession with a downcast expression.

"If you deny this boy his rightful place in fulfilling the last prophecy, then the future of Navarre will cease to exist," Beverly cautions.

"I shall not choose another bride nor entertain any concubine to bear me a son. I shall raise my brother's son as my own. I'll teach him about his father and mother's sacrifice, and groom him to take the throne," Horeb declares. Rachel's countenance brightens. Any doubts that she should be queen disappears.

"We shall love him and raise him as our very own," Rachel confirms as she draws close to Horeb to hold the baby. He gently places him into her waiting arms. As the baby enters her own arms, she too weeps, but her tears are far more profound as this baby represents the life that was lost from her own womb. "Does he have a name?"

"No, the princess didn't give him one."

"My love, allow me the honor of naming him," Rachel requests. Horeb nods his head in agreement.

"Lady Beth has been his wet nurse. I ask that you allow her to continue in that position until he is weaned," Beverly petitions.

"Lady Beth, you'll share my room until my wedding day then it'll be yours."

"Thank you, your majesties." Beth bows respectfully.

"Thank you for keeping him safe and returning him to us," Horeb states appreciatively.

"It wasn't easy to keep him safe. Had it not been for Keevah and Shamilar, we would have lost the prince for sure," Beverly comments.

"Keevah, the merchant?" Horeb inquires further for clarification.

"Yes, the same. He's a portly gentleman with a commanding voice."

"Where is he?"

"He accompanied us here and is staying in our encampment on the southern edge of Indra."

"And Shamilar?"

"He is on his way back to the Port of Salt to repair his tavern.

Now that I have discharged my duties, I'd like to retire for the evening."

Horeb nods his agreement then motions for the guard to come over. He quietly instructs him to fetch Keevah and bring him here to meet with him. The guard nods his understanding and quickly leaves to bring Keevah to the king.

Beverly is leaving with Tubal having discharged her duties to the young prince. She is almost to the door when Horeb calls after them.

"Wait, please, I have a petition for you to consider."

"What can we do for the king?" Beverly asks.

"I would like for you to appoint a representative from Elim to participate in my council. You are the only people that came to our aid during the Great War. I need all the wisdom I can get to take Navarre into a new golden age of enlightenment and prosperity."

"I appoint my son, Tubal. Since my daughter, the Oracle, left with her fiancée, Prince Javan, his purpose as Guardian has been eliminated."

"Mother, are you sure?" Tubal asks with sincere concern for his mother's emotional well being.

"I'm sure my son. You'll make me proud, and you have such

wisdom of your own that you'll be of great help to the king."

"Very well, I accept," Tubal agrees. He drops to one knee in respect of the sovereign he now serves.

"Rise, Tubal of Elim, you'll be my conscience. If someone needs to tell me no and they don't, it'll be your responsibility to do so. I don't want or need peoples' blind obedience to the crown. Too much is at stake. I can't afford a mistake because people are afraid to tell me no. The memory of the way my father ruled as well as my own past behavior is still fresh in the peoples' minds, and I know that subconsciously they'll not want to challenge me for fear of private retribution."

"I'll do my best to keep you on the path of light my king."

"You'll hold the post of the People's Guardian. I charge you this day to be the voice of the people and to look out for their interests at all times. Do you accept this post?"

"I accept. I shall not fail the people, your highness."

"Your first assignment is to go out amongst the people and listen to what they're saying about their fears and aspirations for the future. The task of rebuilding a nation is not a small one, and I don't want fear to take root. Unity is about combining our differences in meaningful ways. The people need to understand that they can agree to disagree and find a solution that will be acceptable to all parties."

"I'll do as you ask."

"Keep the confidence of those that speak things that may seem unsettling. I need to know their fears I don't want to know their names," Horeb orders.

"Understood, my king, I'll keep the people's confidence."

Beverly's chest puffs up with motherly pride and is reassured that Horeb truly has the correct balance of justice and clemency to lead this nation into a new prosperous future where all the people will share in its success and not just the elite.

Rachel catches a glimpse of Hannah out of the corner of her eye. At first glance, nothing was out of the ordinary, but then a glistening tear reflecting the lamplight cascades down Hannah's cheek. Hannah rarely if ever sheds a tear even in the most stressful of situations. Rachel is concerned but doesn't want to embarrass her. Hannah walks down the hall out of sight. This alarms Rachel.

"Beth, would you please take my son and prepare him a bed. The guard will show you to my room. I have something I need to take care of."

"Of course," Beth responds with outstretched arms taking the baby from her.

Horeb is pleased to hear her refer to him as her son and flashes a momentary approving smile as he returns to his glass of wine to await the arrival of Keevah.

Rachel follows after her sister and catches up with her at the end of the hall where she is sitting on a bench staring outside the window. The moonlight shines softly upon her sorrowful face.

"Hannah," Rachel calls tenderly as she takes a seat next to her. "What's wrong?"

"I feel overwhelmed."

"About?"Rachel inquires, but Hannah doesn't respond. "I know I haven't been able to spend much time with you, and I so want to but with the wedding and becoming queen I've just been so busy that I haven't had a moment to myself."

"It's not that. I, too, have been very busy preparing myself to serve in my new role. It's just that I'm different now. The Hannah you knew isn't who I am anymore."

"You've been through a lot. If you're feeling guilty about being used by the enemy, don't. You're not alone, and I know that if you could have, you would have escaped."

"I don't feel guilty about that as I had more control than any of them or are you forgetting the present I left."

A cold chill runs down Rachel's spine when she remembers the charred hair comb that Hannah left on the threshold of the Crossroads Tavern. It's an object that she keeps inside a box by her bed.

"I remember."

"It's what happened after all that which has impacted me most," Hannah explains.

"I don't understand," Rachel admits.

"I know and experienced life on the other side of this current existence bound by time. We all have this vision of eternity as being this never ending perpetual place when time goes on forever, but it's not like that at all. It's the past and future coexisting in the present. In order to be there, you are completely transformed. Everything that was imperfect about you is made perfect. I've seen and lived in eternity and to exist again in this finite place is constricting and unsettling."

"But you said it was a pleasant experience."

"It was, and my heart aches and yearns to return there. In that place, there is a sense of delight that satisfies every desire. There is no hunger, separation, or emptiness. You can't possibly know the depth of contentment that exists there, and I miss it so much."

"I'm sorry. I was selfish. My grief was so consuming, and it was only after I lost you that I realized how much you brought to my life, but I never asked for you to be returned as I didn't know it was possible," Rachel apologizes.

"You weren't being selfish. On the contrary, you were being human and don't apologize, I was willing to come back. I just didn't understand how much of an adjustment it would be."

"Then why are you so sad?"

"When it was just the people of our village, I was able to acclimate which allowed the intensity of the visions to subside. Since we've come to Indra, I can't seem to acclimate. There are too many people."

"What visions? Do you mean like the Matron of Elim?"

"No, mine are far more vivid and complete. I know what the ultimate destination is for each of us and how we get there. I thought it would ease over time. Then when I see someone new, I see their past, their present, and their future in the blink of an eye. I can see what their struggles were, are, or are going to be. Sometimes what I know can save their lives or rescue them from pain."

"Isn't that a good thing?"

"The Most High has forbidden me to interfere with their choices because it would deprive them of their own discovery. It would also put me in a place of such great demand of people wanting to know the future. People have no clue what they ask for. They hope that there is always this positive event that will make life easy, but all too often it's not like that at all."

"I didn't realize that was happening to you. Why didn't you say something?"

"I didn't want to burden you. You have enough on your plate."

"It's going to be okay. No one else has to know. Horeb hasn't placed you in a position of a fortune teller. He's placed you in a position of discerning what could be evil vs. what is still good. I can see where this can be overwhelming, but even if you did try to interfere. How many people would believe you? They make their choices, and nothing will turn them from their course. Even if you were to convince them, perhaps the other choice or choices would take them down a worse road than the one they're on."

"It's a hard burden to manage in silence," Hannah admits.

"Just because you see it, doesn't make you responsible to change it," Rachel encourages wiping away fresh tears falling upon Hannah's face.

The moment Rachel touches Hannah's tears her eyes are opened to a vision of the future. It's brief, powerful, and frightening all at the same time. The power of the vision is so intense that Rachel pulls back hitting her head against the wall. Hannah immediately tries to ease her sister's pain.

"What happened?" Hannah asks. Her concern is evident in her tone and reaction.

"When I touched your tears, I saw a vision of the future that frightened me."

"You saw what I saw when I looked at your adopted son."

"It was of him as a man, but he was near a…"

"Don't utter it. Don't speak it aloud," Hannah warns.

"What do I do? I can't lose him!"

"You can do nothing, but love him and teach him compassion, mercy, and love. Hide nothing from him, so he'll never turn his back on you as some youth are known to do, but never tell him about this vision."

"I said a moment ago that I understood, but I didn't have a clue about what you're feeling," Rachel admits.

"The intensity of the vision will fade over time."

"Since you were able to adjust before, perhaps you can adjust to your new surroundings with time. After the wedding, the population will drop by half. Only those that have been selected by Joss will go with you to obtain the building materials from Ophir's castle. If you need some time alone, I'll make sure that you get it. It's just that this project is so important for the people and to Horeb."

"I agree. I'll not put my needs above the peoples. I can manage. My limited exposure during the project should allow me the time to acclimate. When I return from this task, I'll need some time alone in order to ease myself into being around the people here again."

"You'll have all the time you need," Rachel promises.

"You must never speak of this to anyone especially your new son. The Most High said this knowledge would deprive people of the happy times with worry robbing them of their joy trying to avoid the bad ones. Remember that you're seeing this vision from the vantage point of just having gone through hell, but his future will be different than the glimpse you saw."

"Beverly said that our future is tied to that boy."

"Believe her regardless of what you feel about the vision. Don't give in to fear," Hannah instructs.

"When did you become so wise?"

"I had a good teacher," Hannah responds with her signature beaming smile. The sisters hug and return to their perspective rooms to rest.

***

Horeb waits patiently for Keevah to arrive staring at the fire while sipping on his wine. His mind is a blur of everything that needs to be done and will rest much easier once his cabinet is fully established and functioning.

The guard knocks and enters the room. He announces Keevah and exits the room returning to his post. Horeb stands to his feet to greet his guest. Keevah is already down on one knee showing proper respect for a king.

"Keevah, you old sea dog, it's good to see you!" Horeb greets with arms outstretched.

"It's good to see you too, Sire," Keevah responds carefully not to break protocol. His memories of Horeb are not good ones.

"Rise, to your feet!" Horeb orders and hugs him. Keevah is taken aback by his jovial manner.

"What can I do for you, my king?"

"I need someone to act as my ambassador to other nations. I know you have established relationships with many kingdoms both near and far and would be a good fit."

"Well, I think you over estimate my abilities. My ship and crew left me high and dry when the Dragon unleashed his final fury. If I catch up to them, I'll hang the lot of them."

"They were just scared, Keevah. Show some mercy should you find them again and pardon them."

"Forgive me, Sire, but your reaction is not one that your given reputation would expect."

"I've seen too much death. I'm also not the man I used to be.

Sometime ago I was attacked and left for dead. I was found by the Healer of Tierney, the woman that will be wife come tomorrow. I awoke to her presence and her loving care with no knowledge of who I was. When my memories returned, I couldn't reconcile them to the man I had become, so I started making changes to become the man I had become in that village. The prince you used to know is dead. The king you stand before is a new man who values love, respect, and mercy."

"Then let me say that it'll be my greatest honor to serve the king."

"I'm not yet in a position to grant you a ship, but I do have horses. Although Navarre's lands have been restored and are full of natural resources, we are too weak to defend them adequately. I need someone who is wise and cunning to make sure that our neighbors remain friendly and won't take advantage of our situation."

"I understand."

"Good, we'll be celebrating my wedding for the next three days. Please be sure and enjoy the festivities. Quarters have been prepared for all my cabinet members. You can move into them anytime you like. After the celebration, we shall discuss our plan of action to secure the safety of our borders and establish friendly relations with our neighbors."

"I'm yours to command."

CHAPTER 30

In the heart of the catacombs, the Dwarf Council has been deadlocked for days on whether or not their people should return to the surface. Passionate arguments have been presented on both sides of the issue. Wilhelm, as leader of the council, must remain neutral and weigh all the facts by their own merits. He has been tempted many times in the past to allow his own opinion to sway him, but that has never worked out well in the end. There are too many unknowns on the surface world. In addition, their own long held prejudice of the humans being deceitful and untrustworthy will undoubtedly impact any dealings they have with them. Those that fought alongside the humans will not hold those attitudes, but those that didn't may still struggle with those feelings.

In the catacombs, they control their contact with other races, but on the surface, they'll have no such control. Wilhelm knows what King Horeb knows that Navarre, although healed, is vulnerable should surrounding lands wish to do them harm. If the land has indeed been transformed into the bountiful place that has been reported, Navarre will be a tempting target for marauders and plunderers alike. The general's report confirmed that their numbers, although severely depleted, are still larger than the human population. This will make defending the land from aggressors nearly impossible. And whether his people are willing to admit it or not, what happens on the surface will eventually affect them.

Suddenly, an incessant knocking on the door ensues without abating interrupting the discussion. Although Wilhelm left strict orders for the council not to be disturbed, this intrusion can only mean something terrible has happened and requires their immediate attention. Trepidation fills the room wondering what could have happened.

"Open the door," Wilhelm commands. The honor guards obey. As soon as the doors are open wide enough to allow passage between them, Quimby runs into the room. His face is pale and panic stricken.

"Honorable council, I bring you urgent news that can't wait," Quimby begins panting trying to catch his breath.

"Out with it man," Wilhelm orders.

"It's the underground rivers, they've dried up," Quimby

informs.

"It's an attack!" Thornton yells out. The council begins to murmur loudly amongst themselves. They fear that the humans may have already turned on them, or worse, another nation has invaded.

"No, it's not an attack," Leopold counters as he stands to his feet to calm the council. He waits for them to quiet before finishing his statement. "It is the last sign that marks the end of our habitation of the catacombs."

"Explain," Wilhelm demands.

"In the last pages of the Prophets of Verdoon, it mentions that the Most High will return us to our rightful place on the surface when the renewing springs burst forth from below the broken land to nourish and heal it for all time. If you remember, the General reported that there were several springs that burst forth upon the surface surrounding the battlefield. These springs that have been returned to the surface are the rivers that used to sustain us below the surface. I can show you the passage that contains the last prophecy if you doubt my word."

"That'll not be necessary, Leopold. You're our historian and scribe, and your recounting and interpretation of prophecy has been proven trustworthy many times over."

"Without the underground rivers, we can't live here,"

Thornton adds.

"It would seem that the decision of whether we should return to the surface has been made for us by the Most High and predicted by our own people over millennia ago so we can be assured that it's the correct decision. Our deliberations of whether to go to the surface are closed," Wilhelm informs the council.

"What shall we take with us? It has been reported that the lands along the coast which King Horeb allotted to us were wiped clean," Thornton submits for consideration.

"All that we can, including cannibalizing any structure that will not cause a cave in. Quimby, please have General Rasmussen report to me at once. After you do that, you are to organize the women to start packing our belongings. We'll begin our migration to the surface in two days," Wilhelm responds.

"Yes, sir," Quimby salutes the council and quickly finds the general. The general wastes no time in reporting to the council chambers. Luckily, he was nearby.

"General Rasmussen, reporting as ordered," he declares announcing himself.

"General," Wilhelm addresses. "We have just received confirmation that the disappearance of our water sources to be the final sign of our occupation of the catacombs predicted by our own prophets. We are making preparations to migrate to the surface as soon as possible. What I need from you and your remaining warriors is two-fold. The first is to provide protection for our people until we can establish ourselves on the surface, the second is to oversee the dismantling of any structure that is not part of the support system which keeps the ground from tumbling down on top of us. These materials are to be transported and reassembled on the surface to provide shelter for the people first."

"So what of this place?" Rasmussen inquires.

"When it has been stripped of everything usable, you and your men will seal it so that no one can desecrate these hallowed halls. You are to obscure any sign on the surface that it ever existed."

"Understood... Forgive me your Greatness, but it'll take many moons to do all that you ask. We'll be noticed by passing ships and travelers. It'll be difficult to obscure what is already known."

"Then we shall perform these tasks at night so it'll better obscure the catacombs when we're finished."

"Your orders will be followed to the letter, but how can I simultaneously oversee the dispersion of our people along the coastal lands and the dismantling of the catacombs."

"Get your second, Angus, to oversee the dispersion of the clans along the coast. The people must obey his decisions, based upon their trades and the resources of each area."

"I'll need to send a survey crew ahead of the people, or Angus could make a bad decision."

"Secure Rastus and Oleg to conduct the survey. They have the proper skills."

"Thank you, Sir. I'll do all that you have commanded so that we'll be successful." Rasmussen starts to leave but pauses a moment to inquire about one final piece. "Sir, what about King Horeb. Although he offered us the coastal lands, he'll surely want an official acceptance. He may view the sneaking in during the middle of the night as some type of subterfuge."

"I had no intentions of giving the king the wrong impression of our acceptance or our terms. Instruct Oleg to take this, our terms for peaceful coexistence to King Horeb while Rastus returns to provide Angus with the survey results," Wilhelm instructs handing the general a sealed scroll.

"Your orders will be carried out."

"General, please have Oleg convey the following message to my son. I want him to bring King Horeb's reply to our terms back to me."

The Dwarfs begin the arduous task to migrate their civilization to the surface world. It's a migration that the Builders of Verdoon initially undertook to carve out of the dirt and rocks to create a home below the surface in an effort to hide from the Dragon's fury when he returned. Now, with the Dragon defeated, they're able to take their rightful place back on the surface and peacefully coexist with the humans. Each race has lived independently of each other for so long, but the dark times demonstrated how much they need each other. Their white magic will be an added benefit to the people of the land as they return wonder to nature.

Glenda C. Finkelstein

CHAPTER 31

The wedding day has finally come, and everyone is in good spirits. The city is as festive as it can be considering the recent devastation and what could be cleaned up in thirty days. Flowers are strewn everywhere in beautiful garlands of scent and beauty. The nuptials are to transpire in the city center. Although manufactured goods are in short supply, the women of Indra managed to find and sew a beautiful wedding gown fit for their new queen. This celebration is a welcome distraction from all the work that still lay ahead of the people of Navarre. Only a month ago, every thought was about the ending of an era. Today, it's about the excitement of a new beginning.

King Horeb waits at the fountain with Mordecai, who'll be officiating today's ceremony. His clean-shaven face and neatly combed hair shine brighter than the simple crown that sits upon his brow. His choice of crown is deliberate to demonstrate that his rule will not be consumed with the opulent hording of his father. Trumpeters blast a celebratory chorus as Laban and Samuel exit the Royalty Inn with Rachel between them. This is the second time Laban has given his daughter away, and for Samuel, it's a sign that he, too, is at peace for his late son's wife to re-marry.

Hannah is feeling better than she anticipated. The people are so focused on this joyous occasion that she isn't receiving the overwhelming emotions that accompany her insight. This allows her to enjoy this celebration with her sister without the burden that weighed so heavily upon her just a night or two ago.

The people toss flower petals in front of them as they make their way towards the fountain. As they turn into the garden, Horeb catches a glimpse of Rachel in her fine array. His chest puffs up, and his face beams a great smile of both satisfaction and awe. Her smile disarms him, and he feels a slight blush brush across his face, but no one sees it for all eyes are upon her. It's her grace and genuine sincerity of spirit that elevates her physical beauty. When you look upon her face, you see her heart.

"Who gives this woman to be wed?" Mordecai asks.

"I, her father..." Laban responds.

"And I, her father-in-law..." Samuel responds. Then both men release her into the waiting hands of King Horeb. Rachel takes hold of Horeb's hands with joy.

"People of Navarre, we are gathered here today to celebrate the wedding of our new King, Horeb, to our future Queen, Rachel. You have both played a significant role in bringing our people through the darkest of hours. We've not only survived, but will now thrive in ways we never dreamed of because of your leadership. As a member of your inner circle, I want to make all aware that your new King has only been concerned with one thing, your health, safety, and ability to be prosperous. Taking his bride is the only thing he has done for himself."

"Mordecai…"Horeb starts to interrupt him.

"No, Your Majesty, the people need to know what a good king they are receiving. In the coming days, this king and queen will do things differently with compassion and fairness to all. This type of leadership has not been seen in this land in centuries. This day we celebrate your union and your kingship!"

The people break out in cheers of joy. Rachel looks about the crowd and then turns back to look into Horeb's eyes. Her heart expands breaking any remaining bonds of sorrow that has plagued her for so long. She smiles a loving and joyous smile. Horeb smiles back at her. Their vision in this moment ceases to rest upon what was and is now fully focused on what is, and is to come.

Mordecai completes the ceremony incorporating various traditions from both the Northern and Southern kingdoms. This is yet another example of starting anew as a united people.

Immediately after the wedding concludes with a kiss, Rachel's coronation begins. She kneels before the prophet, and he places upon her head a crown that belonged to Sabrina's mother. The crown glistens in the sun contrasted by Rachel's dark hair. She stands to her feet and turns to face her people.

"Long live the Queen!" The people shout repeatedly. It finally sinks in to her reason that all of these people are hers, not just the small village she came from. She resigns in her heart to serve them well.

"Long live the Queen," Horeb adds joining the people. He then holds up his hands to silence them so that he can speak. "Good people of Navarre, although our future is bright we must remember the ultimate sacrifice of those who led us into this time. My brother, Prince Robert, his wife, Princess Sabrina, her brother, Prince Javan, Queen Rachel's late husband, Seth, the Oracle of Elim, Sasha, and Mark the Redeemer. But these did not fight or sacrifice alone. You the people fought as valiantly and as sacrificially as they. We shall not, however, remember them with sadness, but by honoring them in our lives.'

"Unbeknown to many of you, my brother and his wife had a son. He was protected by the Matron of Elim, Beverly, and Lady Beth of Togarmah's court. Today we will present him to you, and he'll be the heir of a unified Navarre whose veins holds the blood of both former kingdoms." Horeb completes his announcement.

Beverly and Lady Beth take their cue to publicly present the young prince to Queen Rachel. She takes him gently into her arms and then turns him around so that all the people can see his beautiful face.

"Today, I, Queen Rachel bestow upon you your name and to make it known to all the people that your leadership is the key to our future. It's our prayer that you will someday take the throne of Navarre and rule with justice and clemency. I present to you the people, Prince Robert Javan Seth of Navarre."

The people shout for joy. Horeb is pleased with her choice of names for the heir to the throne. Now that the official ceremonies are concluded, the celebration begins in earnest. A great feast has been prepared, and every bottle of wine and ale that can be found is opened, and the people eat and drink until they are full and satisfied. The celebration goes on for three days while the king and queen consummate their union sequestered away in the further most room of the Inn.

***

At the conclusion of the celebration at sunrise on the fourth day before the people disburse, Horeb calls them all to a meeting where he lays out the plans for the rebuilding of their nation. He shares how the unclaimed lands and properties will be divided up and how disputes will be settled should any arise. He announces the newly opened Orphanage giving a hope and a future to many in the crowd. Lastly, he informs them about the dismantling of Ophir's castle which for so long stood as a symbol of oppression.

The people cheer over the wise leadership of King Horeb. The truth of this new way is epitomized in the distribution of needed goods such as blankets, food, and cooking pots, which are given to the people as they leave and distributed to the remainder of those who stay. The coming days will be difficult as they begin the overwhelming task of rebuilding a nation. The people will need to take turns repairing and rebuilding their dwellings. If they're selfish each focusing on their own dwelling, the rebuilding will take a long time. If, however, they focus as a group on one dwelling at a time, the rebuilding will go much faster.

Joss, Hannah, and those that Joss selected make their way to Ophir's castle to begin the dismantling of the castle. Rachel watches her sister leave, but at this moment she is not concerned nor is she filled with any trepidation. Her pain and anguish which lasted so long have finally been vanquished. Her joy is renewed each time Horeb's hand touches hers. In like manner, Horeb is strengthened by the grace and wisdom that is housed so beautifully in Rachel's person.

CHAPTER 32

A few days later while Horeb is holding court, a familiar face shows up in the crowd. It's Oleg, and he's carrying a diplomatic pouch which can only mean that the Dwarf Council has made their decision. He expels a heavy sigh before motioning for Oleg to step forward. Connor sits up straight in his chair wondering what news he brings. He's concerned that his father may still be the stubborn person he's always been, or whether he'll reach out in a new way.

"The Throne recognizes Oleg, ambassador of the Dwarf Council," Horeb announces. The crowd becomes quiet.

"Your Majesty, after the Great War was over you offered the coastal lands to my people. It's my honor to inform you that the Dwarf Council has accepted your offer under the following conditions: Firstly, we will continue to govern ourselves. Secondly, should this land be attacked we will help protect it along side yourselves. Thirdly, we will open trade relations with you.

Fourthly, we ask that you obey our laws as we will obey yours. Lastly, we will ask that you allow us to celebrate our Holy days amongst our own kind. We do not request this of you to offend you, but to allow us to maintain certain traditions that have meaning only to us."

The crowd holds their breath as they're not certain if Horeb perceives a challenge to his authority or not. They can tell that the king is pondering all that Oleg has communicated as he rolls the scroll back up, fastens it with a tie, and extends it towards Horeb. The King stands to his feet and accepts the scroll.

"I, King Horeb, accept your council's terms as an ally and friend to the people of Navarre with whom you hold dual citizenship. Together we will move forward and establish a future that will mutually benefit both peoples."

The crowd erupts into cheers. After Oleg dispenses with the formalities, he meets up with Connor privately. Connor is relieved by this news and is anxious about seeing his father again.

"I can't believe the council agreed to come to the surface," Connor admits to Oleg.

"Well, the underground rivers dried up, so we really didn't have a choice."

"I see. How did my father seem? Was he angry by our water source forcing the decision?"

"No, but he did give me one singular instruction."

"What's that?"

"That you and only you are to return with King Horeb's response."

"He asked for me to bring the response," Connor repeats to make sure his ears weren't playing tricks on him.

"Yes, he not only asked, he demanded. I know things must have been hard for you living in exile all these years, but it's been equally painful for your father. When you see him, don't be harsh with him. He wasn't the same man after you left. I don't think he's slept peacefully these past five decades."

"But he hasn't rescinded my exile. Just because you'll be on the surface doesn't mean I'll be welcome in the towns of our people."

"Did you ever stop to think that this maybe the reason he wants you to bring King Horeb's response back to the council?"

"Maybe you're right. Thanks, Oleg."

The two dwarfs hug each other like brothers. Connor quickly makes his way to tell his wife Rainah who makes arrangements to accompany her husband back to the catacombs to meet with Wilhelm, Connor's father.

The rebuilding of Navarre continues with enthusiasm and

commitment. Much to King Horeb's surprise and relief the surrounding nations are not interested in invading Navarre. They're still reeling from the all the signs and wonders that erupted from this land and choose to leave it be.

The humans and dwarfs were successful in vanquishing their foes thanks to the sacrifice each was willing to make, but far away deep inside the Canyon of Woes where the Dragon's eggs were laid a secret lays hidden amongst the broken shells. Although a small band of human and dwarf warriors led by King Horeb was successful in destroying the vast majority of the eggs prior to them hatching, a single surviving egg begins to hatch. As with all victories, there remains a remnant of the defeated enemy. Will this dragon with no knowledge of what came before wage war on Navarre or will it make peace? Only time will tell…

ABOUT THE AUTHOR

Glenda C. Finkelstein lives in Florida with her husband, Tony, and pet cat. She enjoys the outdoors creating a beautiful flower garden which allows her to escape the everyday stresses of life. She has always been creative both in crafting as well as writing. She enjoys creating these thought provoking and entertaining adventures for her readers and is thrilled to have contributed a smile or just provide a few moments escape from the daily grind for them. She hopes you'll enjoy this final installment of her first epic fantasy series, The Redemption Chronicles.

www.ingramcontent.com/pod-product-compliance
Lightning Source LLC
Chambersburg PA
CBHW070358260626
47161CB00001B/187